A PLANET CALLED TREASON

ORSON SCOTT CARD

ST. MARTIN'S PRESS · NEW YORK

To
MaryJo, who turned me on to Bradbury,
Laura Dene, who loaned me the Foundation Trilogy,
Dale and Maria, who made me read the Chronicles of
Narnia,
and the four thousand people who urged me to read
Tolkien:
It's all your fault.

contents

1 Mueller   1

2 Allison   12

3 Nkumai   25

4 Lanik and Lanik   53

5 Singer   68

6 Schwartz   76

7 Ensel   98

8 Ku Kuei   113

9 Jones   134

10 Britton   141

11 Gill   160

12 Anderson   174

13 Treason   180

14 Lanik in Mueller   195

15 Humping   205

mueller

I've endured having four arms, an extra nose, and two hearts pumping away before the surgeon took me under his knife to cut away the excess. But I could still pretend that it was just adolescence, just the bizarre jumbling of chemicals that could throw a normal Mueller into regenerative patterns. The pretense ended when I began developing a rather voluptuous pair of breasts.

"It's not just breasts," said Homarnoch, the Family surgeon. "Sorry, Lanik. It's ovaries. For life."

"Take 'em out," I said.

"They'll just grow back," he said. "Face it. You're a radical regenerative."

But I didn't want to face it. We bred ourselves for controlled regeneration—it was nothing to us to lose a hand or a foot, to have our eyes put out or our tongue cut off. They would grow back; and as inbreeding became more effective, they grew back faster.

What we feared was when the genetic manipulation resulted in radical regeneration. Body parts grown in before there was a need. And the final test for a radical regenerative was transsexual growth. In my case, ovaries.

"Say that, Homarnoch," I told him, "and you might as well also say that I'm dead."

"Come on, Lanik. It's not the end of the world." He used his buck-up-my-friend voice and slapped me on the back. The impact made my breasts jostle, painfully. It was a pain I wasn't yet used to bearing, and I must have made a sound.

"Lanik, perhaps you ought to—" And he began to suggest a certain item of wearing apparel I needed to acquire. As he spoke I guess my face showed how I felt about it, and he stopped.

"I'm sorry," he said simply. "But I must tell your father immediately."

And he left.

I looked in the large mirror on the wall, where my clothing hung on a hook. My shoulders were still broad from hours and days and weeks with sword, staff, spear, and bow; and more recently with the bellows at the forge. My hips still slim from running and riding. My stomach ridged with muscle, hard and solid and virile. And then, ridiculously soft and inviting, my breasts—

Not mine. Put on me as a cruel joke, but certainly not belonging to me. So strange, in fact, that as I looked at my naked torso I began to be aroused as I was when Saranna came to me at night.

I took my knife from the belt hanging on the wall and pressed its sharp silver edge against my breast. It hurt too badly—I cut only an inch deep and had to stop. There was a sound at the door. I turned.

A little black Cramer bowed her head so she would not see me. I remembered that she had been taken in the last war (which father won), and so belonged to us for life; I spoke gently to her, because she was a slave.

"You're all right, don't worry," I said to her, but she didn't relax.

"My lord Ensel wants to see his son Lanik. He says immediately."

"Damn!" I said, and she knelt to receive my anger. I didn't hit her, though, only touched her head as I walked to my clothing and put it on. I couldn't help but see my reflection as I left—my chest heaving up and down as I strode out of the room. The little Cramer murmured her thanks as I left.

I started to run down the stairs to Father's chambers. After three steps I stopped and leaned on the banister until the pain subsided. When I turned around to go down more slowly, I saw my brother Dinte at the bottom of the stairs. He was smirking, as fine a specimen of budding asshood as the Family had ever produced.

"I see you've heard the news," I said, walking carefully downstairs.

"May I suggest you acquire a halter?" he offered blandly. "I'd loan you one of Mannoah's but hers are far too small."

I put my hand on my knife and he retreated a few steps.

"You mustn't do any more of that, Lanik," Dinte said, still smirking. "I'll be heir now, and head of the family soon enough, and I'll remember."

I walked past him toward Father's room. As I passed he hummed in the back of his throat, as one does to call the prostitutes on Hivvel Street. I did not kill him, however.

"Hello, my son," said Father when I came into his chamber.

"You might advise your second son," I answered, "that I still know how to kill."

"I'm sure you meant to say hello. Greet your mother."

I looked over to where he glanced and saw the Turd, as we children of Daddy's first wife less-than-affectionately called Number Two, who had moved up into my mother's position when she died of a strange and sudden heart attack. Father didn't think it was strange and sudden, but I did. The Turd's official name was Ruva; she was from Schmidt and had been part of a package deal that included an alliance, two forts, and about three million acres. We were compelled by custom, law, and Father's wrath to call her *mother*.

"Hello, Mother," I said coldly. She only smiled her sweet, gentle, murderous smile and tousled the hair of an ugly curly-headed boy that somehow my father had sired on her.

"Well, my son Lanik," Father said, "Homarnoch tells me that you're a radical regenerative."

"I'll kill anyone who tries to put me in the pens," I said. "Even you."

"Someday I'll take your treasonous statements seriously, boy, and have you strangled. But you can remove that fear, at least. I'd never put one of my own sons in the pens, even if he's a rad."

"It's been done before," I pointed out. "I've studied a little Family history."

"Then you'll know what is happening now. Come in, Dinte," Father said, and I turned to see my little brother walking in. It was then that I lost control for the first time.

I shouted: "You're going to let that half-assed moron ruin Mueller, you bastard, when you know damn well that I'm the only one who can hope to hold this flimsy empire together when you've had the courtesy to die! I hope you live long enough to see it all crumble!"

Father leaped to his feet and strode around his table to where I stood. I expected a blow, and braced for it. Instead he put his hands at my throat and I felt a sickening momentary fear that he was at last going to carry out his threat to strangle me. Then he ripped open my tunic, put his hands on my breasts, and pushed them together brutally. I gasped in pain and pulled away.

"You're weak now, Lanik!" he shouted. "You're soft and womanly, and no man of Mueller would follow you anywhere!"

"Except to bed," Dinte added lewdly. Father turned and slapped his ear.

When he turned away I covered my chest with my arms like a virgin girl and spun around, coming face to face with the Turd and her curly-headed creature. She was still smiling, and I watched her eyes move from my face down to my bosom—

Not my breasts! I cried out silently. Not mine, not a part of me, and I felt an overwhelming desire to retreat, to back out of my body completely, let it stay *there* while I went elsewhere, still a man, still an heir with more than a hope for supreme power, still a man, still myself.

"Put on a cloak," Father ordered.

"Yes, my lord Ensel," I murmured, and instead of fading from my body I covered it, and felt the rough fabric of the cloak harsh against my tender nipples. I stood there and watched as Father went through the ritual of declaring me a bastard and my brother Dinte the heir. My brother looked tall and blond and strong and clever, though I knew better than anyone that his cleverness was merely a tendency to be sly; his strength was not equalled by any quickness or skill. When the ceremony was over, Dinte sat naturally in the chair that had for so many years been mine.

I stood before them then, and Father commanded me to swear allegiance to my younger brother.

"I would rather die," I said.

"That's the choice," Father said, and Dinte smiled.

I swore eternal allegiance to Dinte Mueller, heir to the Mueller Family holdings, which included the Mueller estate and the lands my father had conquered: Cramer, Helper, Wizer, and the Island of Huntington. I made the pledge because Dinte so obviously wanted me to refuse and die. Now, with me alive, he would have to worry constantly; I wondered idly how many guards he would post around his bed tonight.

But I knew I wouldn't try to kill him. Removing Dinte wouldn't put me in his place; it would only mean that the Turd's curly-headed larva would inherit. A rad like me could never hope to govern in Mueller. Besides, rads rarely lived past the age of twenty-five, and it was illegal for us to interbreed with ubermen. I felt a sudden pang as I realized what this would do to poor Saranna. They would take the child out of her now, and destroy it. And she would find herself now the concubine of a pariah instead of the potential first wife of the father of the Family.

"Do I see daggers in your eyes, Lanik?" Father asked.

"Never, Father."

"Poison, then. Or deep water. I think my heir is not safe with you here in Mueller."

I glared at him. "Dinte's worst enemy is himself. He needs no help from me to end in disaster."

"I've read Family history, too," Father said, "and I'm sending you on an embassy so that I have a reasonable hope of keeping Dinte alive."

"I'm not afraid of him," Dinte said scornfully.

"Then you *are* a fool," Father said sharply. "Teats or no teats, Lanik is more than a match for you, boy, and I won't trust you with my empire until you show me that you're at least half as clever as your brother."

Dinte was silent then, but I knew that my father had written my death sentence in Dinte's mind. Deliberately? I thought not.

"What embassy?" I asked.

"Nkumai," he answered.

"A kingdom of tree-dwelling savage blacks far to the east," I said. "Why should we send embassies to animals?"

"Not animals," Father said. "They use metal swords in battle. They conquered Drew two years ago. Allison is falling easily even while we talk."

I felt my anger rise to think of tree-dwelling blacks conquering the proud stonecarvers of Drew or the wild horseriders of Allison. "Why are we sending embassies instead of armies?" I asked angrily.

"Am I a fool?" Father asked in return.

"No," I answered. "If they have hard metal, it means that they have found something that the Offworld will buy. We don't know how much metal they have; we don't know what they are selling. Therefore my embassy is not to make a treaty, but rather to find out what they have to sell and what the Ambassador is paying for it."

"Very good," Father said. "Dinte, you may go."

"If these are affairs of the kingdom," Dinte said, "shouldn't I be here to hear them?"

Father didn't answer. Dinte got up and left. And then father waved a hand at the Turd and her child, and they also left the room.

"Lanik," Father said when we were alone, "Lanik I wish to God there was something I could do." And then his eyes filled with tears and I realized with some surprise that Father cared enough to grieve for me. But not for me, after all. For his precious empire, which Dinte could not possibly hold together.

"Lanik, never in the three thousand years of Mueller has there been a mind like yours, in a body like yours, a man truly fit to lead men. And now the body is ruined. Will the mind still serve me? Will the man still love his father?"

"Man? If you saw me on the street you'd want to take me to your bed."

"Lanik!" he cried out. "Can't you believe my grief?" And then he pulled out his golden dagger, raised it high, and then jabbed it through his left hand, pinning it to the table. When he pulled out the weapon the blood spouted and pulsed from the wound, and he rubbed the hand across his forehead, covering his face with blood. Then he wept, while the bleeding stopped and scar tissue formed across the wound.

I sat and watched him in the ritual of grief. We were silent except for his heavy breathing until his hand was healed. Then he looked at me from heavy eyes.

"Even if this hadn't happened," he said, "I would have sent you to Nkumai. For forty years we have been the only ones on our planet to have the hard metals. Nkumai is now our only rival, and we know nothing about that Family. Go secretly; if they know you're from Mueller they'll kill you. Even if you lived they'd be sure you saw nothing of importance."

I laughed. "That much I had already planned."

He smiled back at me. Then his eyes filled with tears again and I wondered if, after all, his love might not be for me.

The interview was over and I left.

I saw to arrangements, setting the grooms to tending my horses and shoeing them for the journey; setting the scullers to preparing a pack for my journey; getting the scholars to make me a map. When the work was in motion, I left the castle proper and walked through the covered corridors to the Genetics Laboratories.

The news had spread quickly—all the high-ranking officers avoided me, and only the students were there to open doors and lead me to the place I wanted to see.

The pens were kept brightly lit twenty-seven hours a day, and I looked through the high observation window at the bodies endlessly scattered across the soft lawns. Here and there dust rose from the wallows. All the flesh was nude, and I watched as the noon food was spread into the feeders. Some of them looked like any other men. Others had small growths here and there on their bodies, or defects barely noticeable from a distance—three breasts, or two noses, or extra toes and fingers.

And then there were those that were ready for harvest. I watched one creature as it awkwardly lumbered toward the troughs. Its five legs didn't move well together, and it flailed its four arms awkwardly, to keep a balance. An extra head dangled useless from its back, and a second spine curved away from the body like a sucking snake cling-ing rigidly to its victim.

"Why have they let this one go so long unharvested?" I asked the student who was near me.

"Because of the head," he said. "Complete heads are very rare, and we didn't dare interfere with the regeneration until it was complete."

"Do we get a good price for heads?" I asked.

"I'm not in merchandising," he answered, which meant that the price was very high indeed.

I looked at the clumsy monster as it struggled to bring food to its mouth with unresponsive arms. I shuddered.

"Are you cold?" asked the student, over-solicitously.

"Very," I answered. "My curiosity is satisfied. I'll go now."

And I wondered why I wasn't even slightly grateful that at least I didn't have to go to the pens. Perhaps because if I were destined for supplying extra parts for the Offworld, I would kill myself. But as it was I was still this side of suicide, and so had no retreat from the terrible knowledge of my loss.

Saranna met me in the greeting room of the Genetics Labora-tories. I couldn't avoid her.

"I thought I would find you here," she said, "being morbid."

"You were right," I said, starting to walk past her. She caught my arm, clung to me and wouldn't let me pull away.

"Do you think it makes any difference to me?" she cried out.

"You're being indecorous," I hissed. Several people were looking at the floor in embarrassment, and the servants were already kneel-ing. "You're causing us shame."

"Come with me, then," she said and to avoid causing any more awkwardness to others in the room I went with her. As we left I could hear the rods being whipped across the servants' backs because they had seen the highborn acting in a low manner. I felt the blows as if they fell on me.

"How could you do that?" I asked her.

"And how could you stay away from me for eight days?"

"Not that long."

"Longer! Lanik, I heard the news, and I already suspected as much. Do you think I care? Do you think it ends anything?"

"It ends everything," I said.

"Cut them off!" she said.

"I'm a Mueller!" I shouted. "They'll grow back in a week!"

"Lanik!" she said, and then put her arms around me and pressed her head to my chest. When her head leaned against soft breasts instead of hard muscle, she pulled her head away for a moment, then resolutely held to me even tighter.

With her head on my bosom I found myself feeling maternal. I wanted to vomit. I pushed her away and ran. I stopped at a turn in the corridor and looked back. She was already slitting her wrists and crying out, the blood dripping onto the stone floor. The cuts were savage—the loss of blood would make her sick for days, with that many lacerations. I left, and went quickly to my room.

I lay on my bed, looking up at the delicate gold inlay on the ceiling. Set in the middle of the gold was a single pearl of iron, black and angry and beautiful. For iron, I said silently. For iron we have bred ourselves into monsters; the "normal" Muellers able to heal from any wound, and the rads serving as domesticated animals, selling their extra parts to the Offworld for more iron. Iron is power in a world with no hard metals. With our arms and legs and hearts and bowels we buy that power.

Put an arm in the Ambassador, and in a half hour a pound of iron appears on the dancing-light grill. Put living frozen sex organs on the grill and five pounds of iron replace it. An entire head? Who knows the price.

And at that rate, how many arms and legs and eyes and livers must we give before we have enough iron to make one starship?

The walls pressed in on me and I felt myself trapped on Treason, our planet forming high walls of poverty that tied us down, that kept us from the Offworld, that made us prisoners as surely as the creatures in the pens. And like them, we lived under watching eyes, Family competing madly against Family in order to produce something (anything!) that the Offworld would buy, paying in precious metals like iron, aluminum, bronze.

We Muellers had been first. The Nkumai were second, perhaps. A battle for supremacy, sooner or later. And whoever the victor, the pyrrhic prize would be a few tons of iron. Could a technology be built on that?

I slept like a prisoner, tied to my bed by the immense manacles of gravity on our poor prison planet; bound to despair by two full and lovely breasts that rose and fell regularly. I slept.

I woke to darkness in the room, and the rasping sound of labored breath. The breath was mine, and in sudden panic I felt liquid in my lungs, and began to cough violently. I threw myself to the edge of the bed, coughing a dark liquid out of my lungs, each cough an agony of pain in my throat. And as I gasped for breath I realized that it came coldly in at my throat, not through my mouth.

I felt my neck, and a huge, gaping wound was open at the throat. My larynx had been cut out, and I could feel the veins and arteries that were covered with scar tissue as they tried to heal, sending blood into my brain whatever the cost. The wound went from ear to ear. But finally my lungs were clear of the liquid, which I now knew was blood, and I lay on the bed and tried to ignore the pain as my body quickly healed the gash.

Not quickly enough, I realized abruptly. Whoever had tried (so clumsily) to kill me would be back to make sure of his work (or her work—Ruva?), and they wouldn't be so careless next time. I stood, breath still hissing in and out of the open wound at my throat. At least the bleeding had stopped, and if I moved carefully the scar tissue working gradually inward from the edges of the wound would eventually close it.

I stepped out into the corridor. No one; but the packs I had ordered were stacked outside my room, awaiting inspection. I dragged them in. The strain caused a little bleeding, so I rested a moment while the blood vessels healed again. Then I sorted through the packs and combined the most essential items in one bundle. My bow and the glass-tipped arrows were the only things I took with me from my room; carrying the single pack I made my way carefully down the corridors and stairways to the stable.

When I passed the sentry stall I was relieved to see that no one was there to challenge me. A few steps later on I realized what that meant, and whirled around, drawing my dagger as I turned.

But it was not an enemy who stood there. Saranna gasped when she saw the wound in my throat.

"What happened to you!" she cried out.

I tried to answer, but my body had not yet rebuilt the larynx I had lost, and so all I could do was shake my head slowly and put a finger to her lips, to silence her.

"Where are you going?" she asked, seeing my pack. "I knew you would leave, Lanik. Take me with you."

I turned my back and went to my horses, which were standing newshod at the woodsmith's bar. Their wooden shoes clumped softly on the stone floor as they moved. I threw the pack over Himmler's back and saddled the stallion, Hitler, to ride.

"Take me with you," Saranna pleaded. I turned to her—even if I could have spoken, what would I have said? So I said nothing, only kissed her and then, because I had to leave in silence and could not hope to persuade her to let me go alone, I struck her sharply with the hilt of my dagger on the back of her head, and she fell softly into the hay and straw on the stable floor.

The horses were quiet as I led them out of the stable, and there was no further incident as I led them to the gate. The high collar of my cloak hid the wound in my throat as I passed the guards. I half expected to be challenged there, but no. And I wondered if it would really make much difference to Dinte whether I was dead or left Mueller. Either way I would not be there to plot against him; and I knew that if I ever tried to return a hundred hired assassins would wait for me behind every corner.

As I mounted Hitler and led Himmler along in the faint light of Dissent, the quick moon, I almost laughed. Only Dinte could have botched the attempt to kill me so badly. But in the moonlight I soon forgot Dinte, and remembered only Saranna, white with loss of blood in grief for me, as she lay on the floor of the stable. I let the reins fall and plunged my hands into my tunic to touch my breasts and so remember hers. Almost I could believe they did not belong to me.

Then the slow moon, Freedom, rose in the east, casting a bright light over the plain. I took the reins again, and urged the horses on, so that daylight would find me far from the castle.

Nkumai. What would I find there?

And who the hell cared?

But I was a dutiful son of Ensel Mueller. I would go, I would see, so that Mueller might, with luck, conquer.

Behind me I saw lights come on in the castle; torches ran along the walls. They had discovered I was gone. I could not count on Dinte being bright enough to realize that killing me would be pointless. I dug my heels into Hitler's flanks. He galloped off, and I clung to the reins with one hand as with the other I tried to ease the pain of the horse's violent footfalls, each one jarring my chest until I realized that I felt no pain in my breasts. Nor in the wound in my throat. The pain was deeper in my chest, and in the back of my throat, and I wept as I sped eastward—not toward the highway as they would surely, knowing my mission, suppose; not toward the surrounding enemies who would be glad to give shelter to a possible tool in their struggle against Mueller imperialism. I went eastward, to the forest of Ku Kuei, where no man went, and so where no man would think to look for me.

allison

The well-farmed plain broke into small canyons and grassy plateaus, and sheep began to be more common than people. Freedom was still low in the west and the sun was well into morning. I was hot.

I was also trapped. Though I could see no one on the trail behind me, I knew where the pursuers were, if there were any (and I had to assume there were): to the south and east of me, guarding the borders with Wong, and to the north of me, patrolling the long hostile border with Epson. Only to the east were there no guards, because no guards were necessary there.

Now the plateaus turned to cliffs and peaks, and I followed the eastward trail carefully. The tracks of a hundred thousand sheep had worn these trails, and this one was easy enough to follow. But sometimes the trail narrowed between a cliff rising on the left and a cliff falling away on the right, and at those times I dismounted and led Hitler along, with Himmler following docilely.

And at noon I came to a house.

A woman stood at the door with a stone-tipped spear. She was in her middle age, her breasts sagging but still full, her hips wide, her belly protuberant. There was fire in her eyes.

"Off the horse and away from my house, ye dammid interloper!" she cried out.

I dismounted, though I found no threat in her silly spear. I was hoping to convince her to let me rest. My legs and back ached from riding.

"Sweet lady," I said in my most unthreatening, gentle voice, "you have nothing to fear from me."

She kept the spear pointed at my chest. "Half the people in these High Hills have been robbed of late, and of a sudden all the troopers have took their bowen off north or south chasing the king's son. How kin I know ye've no weapon and plan to steal?"

I dropped away my cloak and spread my arms wide. By now the scar on my neck would be nothing but a white line, which would disappear by noon. As I spread my arms my breasts rose under my tunic. Her eyes widened.

"I have all I need," I said, "except a bed to rest on and proper clothes. Will you help me?"

She moved the point of the spear and shuffled closer. Suddenly her hand darted out and squeezed my breast. I cried out in surprise and pain.

She laughed. "Why come ye to the house of honest folk all dissembling undressed? Come in, lady, I've a pallet for ye, if ye like."

I liked. But even though it had fooled this woman and earned me a bed, I still found myself darkly ashamed of my transformation. I loathed being taken for a woman, however helpful it might be.

The house was larger inside than it looked from outside. Then I realize it was built right into a cave. I touched the rock wall.

"Ya, lady, cave keeps it right cool all summer, stops the wind good enow in the winter."

"I imagine," I agreed, deliberately letting my voice get even softer and higher. "Why are they chasing the king's son?"

"Ach, child, the king's son's done sommat terrible bad, I guess. Word comes like the wind this morrow early, must be takinn all the troopery of this country here."

"But don't they fear the king's son might come this way?"

She darted me a quick glance. I thought for a moment she guessed who I was, but then she said, "I thinked for a moment here you were having your little fun. Don't ye know not two mile of here starts the forest of Ku Kuei?"

That close. I pretended ignorance. "And what does that mean?"

She shook her head. "They tells it that no man or woman goes into that forest and comes out again alive."

"How could they come out dead?"

"They don't come out, lady. Have a splash of soup, lady, smells like sheep dung but it's true mutton, killed a lamb a week gone and this be simmerinn ever yet."

It was good and strong. It did, however, smell like sheep dung. And after a few swallows I felt ready enough for sleep, and slid from the table, went to the cot she pointed out in the corner.

I woke in darkness. A dim fire crackled in a hearth, and I saw the woman's shape moving back and forth in the room. She was humming a low tune with a melody as monotonous and beautiful as the sea.

"Has it words?" I asked. She didn't hear me, and I fell back asleep. When I woke again there was a candle in my face, and the old woman was gazing intently at me. I opened my eyes wide, and she moved back, a little embarrassed. The cold night air made me realize my tunic was open, my breasts bare, and I covered myself.

"Sorry, wee lady," the woman said. "But a soldier came, he did, looking for a young man of sixteen years named Lanik. I told him none such had been this way, and that only here was me and my daughter. And because your hair is so close-cropped, lady, I had to show him proof ye were a girl, didn't I? So I let your tunic to fall open."

I nodded slowly.

"I thought ye might not want to be known by the soldier, lady. And another bit of news. I had to turn your horses loose."

I sat up quickly. "My horses? Where are they?"

"Soldier found them down the road, a long way, all empty. I hid your things under my own bed."

"Why, woman? How can I travel now?" I felt betrayed, though even then I suspected the woman had saved my life.

"Have ye no feet? And I think ye'll not be wanting to go far now where horses can go."

"And where do you think I'm going?"

She smiled. "Ach, ye've a lovely face, lady. Pretty enough to be or boy or girl, and young, and fair, like a king's child. Happy the woman to have you for a daughter, or the man to have you for a son."

I said nothing then.

"I think," she said, "that there be no place for you now but the forest of Ku Kuei."

I laughed. "So I can go in and never come out?"

"That," she said with a smile, "be the ramshit we tell outlanders and lowlanders. But *we* be knowing right enow that a man can go in a good few leagues and gather roots and berries and other fruit and come out safe. Though odd things do happen there, and a wise man skirts the edge."

I was wide awake now. "How did you know about me?"

"Ye've got royalty in every move ye make, every word ye say, boy. Or girl. Which be ye? I care little. I only know I have little love for the godlike men of the plain who think they rule all Muellerfolk. If ye be running from the king, ye have my blessing and my arm of help."

I had never really suspected that citizens of Mueller would feel that way about my father. But now it was helpful, though I wondered how I would feel about her attitude if I were still heir.

"I've packed ye a bundle easy enough to heft," she said. "And fooded and watered it, hoping ye like cold mutton."

I liked it better than starving.

"Don't eat the white berries in the forest, they'll drop ye dead in a minute, and the fruit with wrinkly bulges, don't even touch that, and be careful not to step on a fungus, or it'll plague you for years."

"I still don't even know if I'm going into the forest."

"And where else, then, if not there?"

I got up and walked to the door. Dissent was high and dim, with clouds across her face. Freedom hadn't risen yet. "How soon must I leave?"

"As soon as Freedom come," she said. "Then I lead you afoot to the edge of the forest, and there ye stay until just before sunrise. Then off and in. Head east but about a third to the south till ye touch a lake. Then they say the true road to safety is due south, into Jones. Follow no paths. Follow no manshape or womanshape ye see. And pay no heed to day and night."

And then she brought out woman's clothing from a trunk and held it up to me. It was shabby enough, and old, but modest and virginal.

"My own," she said, "thought I misdoubt I ever did fit it on my old corpse, what's swoll up with fat these last year and ten." She laughed, and put it in my pack.

Freedom rose, and she led me out the door and along a path leading due east from her house, and not much traveled by. She chattered as we went.

"What be the need of troopery at all, ask I? They flash a bit of hard metal, dip it in another's blood, and then what? Is the world all changed? Do men now fly offworld, as we of Treason now freed by

all the bloodshed? I think we be like dogs that fight an kill over a
bone, and what has the winner got? Just a bone. And no hope of any
more after that. Just the one bone."

And then an arrow swicked out of the darkness and into her
throat and she dropped dead in front of me.

Two soldiers stepped into the moonlight, arrows ready. I ducked
just as the first let fly. He missed. The second one hit me in the
shoulder.

But by then my pack was to the ground, and I buried my dagger
in the first man's heart, then kicked the other to the ground. There
were things they never taught the troops that my father's sons had to
know. Like how to kill without weapons.

When they were both still I cut off their heads, so there was no
hope of their regenerating and telling what they knew. I took the
better of their two bows and all the glass-tipped arrows, then went
back to where the woman lay. I pulled the arrow from her throat,
but saw that she was not regenerating at all. One of the oldest
branches of the family, then, that was too poor to stay in the chain
of genetic advancement that had resulted in masterworks of self-
preservation like the royal family, like the royal troops.

And genetic monsters like the people in the pens. Like me.

I gave her grief, letting the blood drip from my hand onto her
face. Then I put the arrow that had struck my shoulder into her
hand, to give her power in the next world, though I doubted privately that there was such a thing.

The packstraps chafed my wounded shoulder, and the pain was
bad, but I had been trained to endure pain, and I knew that soon
enough it would heal, like the wound in my hand. I walked eastward,
following the trail, and soon came into the shadow of the black trees
of Ku Kuei.

The forest was as sudden as a storm, from the bright light of Freedom into utter darkness. The trees looked eternal, right from the
edge, as if five hundred years ago (or five thousand, the trees are
that large) some great gardener had planted an orchard just *so*, with
the edges neat and crisp along the property line.

Thus it had been, though, three thousand years ago, more or less,
when the ships of the Republic (the damned foul dictatorship of the
working classes, so said the textbooks) took the conspirators and
their families and dumped them on the useless planet called Treason, where they would be exiled until they had ships enough to come

out. Ships, what a laugh, with silver the strongest workable metal on the planet.

Metal we could only buy, and then by selling something that they wanted. For centuries upon centuries every Family would put something on the grid in their Ambassador; for centuries upon centuries the Ambassador took it—and returned it. Until we stumbled upon a way to use the agony of the radical regeneratives.

But some of the Families did not take part in the rush to trade with our captors. The Schwartzes stayed secretly on their desert, where no one went; the Ku Kuei lived somewhere in the bowels of their dark forest, never leaving it and never being troubled by outsiders, who feared the mysteries of the world's most impenetrable forest. The edge of the forest had always been Mueller's eastern border; and in that direction only did my father and his father never try to conquer.

It was cold and silent. Not a bird. Not an insect. And then the sun rose, and so did I, and set off into the depths of the trees, going east but one-third south.

At first there was a breeze, but then that died, and the leaves hung absolutely still. Birds were rare, and when I saw any they were as if asleep in high branches, motionless. No small animals moved underfoot, and I wondered if this were the secret of Ku Kuei—that nothing but plants lived here.

I could not see the sun, and so marked my direction (east and one-third south, I said again and again, trying not to hear it in the woman's voice—why did I grieve for her, whom I did not know?) by noting the trees that went in a line, correcting now and then.

I walked for hours and hours, it seemed, and still it seemed only morning from the vague direction of the brightest light, where I supposed the sun might be. Paths ran left and right, but I followed again the voice of the old woman in my memory, saying, "Follow no paths." I became hungry. I chewed on mutton. I found berries, and ate those (but not the white ones).

At last my legs were so weary I couldn't set one in front of the other, and yet it was still day. I didn't understand my tiredness. In my training I had often been required to walk briskly from sunrise to sunset, until I could do it with little strain. Was there, then, some element in the forest air, some drug that weakened me?

I didn't know. I set down the pack beside a tree and slept without waking, long and hard.

So long that when I awoke it was daylight again, and I got up and pushed on.

Again a day of walking, then exhaustion while the sun was still high. This time I forced myself to go on, farther and farther, until at last I could not make my legs go anymore, and it was only early afternoon, if my guess at the sun's place was correct. And then I came to the lake.

It was not so wide I couldn't see the other shore, but it was long enough that I saw no end, either north or south. The sun dazzled on the bright water. And yes, it could only be two o'clock in the afternoon.

I lay by the water and slept, and woke the next day at what seemed to be the very time I had gone to sleep. Was this going to be the pattern of my whole journey? A few hours' travel, exhaustion, and then twenty-seven hours of sleep?

My legs ached when I started out again, as if I had exerted myself far beyond my training, though I knew I had not.

At the southern tip of the lake I remembered that this was where the woman had told me I should turn south. But what could I hope to accomplish in Jones, where no one would follow a freak like me into battle? My best hope was to go on to Nkumai, complete the mission Father had given me, and perhaps, by proving my loyalty, earn the right to come home.

I went east, toward Nkumai. The journey changed not at all. Until I finally reached the grey-barked slender Ragwit trees that told me I was near "White-tree Allison, of dawn and light among the leaves," and in the afternoon the sun broke through the leaves of the trees, blinding me for a few moments, and I was able, at last, to walk on until dark.

In the morning, a road. I went back among the trees and changed into the girl's clothing that the woman of the High Hills had given me. Counted my wealth: twenty-two rings of gold, eight rings of platinum, and, in case of emergency, two rings of iron. Dagger in the pack.

I was unsure what to do next. The last news we had heard in Mueller was that Nkumai was attacking Allison. Had they won? Was the war still raging?

I stepped onto the road and went east.

"Hey, little lady," said a soft but penetrating voice behind me. I turned and saw two men. Rather larger than I—I still didn't have my full man's weight, though I did have my height since I was fifteen. They looked rough, but their clothing seemed to be the vestiges of a uniform.

"Soldiers of Allison, I see," I answered, trying to sound glad to see them.

The one with his head in a bandage answered with a sick smile. "Ay, if there yet *be* an Allison, with black niggers loose to rule."

So the Nkumai had won, or were winning.

The shorter one, who couldn't take his eyes off my bosom, chimed in with a voice that sounded rusty, as if for lack of use. "Will you travel with two old soldiers?"

I smiled. Mistake. They had me half-stripped before they realized that I knew how to use my dagger and was not playing games. The short one got away, but from the way his leg was bleeding I didn't think he'd get far. The tall one lay on his back in the road with his eyes rolled up in his head, as if to say, "And after all I lived through, I have to die like *this*." I closed his eyes.

But they had given me my entry into the first town.

"Andy Apwit's mother's garter, little woman, you look half dead."

"Oh no," I told the man at the inn. "Half raped, perhaps."

As he put a blanket around my shoulders and led me upstairs, he chuckled to me, "Half dead you may be, but rape's an all or nothing thing, lady."

"Tell that to my bruises," I answered. The room he showed me to was small and poor, but I doubted there was much better in the town. He washed my feet before he left; an unusual custom, and he was so gentle he tickled unbearably, but I felt much better when he was through. A custom we could encourage the lower classes to adopt in Mueller, I thought at the time. Then I imagined Ruva washing somebody's feet, and laughed.

"What's funny?" he asked, looking irritated.

"Nothing. I'm from far parts, and we have no such gracious custom as to wash feet of travelers."

"Be damned if I'd do it for everybody. Where you be from, little woman?"

I smiled. "I'm not sure what's proper diplomatic procedure. Let us say I'm a woman from a land where women are not used to being attacked on the road—but where they're also not used to such kind concern from a stranger."

He lowered his eyes in humility. "As the Book says, 'To the poor give comfort, and cleansing, and care better than to the rich.' I but do my duty, little woman."

"But I'm not poor," I said. He stood up abruptly. I hastened to re-assure him. "At home we have a house with two rooms."

He smiled patronizingly. "Ay, a woman of such a land as yours might well call that comfort." When he left I was relieved that there was a bar on the door.

In the morning I had a pauper's portion at breakfast—larger than anyone else in the family. The innkeeper, his wife, and his two sons, both much younger than I, urged me not to travel alone. "Take one of my lads with you. I wouldn't have you losing your way."

"It won't be hard, from here, to find the capital?"

The innkeeper glowered. "Do you mock us?"

I shrugged, trying to look innocent. "How could such a question be a mockery?"

The woman placated her husband. "She's a stranger, and plainly untaught in the Path."

"We here don't go to the capital," a boy helpfully informed me. "That's lost to God, it is, and we stay away from such gaudy doings."

"Then so shall I," I said.

"Besides," said the father, huffily, "the capital is sure to be full of niggers."

I didn't know the word. I asked him.

"The black sons of Andy Apwit," he answered. "From Nigumai."

Must mean Nkumai. Victory for the blacks, then. Ah well.

I left after breakfast, my clothing mended very neatly by the inn-keeper's wife. The older of the two boys accompanied me. His name was No-fear. For the first mile or so I queried him about his religion. I'd read about that sort of thing, but had never met anyone who actually believed it, aside from burial rituals for the next life. I was surprised at the things his parents had taught him were true—yet he seemed to be disposed to be obedient, and I thought perhaps there was a place for such things among the lowest classes.

At last we came to a fork in the road, with a sign. "Well," I said, "here I send you back to your father."

"You won't go to the capital, will you?" he asked fearfully.

"Of course not," I lied. Then I took a gold ring from my sack. "Did you think your father's kindness would go unrewarded?" I put the ring on his finger. His eyes widened. It was enough, then, for payment.

"But weren't you poor?" he asked.

"When I came I was," I said, trying to sound very mystical. "But after the gifts your family gave me, I am very rich indeed. Tell no man of this, and command your father likewise."

The boy's eyes widened even more. Then he whirled and ran back down the road. I had been able to put his stories to good use; and now I had added to the lore of angels who appeared to be poor men and women at first sight, but who gathered glory to bless or punish according as they had been treated. From man to woman to angel. Next transformation, please?

"Money first," said the man at the counter.

I flashed a platinum ring at him and suddenly his eyes narrowed.

"Stole it, I'll swear!"

"Then you'll commit perjury," I said archly. "I was set upon by rapists on one of your fine highways, and I who have come as ambassador. My guards slew them, but were slain in the process. I must continue in my mission, and I must be dressed as befits a woman of rank."

He backed off. "Pardon, lady." He bowed. "However I may assist." I did not laugh. And when I left the store I was dressed in the gaudy, tight, revealing style of clothing that had surprised me when I saw it on women on the way into the town.

"Ambassador from where?" he asked as I left. "And to who?"

"From Bird," I said, "and to whoever is in authority here."

"Then find the nearest nigger. Because no white person has rank here these days lady, and all the niggers from Nigumai thinks they rules."

My white-blond hair attracted a few glances on the street, but I went on toward the stables, trying to ignore the men who watched me by using the haughty manner of the high-class whores of Mueller as they ignored the men too poor to afford their services.

That was the transformation. Man, woman, angel, and now prostitute. I laughed. I would be surprised at nothing now.

I parted with a platinum ring and got no change, but the carriage the stableman was hitching up belonged to me. The capital of Allison was still a good many kilometers on from this town, and I had to arrive in style.

A thundering of wooden horseshoes on the stone road. I opened the door to the stable and stepped outside. A dozen horses at a walk clopped along the road, raising a deafening din. But I had no eyes for the horses. Instead I watched the riders.

They were as tall as I was—taller, in fact, two meters if anything. And far blacker than any Cramers I had seen. They had narrow noses, not like the flat wide ones of the blacks I had known before. And every one of them carried an iron sword and an iron-studded shield.

Even in Mueller we didn't equip our common soldiers with iron until it was time for battle. How much metal did the Nkumai have?

The stableman spat.

"Niggers," he said, behind me.

But I ignored him and stepped out into the street, raising an arm in salute. The Nkumai soldiers saw me.

Fifteen minutes later I was stripped to the waist and tied to a post in the middle of town. I decided that being a woman was not all it was cracked up to be. A fire was blazing nearby, and an iron brand was already glowing red.

"Be quiet," the captain of the troop said in a mellifluous, educated voice. "You knew you were supposed to register three weeks ago. This won't hurt."

I glared at him. "Let me go from this post or you'll pay with your life," I said. It was hard work to keep my voice high and feminine, and to sound like my threat was just bluster when in point of fact I was certain I could kill him in three minutes if I could get my hands loose—five if I stayed tied.

"I'm an ambassador," I said, for the dozenth time since they took me, "from Bird—"

"So you've said," he answered mildly, and he beckoned to the soldier who was heating the brand. I wasn't sure whether I should submit or not—so I let my instincts take control. In Mueller we only branded sheep and cattle. Even our slaves remained unmarked. So when the grinning Nkumai brought the redhot brand near my stomach, I kicked him in the groin hard enough to castrate a bull. He screamed. I noticed briefly that the kick had torn my skirt. Then the captain hit me in the head with the flat of his sword, and I was out.

I woke in a dark room with no windows—just a small hole in the roof for light and a heavy wooden door. My head ached vaguely, but I could tell that my body had taken care of any damage that might have been done. I was still dressed as I had been, stripped to the waist but otherwise still covered—much to my relief, since a closer examination of my body would have completely shattered my story of being an ambassador from the matriarchal government of Bird.

The door creaked open on its heavy wooden hinges, and a black man in a white robe came in.

"Please," he said, "come out."

He didn't have to ask twice.

He gave me a long robe, which I immediately put on. I liked it better than the trashy looking Allison clothes I had been wearing. I felt more confident now, and less vulnerable. "I demand that I be set free," I said.

"Of course," he answered, "and I hope that you will continue on your journey to Nkumai."

"I doubt that," I said.

"I was afraid so, but I beg you to forgive our ignorant soldiers. We pride ourselves on our learning in Nkumai, but we know very little about nations beyond our borders. The soldiers know far less, of course, than *we* do."

"We?"

"I am a teacher," he said. "And I have been sent to beg your forgiveness and ask you to continue on your way to our capital. When the captain applied for permission to put you to death for maiming one of our soldiers, he told us that you claimed to be an ambassador from Bird. To him the idea of a woman as an ambassador is absurd. He is from the lower social orders, where women's true potential is not always recognized. But I knew that Bird is governed by women, very wisely I am told, and I realized that your story was probably true."

He smiled and spread his hands. "I cannot hope to undo what our soldier has, in ignorance, done. He has, of course, been put to death."

I nodded. That was the least they could do.

"And now, please let me escort you to Nkumai, where I am certain you will be allowed to bring your embassy before the king."

"I wonder," I said, "if our desire to procure alliance with Nkumai was wise after all. We had heard of you as civilized people."

He looked pained. "Not so," he answered. "We are not civilized. But we are at least trying, which is more than can be said of many peoples here in the East. In the West, I am sure, things are different."

I nodded benignly. And then accepted his invitation. For good or ill I was going to try to complete my mission, and find out what the hell they were selling to the Ambassador that gave them iron in greater quantities than even our extra body parts brought us.

And as we got in his carriage and started eastward toward Nkumai, I had the sickening feeling that I was being caught in a whirlpool, and was already so far in that I was irrevocably being sucked down; I could not get out.

The white trees of Allison gradually faded, and the trees became taller, shooting straight upward hundreds and hundreds of meters. The road wound among giant trees that made even those of Ku Kuei look slight. We stopped for sleep twice along the way, and then in the afternoon of the third day, the Nkumai teacher signalled the driver to stop.

"Here we are," he said.

I looked around. I could see no difference between this place and any other part of the forest.

"Where is here?" I asked.

"Nkumai. The capital."

And then I followed his gaze upward, and saw the most incredible system of ramps, bridges, and buildings suspended in the trees, extending as far as I could see upward and outward in every direction.

"Impregnable," he commented.

"Completely," I answered. I didn't comment that a good fire could wipe the entire thing out in a half hour. I was glad I didn't. Because then a terrible rain came, suddenly drenching us and filling the carriage with three inches of water. The Nkumai made no effort to find shelter, and so neither could I.

After only a few minutes the rain stopped, and he turned to me and smiled. "It comes like this nearly every day, often twice a day. If it didn't, we might have to fear a fire. But as it is, our only problem is getting peat dry enough to burn for cooking."

I smiled back and nodded. "I can see that might be a problem." The ground was mud six inches deep, but then we found a rope ladder and left the ground. I didn't touch it again for weeks.

nkumai

"Would you like to rest?" he asked, and for once I was glad that I appeared to be a woman, because the platform was an island of stability in an absurd world of swinging rope ladders and sudden gusts of wind. Lanik Mueller could never have admitted he wanted to rest. But this lady ambassador from Bird could.

I lay down on the platform so that for a few moments I could see only the still-distant roof of green and pretend I was on level ground.

"You don't seem very tired," my guide commented. "You aren't even breathing very heavily."

"Oh, I didn't want the rest because of the exertion. I'm simply— unaccustomed to such heights."

He casually leaned back over the edge of the platform and looked at the ground. "Well, we're only eighty meters off the ground right now. A long way to go."

I stifled a sigh. "Where are you taking me?"

"Where do you want to go?" he countered.

"I want to see the king."

He guffawed, and I wondered if a lady of Bird was supposed to consider it an affront to have someone laugh in her face. What the hell. I just asked, "Is that amusing?"

"Nobody sees the king, lady," he said.

"Is he invisible?"

"When he chooses to be," he answered.

"What are ambassadors supposed to do?"

He smiled and looked indulgent. "We rarely entertain ambassadors. Until recently, I believe that our neighboring nations have regarded us as tree-dwelling, um, 'apes,' I believe the word is. Only now, when our soldiers have begun to call our neighbors to notice, have ambassadors begun arriving. We really aren't equipped to cope."

I wondered how much truth there was to that. On the great Rebel River plain, every nation had exchanged ambassadors with every other nation ever since the Families first divided up the world. But now, surely they had ambassadors from many nations, even if they had been ignored—

"We have only three ambassadors right now, lady," he said. "We had several others, but of course the ambassador from Allison is now a loyal subject, while the ambassadors from Mancowicz, Parker, Underwood, and Sloan were sent home because they seemed far more interested in our Ambassador—the one from the Watchers, you understand—than they were in promoting good relations with Nkumai. Now only Johnston, Cummings, and Dyal have embassies here. And since we're quite economical with living space, we've had to house them together. We're a backwater of the world, I'm afraid. Very provincial."

And you're overdoing it a bit, I commented silently. But however unsubtle he had been, I had got the warning well enough. They were alert to what ambassadors were probably looking for. So I would have to be careful.

"But why can't I see the king?"

"Oh, perhaps you can. But you have to make application at the office of social services, and where that will lead you who can say. Bureaucracy. I believe the colorful word has always been 'red tape.' Well, we don't bother with that here in Nkumai. We have our own system, which could be called, I imagine, black tape." He laughed at his little racial joke, and I began to wonder how sensitive they were about their color. Cramers were more sensitive about their height than their tint—but the Allisons had seemed a bit snide about the Nkumai's blackness.

"Shall we go?" he suggested.

I advanced warily to the rope ladder that still swung gently in the breeze, moored loosely to the platform by a thin rope tied around a post.

"Not that," he said. "We're going another way." And he took off running away from the platform along one of the branches. If you could call them branches—neither of them less than ten meters thick. I walked slowly to where he had climbed up the branch, and sure enough, there were some subtle handholds that seemed more to have been worn than cut into the wood. I clumsily got myself from the platform to the place were my guide waited impatiently. Where he was the branch had leveled out a little more and now rose more obliquely up into the distance, criss-crossed by branches from other trees.

"All right?" he asked.

"No," I answered. "But let's go on."

"I'll walk for a while," he said, "until you're more accustomed to the treeway. What's your name, lady?"

Name? Hadn't I prepared myself with a name? Surely I had—but for a moment I couldn't remember what it was—can't remember even now what name I had chosen. And since my confusion was obvious, there was no way I could simply make another one up without arousing his suspicion.

"Name, sir? Either you are no gentleman, or you do not think me a lady."

He looked momentarily abashed. Then he laughed. "You must forgive me, lady. Customs vary. In my land only ladies *have* names. Men are called only for their duties. I am, as I told you, Teacher. But I meant you no disrespect."

"Fine," I said, forgiving him curtly. The game was becoming amusing, trying to assert some superiority over him in a situation in which I couldn't help but be inferior. It almost let me forget the fact that though the path we followed was no more difficult than climbing a steep hill, this hill sloped away quickly on both sides, and if I were to stray from the path I would soon find myself hurtling down "how many meters to the ground?"

"Now I would say about a hundred and thirty, lady. But I'm really not sure. We don't measure it, much. Once you're high enough to kill yourself falling, it really doesn't matter how far the ground is, does it? But I can tell you how much higher we have to go."

"How much?"

"About three hundred meters."

I gasped. "Where are we going?"

He laughed again, and this time he made no effort to conceal his enjoyment at my dislike of heights. His way of getting back at me for the little trouble over names. "We're going," he said, "to the place where you're going to live. We thought you'd appreciate visiting the very top. Few outsiders ever have."

"I'm going to *live* at the top?"

"Well, we couldn't very well keep you with the other embassies, could we? They're men. So Mwabao Mawa has consented to take you in."

Our conversation was interrupted as he lightly trotted across a rope bridge, only occasionally using his hands. It looked easy, particularly since the tread of the bridge was wooden. But as I stepped on it, it swayed, and the farther out I got, the worse the swaying was. At the apex of each swing, I could see the trunks of the trees dropping down to a ground so distant that I couldn't be sure exactly where it was, in the heavy shade. I vomited at one point. But then I felt better and made it across the bridge without further incident. And from then on, since I was already utterly disgraced, I made no further attempt to conceal my fear—and found that it therefore became easier to bear. My guide, Teacher, was more helpful, too, and I was more than willing to lean on him.

And as we finally got to the level where the leaves grew, giant fans as much as two meters broad, the realization sank in that even if I found out what Nkumai was selling to the Ambassador for iron, it would do us little good. How could the landbound, plains-dwelling men of Mueller ever invade, let alone conquer, a people like this? The Nkumai woud only pull up their rope ladders and sneer. Or drop deadly rocks.

I was depressed.

I was even more depressed when we finally walked gingerly along a narrow branch to a rather involved house—though in fact I would never have considered it that back in Mueller. Teacher spoke softly, but penetratingly, saying, "From the earth to the air."

"And to the nest, Teacher. Come in," and the husky but beautiful voice of Mwabao Mawa drew us into the house.

It was basically five platforms, not much different from those I had already rested on, though two of them were quite a bit larger. They had roofs, however, of leaves, and a rather complicated system of gathering all the roofwater into barrels in the corners of the rooms.

If they could be called rooms. Each platform was a separate room. And I could detect no hint of a wall anywhere. Only curtains of brightly colored cloth hanging from the roofline to the floor. Breezes opened the walls easily.

I chose to stand in the center of the room.

Mwabao Mawa was, in a way, disappointing. She should have been beautiful, from her voice, but she was not—at least not by any standard of beauty I have ever known—even by Nkumai standards. But she was tall, and her face, however unlovely, was expressive and lively. When I say tall, the word does not convey: in Nkumai, nearly everyone is at least as tall as I am, and in Mueller I am much above average. Among the Nkumai, Mwabao Mawa was towering. Yet she moved gracefully, and I didn't feel intimidated. I felt, in fact, protected.

"Teacher, whom have you brought me?"

I noticed the archaic speech and was surprised that it didn't sound like an affectation.

"She won't give me a name," Teacher said. "A gentleman, it appears, does not ask a lady."

"I'm the ambassador from Bird," I said, trying to sound impressive without sounding pompous, "and to another lady I will tell my name." By then, of course, I had decided a new name, and from then on throughout my stay in Nkumai, I was Lark. It was the closest I could come to Lanik and still be plausible as a woman from Bird.

"Lark," Mwabao Mawa said, making the name sound musical. "Come in."

I thought I already was.

"In here," she said, instantly trying to soothe my confusion. "And you, Teacher, can go."

He turned and left, trotting easily along the narrow branch that had so frightened me.

I followed Mwabao Mawa through the curtain she had entered from. There was no path—just a space about 150 centimeters across to the next room. Miss the jump, and meet the earth. Not exactly a record-setting leap—but the competitive jumping in Mueller offers no further penalty for missing the goal than the scorn of the observers.

This time the wall curtains were subdued and darker, and the floor was, thank heaven, not level. It sank in two steps to a large center arena, which was liberally sprinkled with cushions. When I stepped down, I found that my eyes were willing to believe that I was surrounded by real walls, and I relaxed.

"Go ahead and sit," she said. "This is the room where we relax. Where we sleep at night. I'm sure Teacher showed off all the way up here—but we're not immune to fear of heights. Everyone sleeps in a room like this. We don't like the thought of rolling off at night."

She laughed, a rich, low laugh, but I didn't join in. I just lay back and let my body tremble, releasing the stored-up tension of the climb.

"My name is Mwabao Mawa," she said. "And I should tell you who I am. You'll doubtless hear stories about me. There are rumors that I have been the king's mistress, and I do nothing to discourage them, since it gives me a great deal of petty power. There are also rumors that I am a murderess—and those are even more charming. The truth is, of course, that I'm nothing but a consummate hostess and a great singer of songs. Perhaps the greatest who ever lived in a land of singers. I'm also vain," she said, smiling. "But I believe that true humility consists of recognizing the truth about yourself."

I mumbled acquiescence, content to bask in the warmth of her conversation and the security of the floor. She talked on, and sang me some songs. I remember almost nothing of the conversation. I remember even less of the songs, except that, though I understood no lyrics and detected no particular melody, the songs carried me off into my imagination, and I could almost see the things she sang of—though why I knew what she was singing of I don't know. Though terrible things have happened since, and I myself silenced Mwabao's music, I'd give up much to be able to hear those songs again.

That night she lit a torch outside her main door and told me that guests would come. I later learned that a torch meant that a person was willing to receive guests, an open invitation to all who might see the glowing in the night. It was a measure of Mwabao Mawa's power over other people (or, less cynically, their devotion to and delight in her) that whenever she put the torch outside, it was only a matter of an hour before her house was full, and she had to douse the light.

The guests were mostly men—not uncommon, either, in Nkumai, since women rarely travelled at night. And the talk was mostly small, though by listening carefully I hoped to learn. Unfortunately, Nkumai courtesy forced the guests to spend as much time talking to me as they spent talking to each other. It would have been nicer, I thought at the time, if they had shared Mueller's custom of letting a guest sit in silence until he wished to join a conversation. Of course, Nkumai's custom keeps a guest from learning much—and I was kept from learning anything I thought significant that night.

I only learned that all her guests were men of education—

scientists of one kind or another. And I got the feeling from the way they talked and argued that these were men little concerned with science as Mueller used it, as a means to an end. Instead, science was the end in itself.

"Good evening, Lady," a small, softspoken man said. "I'm Teacher, and I'm eager to be of service to you."

A standard greeting, but at last I gave in to my curiosity and asked, "How can you be named Teacher, and also three other men in this room, and also the guide who led me here? How can you tell one another apart?"

He laughed, with that superior laugh that already irritated me and which I soon learned was a national custom, and said, "Because I'm myself, and they are not."

"But when you talk *about* each other?"

"Well," he patiently explained, "I hope that when men talk about me, they call me Teacher Who Taught the Stars to Dance, because that's what I did. The man who guided you here this morning—he's Teacher of True Sight. That's because he made that particular discovery."

"True sight?"

"You wouldn't understand," he said. "Very technical. But when someone wants to talk about us, he refers to our greatest accomplishment, and then everybody who matters knows who he's talking about."

"What about someone who hasn't made a great discovery yet?"

He laughed again. "Who would want to talk about such a person?"

"But women have names."

"So do dogs and little children," he said, and I could almost believe he hadn't intended to be insulting. "But no one expects great accomplishments from women and it would be demeaning to speak of a woman by referring to her greatest gifts. Imagine calling someone 'Prostitute of the Huge Buttocks' or 'Woman Who Always Scorches Soup.' He laughed at his own joke, and several others, who had been vaguely listening in, suggested other titles. I thought they were hilarious, but as a woman I had to pretend to find them insulting, and in fact I was a bit annoyed when one of them suggested that I might be called "Ambassador with the Freckled Breasts."

"How would you know to call me that?" I asked archly. I was getting better at sounding arch; all I had to do was imitate the

Turd (though at the thought of her—even *her*—I felt a slight stab of nostalgia for Mueller and my old, ever-vanished life there) and raise one eyebrow, which I've been able to do since childhood, to the amusement of my parents and the terror of the troops under my command.

"I don't," the black named Stargazer (like two others in the room) answered. "But I'd be willing to find out."

It was something I hadn't really been prepared for. Rapists on the road I could cope with by killing them. But how does a woman say no to a man in polite company without offending? As a king's son, I was not used to hearing women say no.

Fortunately, I didn't have to invent a way.

"The Lady from Bird is not here to find out what's hidden under your robe," Mwabao Mawa said, "especially since most of us know how little is there." The laughter was loud, especially from the man insulted, and I was allowed a few moments to myself, to observe.

There was, amid all the chatter of science and court gossip—more of the latter than of the former, of course—a detectable pattern that amused me. I watched as one man at a time took Mwabao aside for just a moment of quiet, unheard conversation. And one of them I overheard. "At noon," he said, and she nodded. Little enough to generalize on, but I was willing to believe that they were making appointments. For what? I could think of several obvious purposes. She might be a whore; though I doubted it, both because of her lack of beauty and because of the obvious respect these men had for her mind, never leaving her out of their conversations or ignoring a remark she made. Or she might really be a mistress of the king, in which case she could be selling influence—though again I doubted it, because it seemed so unlikely that an ambassador would be placed with a woman who had that kind of power.

A third possibility was that she was somehow involved with a rebellion or a secret party, at least. This didn't contradict either fact or logic, and I began to wonder if there was something there that might be exploited.

But not that night, at least. I was tired, and though my body had long since healed from the strain of climbing to Mwabao Mawa's house—and, for that matter, from the beating of the Nkumai soldiers only a short time before—I was still emotionally drained. I needed to sleep. I dozed for a moment and woke to find the last of the men leaving.

"Oh," I said, startled. "Did I sleep so long?"

"Only a few moments," Mwabao Mawa told me, "but they realized it was late, and went. So you could sleep."

And she went to a corner, dipped her hand into a barrel, and drank.

I would have done the same, but as I thought of water a horrible realization came over me. In prison I had had privacy to eliminate wastes, and while traveling with Teacher he had delicately let me take care of those needs on the other side of the carriage, forbidding anyone to watch. But alone here in the house with another—another?—woman, there might be no such fastidiousness.

"Is there a room particularly for—" For what, I wondered. Was there a delicate way of putting it? "I mean, what are the other three rooms of your house used for?"

She turned to me and smiled slightly, but there was something other than a smile behind her eyes. "That I will tell to those who have a practical reason for such knowledge."

Didn't work. And worse, I had to watch as Mwabao Mawa casually took off her robe and walked naked across the room toward me.

"Aren't you going to sleep?" she asked me.

"Yes," I said, not bothering to hide how flustered I was. Her body was not particularly attractive, but it *was* the first time I had ever seen a black woman undressed, and I also had to figure out a way to keep from getting undressed myself, since my modesty was essential to my survival in a nation which took me for a woman.

"Then why aren't you undressing?" she asked, puzzled.

"Because in my nation we don't undress to sleep."

She laughed aloud. "You mean you wear clothing even in front of other women?"

"This body is one's most private possession," I said, "and the most important. Do you wear all your jewels all the time?"

She shook her head, still amused. "Well, at least I hope you'll take it off to drop."

"Drop?"

She laughed again (that damned superior laugh) and said, "I guess a soiler would have a different word for it, wouldn't you? Well, you might as well watch the technique—it's easier to show it than to explain it."

And so I followed her to the corner of the room. She grasped the corner pole and then swung out, through the curtain. I gasped at the suddenness of the way she lurched out over the vast distance to the ground. But she sounded calm as she said, "Well, open the curtain, Lark. You can't learn if you don't look!"

So I opened the curtain and watched as she defecated over empty space. Then she swung back in and walked over to another water bucket—*not* the one she had drunk out of—and cleaned herself.

"You've got to learn quickly which bucket is which," she said with a smile. "And also—don't ever drop in a wind, especially in a wind with rain. There's nobody directly below us, but there are plenty of houses off at an angle below my home, and they have strong opinions about feces on their roofs and urine in their drinking water." Then she lay down on a pile of cushions on the floor.

I hitched up my robe until the skirt was very short, and then grasped the pole tightly and delicately tiptoed through the curtain. I began to tremble as I glanced down and saw how far below me the few torches still burning seemed to be. But I bowed—or rather squatted—to the inevitable, trying to pretend that I was not where I was.

When I finished I came back and walked awkwardly to the water barrel. Then, for a difficult moment, I wondered if I was at the wrong one.

"That's the one," came Mwabao Mawa's voice from the cushions on the floor. I cleaned myself and lay down on another pile. They were too soft, and soon I pushed them aside and slept on the wooden floor, which was more comfortable, though something in between would have been nicer.

Before I slept, though, Mwabao Mawa asked me sleepily, "If you don't undress to sleep, and you don't undress to drop, do you undress for sex?"

To which I just as drowsily replied, "That I will tell to those who have a practical reason for such knowledge." Her laughter this time told me that I had a friend, and I slept peacefully all night.

I woke because of a sound. In a building where there is not only a north, south, east, and west, but also an up and down, I couldn't tell where the sound was coming from. But it was, I realized, music.

Singing, and the voice, which was distant, was soon joined by another, which was closer. The words were not clear. There may have been no words. But I found myself listening, pleased by the sound of it. There was no harmony, at least nothing that I could recognize. Instead, each voice seemed to seek its own pleasure, without relation to the other. But there was still some interaction, on some subtle—

or perhaps merely rhythmic—level, and as more voices joined in, the music became very full and lovely.

I noticed a motion, and turned to see Mwabao Mawa looking at me.

"Morningsong," she whispered. "Do you like it?"

I nodded, and she nodded back, beckoned to me, and walked to a curtain. She drew it aside, and stood on the edge of the platform, naked, as the song continued. I held to the corner pole, and watched where she was watching.

It was the east, and the song was to the sun. And as I watched, Mwabao Mawa opened her mouth and began to sing. Not softly, as she had yesterday, but with full voice, a voice that rang among the trees, that seemed to find the same mellow chord that had originally been tuned into the wood, and after a while I noticed that silence had fallen except for her voice. And as she sang an intricate series of rapid notes, which seemed to bear no pattern but which, nevertheless, imprinted themselves indelibly in my memory and in my dreams ever since, the sun topped a horizon somewhere, and though I couldn't see it because of the leaves above me, I knew from the sudden brightening of the green ceiling that the sun had risen.

Then all the voices arose again, singing together for a few moments. And then, as if by a signal, silence.

I stood, leaning on the pole, until Mwabao Mawa closed the curtains.

"Morningsong," she said, smiling. "It was too good an evening not to celebrate it today."

And then she cooked breakfast—the meat of a small bird, and a thin-sliced fruit of some kind.

I asked; she told me that the fruit was the fruit of the trees the Nkumai lived in. "We eat it as soilers eat bread or potatoes." It had a strange tang. I didn't like it, but it was edible.

"How do you catch birds?" I asked. "Do you use hawks? If you shot the bird, it would fall forever to the ground."

She shook her head, waiting to answer until her mouth was empty. "I'll have Teacher take you to where the birdnets are."

"Teacher?" I asked, and as if my question had been his cue, he was standing outside the house, calling softly, "From the earth to the air."

"And to the nest, Teacher," Mwabao Mawa answered, and she walked out of the room, on to the next room where Teacher would be waiting. Reluctantly I followed, making the short jump to the other room, and then without even a good-bye following Teacher away from Mwabao Mawa's house. No good-bye because I had no idea how women who barely knew each other should say it, and because she was already gone from the curtain before I thought to turn and say something.

Up was terrible, but down was infinitely worse. Coming up a rope ladder, you reach the platforms with your hands first, pulling yourself to security. But going down you have to lie on your stomach and extend your feet downward, hunting for a rung with your toes, knowing that if you go any farther you won't be able to pull yourself up.

But I knew that my achieving my purpose in Nkumai depended on my ability to get from place to place, and so I refused to let my fear rule me. If I fall, I fall, I told myself. And then I blanked out my peripheral vision and trotted along after Teacher. He, for his part, didn't try to show off as much today as yesterday, and so the going *was* easier. And I discovered that maneuvers which were difficult and frightening when done slowly were much easier—and much less frightening when done quickly. A rope bridge is easy when you run across it—but when you walk timidly it sways at every step. And when Teacher took a suspended rope with a knot in the end and swung easily from one platform to another, across an abyss that no one in his right mind would ever cross, I simply laughed, caught the rope he threw at me, and swung across just as quickly. It wasn't hard after all, and I said so.

"Of course not. Glad you're learning so fast."

But as we trotted along a sloping branch, I asked, "What would have happened if I hadn't reached the other platform? If my aim had been wrong, or if I hadn't swung hard enough?"

He didn't answer for a moment, and then said, "We would have sent a boy down from the top, swinging all the way, to get the rope back to one platform or another."

"Could the rope support two people, doing that?" I asked.

"No," he answered, "but we wouldn't do it right away."

I tried not to think of myself swinging helplessly over nothing as dozens of Nkumai waited impatiently for me to let go and drop (that word no longer had the same meaning for me) so that they could get their highway working again.

"Don't worry," Teacher said at last. "A lot of those swings have a guy rope on them, so they can be pulled back."

I believed him, but I never saw a swing with a guy rope. Must be in another part of Nkumai.

Our first stop was at the Office of Social Services.

"I want to see the king," I said, after explaining who I was.

"Wonderful," said the ancient Nkumai who sat on a cushion near the corner pole of the house. "I'm glad for you."

That was all, and apparently he meant to say no more. "Why are you so glad?" I asked.

"Because it's good for every human being to have an unfulfilled wish. It makes life so much more meaningful."

I was nonplussed. At this point in Mueller, if I had been taking an ambassador to a government office, I would have ordered such a recalcitrant official's strangulation. But Teacher just stood there smiling. Thanks for the help, friend, I said silently, and proceeded to ask if this was the right place.

"For what?"

"For getting permission to see the king."

"Persistent, aren't you?" he asked.

"Yes," I answered, determined to play the game by his rules, if necessary, but to win whatever the rules might be.

And so it went all morning, until finally the man grimaced and said, "I'm hungry and a man as poor and underpaid as I must take every opportunity to eat that he can get."

The hint was clear, and I took a gold ring from my pocket. "By chance, sir," I said, "I was given this as a gift. But I couldn't bear to own it, when a man such as you would make so much better use of it."

"I couldn't take that," he said, "poor and underpaid though I am. For my work is to feed those even less fortunate than I, in the name of the king. I will accept your gift in order to pass it along to the poor."

And then he excused himself and went to another room to eat lunch.

"What do we do?" I asked Teacher. "Do we go? Do we wait? Did I just waste a perfectly good bribe?"

"Bribe?" he asked suspiciously. "What bribe? Bribery is punishable by death."

I sighed. Who could understand these people?

The official came back into the room, smiling. "Oh, my friend," he said to me, "dear Lady, I have just thought of something. Even though I can't help you, I know a man who can. He lives over there, and he sells carved wooden spoons. Just ask for Spooncarver Who Made the Spoon You Can See Light Through."

We left, and Teacher patted me on the shoulder. "Very well done. It only took you one day."

I was a bit angry. "If you knew this Spooncarver was the man I had to see, why did you bring me here?"

"Because," he said, smiling patiently, "Spooncarver won't bother talking to anyone who wasn't sent by Officer Who Earns Foreign Exchange."

And how he earned it, I knew too well.

Spooncarver Who Made the Spoon You Can See Light Through didn't have time to see me that day, but urged me to return tomorrow. And so I followed Teacher through the maze of trees, and he showed me a birdnet being strung among the trees. "In a week or so it'll be ready to drop. It looks thick enough while it's rolled up, but when it's unrolled among the trees, the net is so fine it can hardly be seen." He showed me how the gaps in the net were just wide enough for a bird's head to pass through, and just small enough that unless the bird withdrew its head exactly backward, which was impossible for most birds, it would break its neck or strangle. "And at the end of the day, we draw up the net and distribute the food."

"Distribute?" I asked.

And then got a lecture about how in Nkumai, everything belonged to everybody, and no money was ever used because nobody was ever paid.

However, I learned quickly that in fact everybody was paid. I could go to Spooncarver, for instance, and ask for a spoon, and he would readily agree, promising it to me within a week. But at the end of the week, he would have forgotten, or had so much other work to do that he just couldn't get to mine yet. He would keep promising and keep putting me off—until I did him some favor, out of the goodness of my heart.

Mwabao Mawa's favor was that every now and then she stood at the edge of her house and sang morningsong, or eveningsong, or birdsong, or who knows what else. It was enough—she was never hungry, and often had so much food and so many possessions she gave them away.

The poor were those who had nothing of value to give. The stupid. The untalented. The lazy. They were tolerated; they were fed—barely. They were not, however, considered to have any importance in life. And they all had names.

I was in Nkumai almost two weeks, and life was becoming normal, when I finally got to see someone who had real power. He was

Official Who Feeds All the Poor, and Teacher actually bowed slightly to him when we entered his house.

But the interview was pointless. Small talk, questions about my homeland (I had long since invented my own idea of what Bird was like, since I had no other way of answering the questions so many Nkumai put to me about the country), and a discussion of Nkumai's social conscience. And an invitation to dinner a few days hence. "When I burn two torches," he said, and I left unsatisfied.

I was more unsatisfied when Teacher laughed at me and said that it looked like my climb upward through the government had reached an end. "What will you give *him?*" he asked. I didn't point out that he was tacitly admitting that I *was* bribing Nkumai officials after all. I just smiled and showed him one of my precious iron rings.

He only smiled and pulled open his robe to reveal a heavy amulet of iron hanging from his neck. "Iron? We have so much of that. Iron would do with Spooncarver and Birdmaster, but with Official Who Feeds All the Poor?"

"What kind of gift would he appreciate?"

"Who knows?" Teacher answered. "No one's ever given him one that did any good. But you should be proud of yourself, Lady. You spoke to him at all—which is more than most ambassadors have been able to do."

"How wonderful," I said, "to have spoken to him."

I insisted to Teacher that I knew the way back to Mwabao Mawa's house without his help, and at last he shrugged and let me go alone. I covered the space quickly, and was pleased to see how well I was doing at traveling among the treetops. I even took a few moments to climb some unmarked branches, for the fun of it, and though I still avoided looking down, I found it a pleasant challenge to conquer a difficult approach. It was nearly dark when I got to Mwabao's house and called to her.

"Come into the nest," she said, smiling. "I hear you got to Official Who Feeds All the Poor," she commented, as she served me supper.

"Someday you have to let me cook you a dinner such as we have in Bird," I said, but she laughed. And so I asked her, "Why did you take me in, Mwabao Mawa, if there was never any intention for me to see the king?"

"King?" she asked, smiling. "No one has any intentions at all. They asked who would let you live with them, and because I have food enough to spare, I offered. They let me."

"How can you of Nkumai expect to deal with the world," I said angrily, as I ate, "if you refuse to allow ambassadors to see your king?"

She reached out her hand and gently stroked my cheek, to which no beard had come. "We don't refuse you anything, little Lark," she said, and smiled. "Don't be impatient. We Nkumai do things our way."

I pulled away from her hand, deciding that it was time I let someone see me get angry. "You all tell me that bribery is forbidden, and yet I've bribed my way through a dozen interviews. You all tell me that you all share everything, and no one has to buy or sell, and yet I've seen purchases and sales just like bartering peddlers. And then you tell me that you don't refuse me anything, but I've met with nothing but impediments."

And I stood and walked from her angrily.

She didn't say anything for a while, and I couldn't turn and say more, or I'd lose something, lose the moment of impact. It was an impasse, until she began to sing in a little-girl voice, nothing like her real songs, "Robber bird hunts for berries, but only catches bees; she says 'I know how to eat and sleep, but what do I do with these?' "

"One follows them," I said, my back still turned, "until one finds their honey." And then I faced her, and said, "But what are the bees, Mwabao Mawa? Whom do I follow, and where is the honey?"

She didn't answer, just got up and walked out of the room—but not toward the front room where I had often been. Instead she went into one of the forbidden back rooms, and because she didn't say anything else, I followed.

I found myself—after a short run along a branch not even a meter thick—in a brightly curtained room lined with wooden boxes. She had one open, and was rummaging through it.

"Here," she said, finding what she was looking for. "Read this." And she lent me a book.

I read it that night. It was a history of Nkumai, and it was the strangest history I had ever read. It wasn't long, and there were no stories of war in it, and no records of invasions or conquests. Instead it was a list of Singers and their life stories, of Woodcarvers and Treedancers, of Teachers and Housemakers. It was, in fact, a record of names and their explanations. Why Woodcarver Who Taught the Tree to Color Its Wood got his name. How Seeker Who Saw the Cold Sea and Brought It Home in a Bucket earned his title. And as I read the brief stories, I began to understand the Nkumai. A peaceful people who were sincere in their belief in equality, despite their tendency to despise those with little to offer. A people who were utterly at one with their world of tall trees and flitting birds.

But as I read in the light of a thick candle, I began to sense the contradictions. What could such a people possibly have developed to sell to the Ambassador? And what caused them to come down from the trees and go to war, using their iron to conquer Drew and Allison, and perhaps more, by now?

And as I thought that way, I began to realize other contradictions. This was the capital of Nkumai, and yet no one seemed aware or even interested in the fact that a war had just been won. There were no slaves from Allison or Drew making their way carefully among the trees. There was no sudden wealth from the tribute and taxes. There wasn't even any pride in the accomplishment, though no one denied it when I mentioned their victories.

"You're still reading?" Mwabao Mawa whispered in the darkness.

"No," I said. "Thinking."

"Ah," she answered. "Of what?"

"Of your strange, strange nation, Mwabao."

"Strange? I find it comfortable." She was amused; her voice hinted at a smile.

"You've conquered an empire larger than most other nations, and yet your people aren't military, aren't even violent."

She chuckled. "Not violent. That's true enough. You're violent, though. Teacher tells me that you killed two would-be rapists on a country road in Allison."

I was startled. So they had been checking on my stories. It made me uneasy. How far would they go? I should have said I was from Stanley, at the other end of the world from Nkumai—but only Bird had women for rulers. Then I realized that a tall black Nkumai could no more get through Robles or Jones to make inquiries in Bird than I could jump from Mwabao's house and land running.

"Yes," I admitted. "In Bird women are trained to kill in secret ways, or men would soon have power over us. But Mwabao, why have the Nkumai gone to war?"

It was her turn to be silent for a moment, and then she said simply, "I don't know. No one asked me. I wouldn't have gone."

"Where did they find the soldiers, then?"

"From among the poor, of course. They have nothing to offer that anyone wants. But I suppose the war has allowed them to give the only thing they have. Their lives. And their strength. War is easy, after all. Even a fool can be a soldier."

And I remembered the strutting, too-brave men of Nkumai armed with iron and quick to abuse the cowering populace of Allison. Of course. The worst of Nkumai, those used to being despised by all, at last in a position of power over others. No wonder they used it, and then abused it.

"But that isn't what you want to know," said Mwabao Mawa.

"Oh?"

"You came here for something else."

"What?" I asked, feeling that sickening fear that children feel when they are just about to be found in hide-and-go-find.

"You came here to find out where we got our iron." •

The sentence hung there in the air. If I said yes, I could imagine her crying out in the darkness of night, and a thousand voices hearinp her, and my being cast off the platform into the darkness that led to the ground. But if I denied it, then would I be missing a chance, perhaps the only chance, to learn what I wanted to know? If Mwabao was indeed a rebel, as I had suspected, she might be willing to tell me the truth. But if she was working for the king (her lover?) she might be leading me on to trap me.

Be ambiguous, my father always taught me.

"Everyone knows where you get the iron," I said easily. "From your Ambassador, from the Watchers, just like everyone else."

She laughed. "Clever, my girl. But you have a ring of iron, and you thought it had great value"—did she know *everything* I had said and done these two weeks?—"and if your people are getting iron, in however small a quantity, you must be eager to find out what *we're* selling to the Ambassador."

"I've asked no one any questions about such matters."

She chuckled. "Of course not. That's why you're still here."

"Of course I'm curious. But I'm here to see the king."

"The king, the king, the king, there you go like everyone else, always chasing after lies and empty dreams. Iron. You want to know what we do to get iron. Why, so you can stop us? Or so you can do it yourselves, and so get as much iron as we?"

"Neither, Mwabao Mawa, and perhaps we shouldn't speak of such things," I said, though I was sure she would go on, was eager to go on.

"But that's where it's all so silly," she said, and I heard a mischievous little girl creep into her voice. "They take all these precautions, keep you imprisoned either with me or with Teacher all day, every

day, and yet it's so impossible for you, either to stop us or to duplicate what we do."

"If it's impossible, why do you worry?"

She laughed—giggled, this time, like a child—and said, "Just in
case. Just in case, Lady Lark." And then she stood up suddenly,
though she had already undressed for bed, and strode out of the
room, back toward the room with the chests of books and other
things. She was after other things. I followed her, and arrived just in
time to catch a black robe she threw at me.

"I'll leave the room so you can dress," she said.

When I got back to the sleeping room, she was waiting—impatiently, walking up and down, humming softly to herself. When I
came in, she came to me, and put her hands on my cheeks. Something warm and sticky was on them, and she giggled when she
looked at me.

"Now you're black!" she whispered, and proceeded to decorate my
hands and wrists, and then my ankles and feet. As she painted my
feet, she ran one hand up the inside of my leg, past the knee, and I
stepped back abruptly, frightened that in playfulness she might find
out not too playful facts.

"Careful!" she cried out. I looked behind me, and realized that I
was standing right at the lip of the platform. I stepped forward.

"Sorry," she said. "I won't offend your modesty again! Just playing, just playing."

"What's going on?" I asked. "Why are you doing this?"

"I can travel at night like this," she said, spinning her naked body
around in front of me, "and no one sees from very far away. But you
—lily-white and hair so light, Lady Lark—you they could see from a
mile off." And then she pulled a snug black cap over my head, and
took me by the hand to the edge of her house.

"I'm taking you," she said, "and if you like what you see, you must
do me a favor in return."

"All right," I said. "What's the favor."

"Nothing hard," she said, "nothing hard." And then she stepped
off into the night. I followed.

It was the first time I had tried to travel in the darkness, and suddenly my old panic returned. Now on the broad branches I was too
frightened to run—what if I veered only slightly from the path?
How could I see to jump with the singing ropes? How could I hope
to keep my footing anywhere?

But Mwabao Mawa led well, and on the hard places she took my hand. "Don't try to see," she kept whispering. "Just follow me."

She was right. The light, which was only starlight and the dim light of Dissent, did more harm that good, diffused as it was by the leaves. And the lower we got, the darker it became.

There were no swings. For that I was grateful.

And at last we came to a place where she told me to stop. I did, and then she asked me, "Well?"

"Well what?" I responded.

"Can you smell it?"

I hadn't thought to smell. So I breathed slowly, and opened my mouth, and tasted the air through my nose and tongue, and it was delicious.

It was exquisite.

It was a dream of lovemaking, with a woman I had wanted forever but never hoped to have.

It was a memory of warfare, with the lust of blood and the joy of surviving through a sea of dancing spears and obsidian axes.

It was the essence of rest after a long journey at sea, when land smells welcome and the grain waving on the plains seems to be another sea, but one you could walk on without a boat, one you could drown in and live, and I turned to Mwabao Mawa and I know my eyes were wide with astonishment, because she laughed.

"The air of Nkumai," she said.

"What is it?" I asked her.

"Many things combined," she said. "The air rising from a noxious swamp below us. The falling fragrance of the leaves. The smell of old wood. The last vestiges of rain. Spent sunlight. Does it matter?"

"And this is what you sell," I said.

"Of course," she answered. "Why else would I bring you? Only the smell is much stronger in daylight, when we capture it in bottles."

"Smells," I said, and it seemed funny. "Smells from a gassy swamp. Can't the Watchers synthesize it?"

"They haven't yet," she said. "At least, they keep buying it. It's funny, Lady Lark, that mankind can speed between the stars faster than light itself, and yet we still don't know what causes smells."

"Of course we know," I said.

"We know what different things smell like," she answered, "but no one knows what it is that travels from the substance to the olfactory nerves."

No arguing that, since I didn't really know an olfactory nerve from an occipital ridge. Then, anyway. Another thing she had said intrigued me: "Faster than light? Any schoolchild knows that's impossible. Our ancestors were brought to Treason in starships that took a hundred years of sleep to arrive."

"Did you think men would stop learning, just because our ancestors left them? In three thousand years of isolation, we've missed the great things of humanity."

"But faster than light," I said. "How could they have done that?"

She shook her head, a faint grey in the grey of night moving faintly. "I was just talking," she said. "Just chattering on. Let's go back."

And so we retraced our steps. But we were halfway up a rope ladder when a voice above us whispered faintly in the night.

"Someone's on the ladder."

Mwabao Mawa ahead of me froze, and I did the same. Then I felt the rope jiggle slightly, and her foot came down near my face. So we were going down, I realized, and would have descended except that her foot twisted and hooked under my arm, stopping my descent. So I waited, until she climbed down the opposite side of the ladder to be at the same height as me—her feet on the rung below mine, and so her lips not far below my ear.

The sound wouldn't have been audible three feet away. "First platform. Wash face. Going to visit Official Who Feeds All the Poor. Two Torches."

So we went on climbing, and reached the first platform, which by chance—an odd chance, too, since it was not common—had a barrel of water. I washed my face as silently as possible, while Mwabao Mawa kept climbing up and down the same three meters of rope ladder, so that anyone observing the strand in the night wouldn't know we had stopped.

I got my face as clean as possible, and also my hands and feet. Then I climbed on the ladder behind her.

"No," she whispered, and then we were both standing on the platform, as she demanded, quietly of course, that I give her my robe.

"I can't," I whispered.

"You're wearing clothing underneath, aren't you?" she asked, and I nodded. "Well, I can't be caught naked on the treeways. I can't."

But still I refused, until finally she said, "Then give me your underclothing." I agreed to that, and reached under the robe to strip off the pants and halter. The pants were too tight for her hips, but she struggled into them anyway. The halter, however, fit nicely—a disgusting proof of exactly how buxom I had become.

I had a worse realization, however, at the same time. The halter, as I slipped it off my shoulder inside my robe, had snagged on something on my shoulder. There was nothing there to snag on. Which meant that something new was growing.

An arm? Then I had less than a week before I'd have to cut it off, and it wasn't in a good position for me to get at alone. How could I go to an Nkumai surgeon (were there any Nkumai surgeons?) and ask him to remove an extra arm?

But the momentary alarm that gave me turned into relief as I realized that of course I could go. Of course, of course, I had all that I had hoped for. I could now make a great show of leaving Nkumai in disgust; I could return to my father, and tell him what the Nkumai sold to the Ambassador.

Smelly air.

I might have laughed, except that we were climbing the ladder again. And as I realized how close I had come to laughing, it occurred to me that whiffs of Nkumai forest air above noxious swamps could be dangerous. Restraints that I could normally count on, reflexes that were sure, didn't function as well tonight.

Finally we reached the platform where the guards were watching.

"Stop," said the sharp whisper, and then hands grabbed my wrist and pulled me toward the platform. Unfortunately, I wasn't ready for the movement, and it was only with luck that I kept my feet on the rope ladder. As it was, I hung over the abyss, my feet on the ladder and my one arm suspended in the firm grasp of a guard.

"Careful," said Mwabao. "Careful, she's a soiler, she might fall."

"Who are you?"

"Mwabao Mawa and Lady Lark, the soiler ambassador from Bird."

A grunt of recognition, and I found myself being pulled toward the platform, until my shin struck the edge. I stepped clumsily onto the wood, falling to one knee.

"What are you doing, wandering in the dark like this?" the voice insisted. I decided to let Mwabao answer. She explained that she was leading me to meet with Official Who Feeds All the Poor.

"Nobody has torches out now," said the voice.

"He will."

"Will he now?"

"Two torches," she insisted. "He is expecting a guest."

Whispers, and then we waited while quiet feet scampered off. A guard—or two, I realized, as the breathing patterns broke up—stayed with us, while another ran to check. It wasn't long before he returned and said, "Two torches."

"All right then," said the voice. "Go on. But in the future, Mwabao Mawa, carry a torch. You are trusted, but not infallible."

Mwabao mumbled her thanks, and so did I, and we were on our way again.

When two torches shone in the distance, Mwabao Mawa said good-bye.

"What?" I said, rather loudly.

"Quiet," she insisted. "Official must not know that I brought you."

"But how do I get there from here?"

"Can't you see the path?"

I couldn't, so she took me closer, until the dim light of the torches illuminated the rest of the way. I was glad that Official didn't have the same penchant for narrow approaches that Mwabao did. I felt safe enough following the path in the dark; as Mwabao Mawa slipped off into the night of the trees.

I came to the door and said, very softly, "From the earth to the air."

"And to the nest, come in," said a soft voice, and I stepped through the curtains. Official sat there looking very, well, *official* in his red robe in the flickering light of two candles.

"You came at last," said Official.

"Yes," I said, and added truthfully, "I'm not very good at traveling in the dark."

"Speak softly," he said, "for the curtains conceal little, and the night air carries sounds a long way."

And so we spoke softly, and he asked me questions about why I wanted to see the king, and what I wanted to accomplish. What could I say? No need to see the old boy now, Official, already got what I wanted? So I answered all his questions, and at last he sighed deeply and said, "Well, Lady Lark, I've been told that if you passed my screening, I was in no way to impede you from further approach to the king."

I couldn't believe it. Yesterday I would have been delighted. But tonight—tonight I just wanted to take my body and the new arm I was growing and get out of Nkumai.

"I'm grateful, Official."

"Of course you don't go straight from me to him. A guide will come and take you to the very highly placed person who gave me my instructions, and that very highly placed person will take you higher."

"To the king?"

"I don't know exactly how highly placed this person is," Official said, not smiling. How could they conduct government this way, I wondered.

But a boy appeared when Official snapped his fingers, and led me off another way. I followed gingerly, and this time there was a swing —but the boy lit a torch at the other end, and I made it, though I landed clumsily and twisted my ankle. The sprain was mild, and it had healed and lost its soreness in a matter of minutes.

The boy left me at a house which had no light, and he told me to say nothing. So I waited in front of the house, until finally a low whisper said, "Come in," and I went in.

The house was absolutely dark, but once again I was asked questions, and once again I answered, not having any idea who I was speaking to or even where, precisely he was. But after a half hour of this, he finally said, "I will leave now."

"What about me?" I asked idiotically.

"You'll stay. Someone else will come."

"The king?"

"The person next to the king," he said, even more softly, and left through the gap in the curtains I had entered by.

Then I heard soft steps in another direction, and someone came in and sat beside me. Close beside me. And then chuckled softly.

"Mwabao Mawa," I said, incredulous.

"Lady Lark," she whispered back to me.

"But they told me—"

"That you would meet the person closest to the king."

"And it's you?"

She chuckled again.

"So you are the king's mistress."

"In a way," she said. "If only there were a king."

That one took awhile to sink in.

"No king?"

"No *one* king," she answered, "but I can speak for those who rule as well as anyone. Better than most. Better than some of *them*."

"But why did I have to go through all of this? Why did I have to —bribe my way up to you? I was with you all along!"

"Softly," she said. "Softly. The night listens. Yes, Lark, you were with me all along. I had to know that I could trust you. That you weren't a spy."

"But you showed me the place yourself. Let me smell the smells."

"I also showed you how impossible it was to stop us, or duplicate it. Near the ground, Lark, the air smells foul. And your people could never climb our trees, you know that."

I agreed. "But why did you show me, anyway? It's so useless."

"Not useless," she said. "The smell has other effects. I wanted you to breathe that air."

And then I felt her hand pull the cap off my hair. She gently pulled at a single lock of it. "You owe me a favor," she said, and I suddenly felt dead.

Her breath was hot on my cheek and her hand was stroking my throat when I finally thought of a way out of this. At least a way to postpone it. My inhibitions had been, to say the least, inhibited. But the inhibition against dying is very strong, and hadn't weakened anywhere near as much as my inhibition against making love to a woman, which had been my habit for years. The trouble was that it was a habit my body still had, and I knew that if things went on discovery of my rather odd physique would be inevitable.

"I can't," I said.

"You will," she said, and her cold hand slid inside my robe. "I can help you," she said. "I can pretend to be man for you, if you like," and she began humming and singing a soft, strange song. Almost immediately that hand inside the robe became rougher, stronger, and the face that kissed my cheek was rough and bearded. All through her song. How did she do it, I wondered, even as another part of my mind laughed hysterically and shouted silently to her that it didn't help things one bit for her to pretend to be male, I had no tendency yet to desire members of that particular sex.

Except that my breasts reacted like any woman's, and I began to be very afraid as the song began to become too rhythmic, to pull me too deeply into a trance.

"I mustn't," I said, and I pulled away. She followed. Or he? The illusion was powerful. I only wished I could do the same, and fool her into thinking I was a woman. But I couldn't. "If you do," I said, "I'll kill myself afterward."

"Nonsense," she answered.

"I haven't been purified." I tried to sound desperate. It wasn't hard.

"Nonsense," she said.

"If I didn't kill myself, my people would," I said. "If I haven't been purified first."

And finally she stopped, or rather paused, and asked, "What is it, this purification?"

I made up a jumble of religious ritual, half stolen from the practices of the people of Ryan and half a product of my need for solitude. And so I made another journey in the dark, and found myself alone in Mwabao Mawa's room, the one with the chests and boxes, "meditating."

I had given myself a morning and an evening and a night.

And I had no idea what I would do after that. Mwabao was in the other room, the one we had shared for two weeks, humming softly an erotic song—one that kept me almost constantly aroused.

I toyed with the idea of cutting off my genitals, but I wasn't sure how long regeneration would take, or what sex would regenerate. Besides, there are limits to what a man can do to himself.

I also thought of escape, of course, but I knew perfectly well that the only escape route lay through the room where Mwabao Mawa cheerfully waited. I cursed again and again, very softly, of course, wondering why I had the miserable fortune to end up imprisoned in a woman's body, with a lesbian for a jailer, and hundreds of meters of gravity serving as the bars for my cell.

And at last I realized that my only hope, thin as it was, was to escape, not as a woman, but as a man. Tomorrow night, in the darkness, if I painted myself black, I might elude the guards. If I didn't, and I was taken, all I'd need to do is fall. Drop, I thought ironically. And my identity as a Mueller would be safe.

Getting past Mwabao? Simple. Kill her.

Could I do it? Not so simple. Perverted or not (and there were plenty of perverts in Mueller—I had read Family history), I liked her.

But breaking a few bones should suffice. To silence her for long enough—

All that remained was to hide who I was. The blacking of my skin could come later, after I finished with Mwabao. But the other preparations would be good for shock value.

I began searching quietly through her boxes, hoping to find a knife. With it I would cut off my breasts. They'd grow back, of course, but by tonight the scar tissue would only have turned back into normal flesh, and the breasts would still not have begun noticeably to grow. The most sex change I could hope to accomplish, I realized bitterly.

I didn't find a knife. Instead I found several more books, and a moment's curiosity turned into a half-hour's concentration.

It was a history of Treason. I had read *our* history of the planet, of course, but this was more complete in some ways. In some very important ways, and I began to realize that I had been almost completely fooled. And yet it was so obvious.

What Mueller's history left out, and what Nkumai's history dwelt on, was the entire group—all the members of the conspiracy who were exiled to this metalless planet as a horrible example to the rest of the Republic of what happened to people who tried to establish a government of the intellectual elite. The long-dead issues that had brought the Families here always seemed laughable to me, and still do. Who should rule whom? The answer was always, eternally, "I should." Whoever "I" might be, "I" would seek power.

But the Nkumai history went over the roster of names. I hunted for Mueller, and found it. Han Mueller, a geneticist specializing in the hyperdevelopment of human regeneration. I found others. But the interesting one was Nkumai. Ngago Nkumai, who had adopted a pseudo-African name as a gesture of defiance, and who had made his name in the development of theoretical physical constructs of the universe. Making new ways of looking at the universe that would enable men to do new things.

It all came together at once, each part so flimsy that alone it proved nothing, but all the events of the weeks I had spent in Nkumai fitting so well that I couldn't doubt my conclusion.

The smelly air above the swamp was nothing, was a decoy, was Mwabao Mawa's device for getting the slim, pretty blond girl from Bird into bed. But other things were true. There was no king, for instance. Mwabao had told the truth: a group governed. But not a group of politicians. A group of men like the founder, Ngago Nkumai. A group of scientists who made up new ways of looking at the universe—scientists who invented things like True Sight and Making the Stars Dance. And they used Mwabao Mawa as their liaison with the army? With the guards? It hardly mattered. And why did all the Nkumai believe there was a king? There undoubtedly had been—or still was, as a figurehead. Again, it hardly mattered.

What mattered was that Nkumai wasn't selling smells to the Ambassador at all. It was selling physics. It was selling new ways of looking at the universe. It was selling, of course, faster-than-light travel, as Mwabao Mawa had so blandly let slip and then covered so well. And other things. Things worth far more to the Watchers than arms, legs, hearts, and heads that were carved off the bodies of radical regeneratives.

Each Family would, if it had any hope of creating anything to sell to the Ambassador, try to develop what its founder had known best. Mueller, human genetic manipulation. Nkumai, physics. I looked up Bird, and laughed. The original Bird had been a wealthy socialite, a woman with no skills and abilities at all. They didn't have a chance. But then, there was an ironic symmetry to it: she had been used to manipulating men all her life, and her female descendents did it still. She had passed on her knowledge of what she was best at.

I closed the book. Now it was even more urgent that I escape, because *this* particular discovery could be the key to a Mueller victory over Nkumai. And I could—I was sure of it—train a Mueller army to be able to fight in the trees. And we could—I had hope for it— win a victory and capture at least some of those minds, and destroy their Ambassador. After all, the basic population of Nkumai was ill- equipped for fighting, but the basic population of Mueller was raised to the knife and the spear and the bow. We could do it.

We *had* to do it. Because Nkumai was getting metal faster, and when they had enough of it, they had the technology to build a ship and get offplanet. Get off Treason—and Mueller had no hope of that. And once the Nkumai could reach the Republic, and come back with all the metal their ships could carry, no Family could hope to stand against them. They would rule.

I would stop them.

And I put away the book and searched again for a knife. I was still searching when the curtains parted and five Nkumai guards came into the room.

"Our spies just got back from Bird," one of them said.

"Do tell," I answered, and I killed two before the others were able to knock me unconscious.

4

Ianik and Ianik

I awoke lying on a platform so small that with my head on the platform my feet dangled off it. Two Nkumai guards were standing nearby, and when they saw that I was awake, they quickly threaded their way to me along narrow branches. We were so high that leaves were thick around us, and I could see splotches of sky. The branches were so slender that my platform bounced wildly as the guards walked toward me.

When they were standing on the branch that passed under my platform, they reached out hooks and snagged two ropes dangling from even higher, thinner branches. On the ends of the ropes were the most ingenious manacles I had ever seen. Instead of the clumsy and quick-to-rot wooden manacles we used in Mueller, these were made of glass bound in rope. Two half cylinders of glass were slipped around my wrists. They did not quite meet on either side. Then the rope was tied tightly around them, held in place by a groove in the glass. When the guards were through trying the ropes, the glass half cylinders met tightly.

And then, as a parting gesture in our wordless interplay, the guards jerked the manacles on my arms. The guard on the right pulled the manacle down, toward my elbow. The other pulled his manacle up, toward my hand. The pain was sharp and immediate, and I cried out in surprise. They smiled grimly and left.

Around my right arm and around my left hand the manacles had cut deep enough to draw blood. I looked carefully at them, and it was clear that the glass had been ground or chipped sharp. The only way out of these manacles was to cut off your hands, in which case climbing down from the tree would be rather difficult.

The manacles were also tied just far enough apart that I couldn't bring them together to break them. Furthermore, because they were tied to branches with a great deal of spring, when I pulled them down, they had a tendency to spring back, cutting my arms. I couldn't lie down—couldn't even kneel.

They didn't want me to get away.

So, having satisfied myself that there was no simple means of escape, I looked around. It was early evening—the sun was still high off the horizon. Clouds were rolling in from the northwest. I must have been out for hours.

My platform rested on a single branch—but that branch not only connected to many others, but also rested on others that touched still others. All in an intertwining network. I bounced lightly on my platform. Immediately the guards felt the movement and looked around.

There were other platforms near me, but none occupied. Farther away I thought I could see someone else standing in manacles, but I couldn't be sure. Leaves kept me from seeing too far.

And then it began to rain. I was immediately soaked; and here, where fewer leaves and branches could dissipate the storm, the heavy drops were almost painful. It fell with such force that every gust of wind jerked and jiggled the branches, and it felt like the first time I had walked on a rope bridge—worse than seasickness. During the rain I could see that the guards huddled under two small roofs, watching no one.

The plan formed quickly and easily, but it would only get me away from this prison area. How I would get to the ground alive—and from there, how I would get through the forest to safety (and where was that?)—those were questions too esoteric to be handled right then.

"Lady Lark," said a distant voice I recognized. Mwabao Mawa was making her way along the network of small branches. The guards stood and nodded to her as she approached me.

"Mwabao Mawa," I said and, in a feeble attempt to sound self-confident, I added, "I've changed my mind. I'd rather continue living with you after all."

No one was fooled. She only looked at me with pursed lips and said, "We've had the full report from our spies. They're a rather treacherous pair—mercenaries from Allison—and they had the mistaken notion that we'd continue to pay more and more for every bit of information they eked out. I hope you don't have any such mistaken notion, Lark, or whoever you are. We will do no bargaining, except for your life."

I smiled, but I'm sure I didn't look particularly jovial.

"Lady Lark, you are not from Bird. Not only that, but the absurd stories you told us about that Family's culture were so far from the truth as to imply that you have never even been there. Nevertheless, it is obvious from your speech that you are from the Rebel River plain. It is also obvious from the iron coin you used that you are from a Family that uses money. And it is equally obvious that since the iron could not have come from us, it must have come from some other Family that is selling to the Ambassador. Who is it?"

I smiled more widely.

"Oh well," she said. "I know perfectly well that you're from Mueller. Precisely who you are I will know within a week, from more reliable spies than the pair of Allisons we used before. I will get to more practical things. What are your people selling to the Ambassador?"

"Air," I answered, "from the swamps at the mouth of the Rebel River."

She glared at me. "I truly did like you," she pointed out.

"And I truly did like you," I responded. "My liking for you, however, ended night before last, when I found out that our sexual tastes are, shall we say, divergent." An out-and-out lie—we both liked women.

"I still do like you, Lark," she said, though her tone of voice spoke of other desires and preferences.

"How nice, that we should be so mutually pleasing."

"I'm not a sadist," she said sharply, "and so I won't stay to watch."

She didn't stay to watch.

The guards came and lifted me into the air. I thought at first they would simply drop me, letting the manacles do the work. But apparently not—if they accidently cut off a major portion of my hand, manacles couldn't hold me any more. Instead, as I was in the air, they spoke for the first time and urged me to take hold of the ropes, which were now slack enough for me to do so.

I held onto the ropes as they swung my feet forward. In that position I couldn't let go of the ropes without slashing my wrists on the manacles, and the ropes were tied to such bouncy branches (like a child's swing) that I couldn't get leverage to kick at the guards. They proceeded to carve up my feet, in a delightful criss-cross pattern about half an inch deep, getting to bone in several places. It was, shall I admit, agonizing, and because it was expected of me I ignored my Mueller training and moaned and screamed in agony. I'm sure I gave a very convincing performance. At last they lifted me again, told me to let go of the ropes, and set me gently down.

On my feet.

It would have been a very convincing torture, except for one thing. I was a Mueller, and the feet were healed in half an hour. A simple, uncomplicated cut like those could heal before your eyes—when there were many, it just took a little longer.

The trouble with healing so fast in a place like that was that if it was noticed, as it surely would be, there would be no further need for me to hide what it was that Mueller sold to the Ambassador.

I began to pray for rain. Or at least wish for it, since my pantheon didn't include anyone in charge of weather.

It came an hour after nightfall. The clouds rolled across the sky, blotting out the stars and the light of Dissent. The wind came up, bouncing the platform around. That was my signal to begin.

It was excruciating, but I had been raised to endure excruciating pain. The hardest thing was keeping the pressure on the manacles strong enough in the right direction so that the little finger on each hand was ripped off by the glass, and not the thumb. I needed the thumb for climbing.

There was a horrifying moment when both hands came free at once, right when a gust of wind jerked the platform under me. I fell flat on my face—but luck had it kindly for me that day, and I fell on the supporting branch rather than into empty space.

I lay there for a moment, dripping blood from my maimed hands, and the rain began to pour.

Only a few minutes left. It was, quite possibly, the hardest thing I ever had to do in my life until then, with the greatest personal risk. Even now, as I think about it, I wonder at what kind of madness caused me even to attempt it. But I was still young then, and life didn't have quite the high price on it that it has now.

It was an infinitely long ten-minute rainstorm. Even though the rain was pummeling me unmercifully and the wind threatened to toss me off the branches at any time, I knew that the moment they ceased, if I wasn't on solid wood the guards would feel the bouncing of the branches and I'd have no chance.

The wood was slippery, and I was choosing my way by dead reckoning, going far faster than was safe, but trying to stay on the branches in the direction they forked from, knowing that eventually I would find firm footing. I mostly kept my eyes closed, because even in the pitch darkness as long as they were open my mind kept wanting to see, and tended to panic when it couldn't.

Once I came to a platform, and was afraid for a moment it might be occupied. It wasn't, and from that platform to solid wood was only a matter of moments.

I still didn't get up and run, however. I had no guide, and the wood was slick. But it was a relief not to be tossed back and forth, and I let myself descend into the darkness.

The rain stopped. The wind stopped. And just as I sighed in relief, the path I was following suddenly became very steep, and I lost my hold and fell.

"What the hell!" said an angry voice as I got up from the platform. I had knocked somebody down.

"What in the world is falling from the sky these days?" asked a woman's voice, amused.

I doubt they were amused when I took them apart. I had no time to be gentle and persuasive. But I don't think I killed them. Their instincts and my desires coincided far enough that neither of them came close to falling off the platform and I took a moment to search them for anything I might be able to steal. I had some vague notion of pretending to be a thief, to throw off the chase.

The man did have a knife, and I took it, along with an iron amulet the woman wore around her neck. And then I found a rope ladder that began at the platform, held my breath, and let myself over the side and down into the darkness.

I descended silently, listening for any tell-tale noise that might come through the night air, telling me that my escape had been discovered, but the night was silent. And a dim light began to filter down to my level as the clouds moved away and Dissent came higher into the sky.

As I passed a platform that connected with a rope bridge, I toyed with the idea of getting off the ladder then. But I decided to go down at least one more level, putting as much vertical distance between me and my pursuers as possible.

It was a bad decision. I had no sooner passed the platform than the rope ladder began to swing violently, pendulum-fashion. And then it began to rise. They had found me.

My reflexes on the treeway were still slow. It took me a moment to decide to turn around on the ladder, get on the other side, the same side as the platform. By then I was a good three meters above it, and rising fast. I couldn't wait to get the range. I jumped backward when a dead guess told me I should.

It nearly was a dead guess. I landed on my back, and I slid in the direction of the grain of the wood, filling my back with splinters. I had so much momentum that I slid right off the platform and down the steep beginning of the rope bridge.

It's one thing to run madly down a rope bridge and up the other side. Sliding down headfirst on your back offers far less control. I spread my feet to try to stop myself by hooking onto the ropes on either side. Unfortunately, my right leg caught first, jerking me in that direction. The side ropes stopped me from falling, but my impact had enough force to tip the entire bridge to the side, spilling me over.

I caught the ropes, and my grip held with a sickening jerk. The bridge was virtually upside down where I hung—and the situation became worse as the wooden treads fell out of position. One of them struck me in the shoulder, and by reflex that hand let go. I held with the other, and quickly recovered my grip. But I could see no way of righting the bridge—it was not like a boat that had capsized. There was no water to support me while I turned up the bridge; in fact, the only way to right the bridge was to let go. And that wouldn't help me a bit.

I toyed with the idea of going back, hand-over-hand, to the platform I had left because it was much closer than the other side. But I knew that it wouldn't be long before my followers, undoubtedly guards, were on that platform—and besides, they controlled the only other escape from it, the rope ladder.

So I began to go hand over hand toward the other end of the bridge. I was grateful for my thumbs. Even though the bleeding from my amputated fingers had stopped, my hands were still sore. But I had a grip. At first, at least. After a while I had to twist an arm into the ropes to help support my weight. It slowed me down more, but I still made fair time.

Toward the end of the bridge, the position of the main hawsers forced the bridge to a more normal level, despite my body weight, and I gratefully pulled myself up onto the treads.

Then I felt a bouncing that was not caused by my own motion—someone else was coming along the bridge. Now that it was upright again, they'd make good time, except in the section where the treads had fallen out. And sure enough, I heard a cry of surprise and a sudden lurching of the bridge. Did the man fall through, or catch himself in time? I had no way of knowing, and even in the dim light I couldn't see more than two meters ahead of me.

Two meters was enough, however, for me to see that the platform I was approaching was occupied. However, they were obviously not part of the chase—both men were facing away from me. I had not time to waste, and there was no longer any point—if there ever had been—in trying to mask the fact that I was escaping. The knife I had stolen from the Nkumai found one man's heart as he turned around to face me, even as the other men fell forever into the night from a sharp kick I landed on the small of his back. He made no sound as he fell.

Pulling the knife out of the Nkumai, I looked around for another escape, and discovered that I was at the crotch of a main trunk and a major branch, not two branches. There was no downward slope—only the straight-down plunge of the trunk. The branch led upward—not the direction I wanted to go. And the bridge was still bouncing with my pursuers' travel. If they hadn't been slowed by the missing treads, they would certainly have reached me by then, accustomed as they were to travel in the dark.

I thought of cutting the rope bridge, but the hawsers were far too thick and I didn't try.

Instead, I decided to go up the branch and hope it led to a route I could use. I was starting the climb when I noticed what the two Nkumai had been working on: a birdnet.

They had been securing the end—the rolled-up net swung out taut into the darkness. At least one other point was secured—and that might be enough.

I tested their knots—they were secure. Then I slithered out feet-first onto the thick roll of the netting. It was rough, and provided enough purchase that I didn't fall, or even swing over to hang from the bottom. And as I crept backward along the net, I cut the strings that held the net in a roll.

When I reached the next tie point, I tested, and found to my relief that the net was tied at the point beyond. I could hear—not very far away—the sound of footsteps reaching the platform I had just left.

Cutting every string as I passed, I continued backward along the net. I could see the net unfolding, falling open along the route I had just traveled. Would my followers try to follow my path along the net? With it open, they would find it considerably harder. Or would they cut the net? It wouldn't hurt me—there was a tie point between me and them. And it would make pursuit impossible.

I could almost hear them trying to decide in the darkness and stillness of the Nkumai night.

How far would the net go down? How far, for that matter, had I descended? What good would it do me to unroll the net if, once I chambered to the bottom, there were still a hundred meters between me and the ground?

The net was long, and when I reached the seventh tie point, it occurred to me that the Nkumai might be waiting at the platform where the net ended, ready for me to back into them and return to captivity. So I laboriously turned around on the net. It was harder, going face first, but I felt more secure about the chances of surprise. And it was a good thing I did. I was at the ninth tie point when I felt a jiggling on the net. It couldn't be coming from behind me—I would have felt it long ago if someone were pursuing me along the route I had followed. All my training in logic was not required for me to conclude that someone was coming in front of me.

I kept slicing knots in the strings as I proceeded forward. And at the next point, I decided to end my journey along the net. Just beyond the tie I began slicing the net itself. Each strand cut easily, even five or six strands together, but there were hundreds in the rolled-up net. And I was so involved that I didn't see my enemy until he was nearly with me.

He had not been cutting knots, of course, and so the net was still thick beneath him, while under and behind me the net fell away, leaving me on a much thinner and so less stable strand. I was half-way—or more—through cutting the net, but he had a knife, too, and I prudently decided that fighting him had a higher priority than cutting string.

That battle was rather one-sided. In good condition on level ground—even on a level platform—I'm sure I could have killed him easily. But on a net, high above the ground, in darkness only faintly relieved by dim and dissipated moonlight, and weakened by loss of blood and the still throbbing amputations on my hands, I was not particularly better than he. In fact, I was more than a little worse at such a fight, and he pressed his advantage to win.

It didn't take much guesswork to realize that apparently I was as valuable dead as alive—he was not trying to capture me. And the brief battle would have ended summarily when he finally pressed his knife into my bowels, if the top of the net hadn't been within reach.

He passed the knife back and forth, and the agony was intense. I cut down at his arm, and struck flesh, but a moment afterward his hand was back, the knife again stabbing to disembowel me. It was clear that such a trade-off—his arm for my guts—would quickly end my struggle, I hacked wildly at the net above, where I had already been cutting. Pain and desperation gave me greater strength, or else the time was actually longer than I thought, but the net soon snapped, and my enemy gave a grunt of surprise as the portion he had been holding to fell away and down. He quickly disappeared into darkness, leaving me alone on the net.

It was now open along the entire remaining length, and I clung to the thin mesh by fingers and toes. The air was cold on my open abdomen. Something hot and wet brushed by my knee, and I realized that some intestine had fallen out.

Disguise of my true sex was hardly important now, and I cut off my black robe at the shoulders, to free me for a scramble down the net. Naked now, and becoming numb to the pain, I began to climb down the net.

I felt like a crippled spider on a broken web. More than once a strand gave way and I had to grasp for another handhold. Constantly the thin mesh cut into my fingers and toes.

After an eon of descent my foot found nothing under it.

I had reached the bottom of the net, and under it was air.

How much air? Fifty centimeters? Or two hundred meters?

After all this, I was not in the mood to gamble on a blind jump, not if there was another chance.

I moved left. I wasn't far from that edge of the net, which was ragged from my cutting it.

I took the knife from my teeth into my left hand and cut the individual strands above me from the left edge. The strands directly above me were tauter and as I cut each one, the next cut became easier as my own body weight on the net helped break the strands apart. And before I had finished cutting all I could reach, the strands began to snap of their own accord, one at a time, each sending me lurching farther downward, my portion of the net coming closer to ground.

The strands snapped faster and faster, and the sound of their ripping grew louder and louder, until at last I was falling and moving to the right fast enough that I could feel wind from my own motion, fast enough that the ripping sounded like heavy fabric being violently torn all at once.

But my speed was as much to the right as down, and I hoped that when the net brought me to the ground, I could survive the impact by rolling.

A sickening thought was that even after exploiting the whole width as well as length of the net, I might be a hundred meters up after all.

And that sickening thought turned to reality as I heard the ripping noise stop, and my direction abruptly changed to straight down. The last of the net had given way, and I heard a brief whimper—mine—just before I hit the ground.

I had only fallen free for a second, but I hadn't exactly been going slowly before that. I rolled, the breath knocked out of me by the impact. And because I hadn't let go of the net, I got tangled up in it, meter after meter wrapped around me.

For just a moment I lay there, almost stunned, tempted by the welcome release of unconsciousness. But I refused. The fact that I had lived to get to the bottom of the Nkumai forest made me determined to try to make good the escape. How long would it take the Nkumai to reach the bottom, going by ladder? And once down here, how long would it take them to reach me? Not long, I decided, and struggled free of the net.

I left some intestine with the net, and the gut still connected to me tried to lurch forward out of the gaping wound with every step I took. Only a hand constantly pressed to my belly held it in. And I staggered off in a direction that would take me, I hoped, to the sea. If I had kept my sense of direction during my night travels.

Even though my mind was not functioning brilliantly, I remember being at least moderately clever in trying to hide my trail. I found a brook, and pausing long enough to rinse my wound (the cold water struck my bowel like a club), I followed it downstream a long way. The drinks I occasionally took seemed to refresh me, until the sickening moment when the water reached the disrupted gut. I soon gave up drinking.

And then, suddenly, the brook tumbled off into darkness, and I fell with a huge splash into a river. I almost lost consciousness there, and might have drowned, except that the current was swift, and I was able to keep awake and afloat long enough to reach the other shore. But in the river I lost the knife I had managed to keep in the fall; I cared little at the time, and slept on the far side of the river, in plain sight on the bank.

I woke with the sun shining dimly through the leaves at the top of the forest, and stayed awake long enough to crawl into some thick brush, where I couldn't be seen from above.

I woke again in darkness, panting with thirst, and though I remembered the agony of the last drink I had taken, I slid painfully down to the river, my intestine trailing limply behind me, and drank the murky water there. It did not turn to torture in my bowel; apparently my Mueller body was trying to cope even with that massive a wound, and had closed a connection somewhere that let the water through. The connection had bypassed much of my gut, however. It still slopped and dragged in the grass and dirt, and I was too tired to try to clean it.

Again in daylight the sun roused me. And this time I heard talking and calling. The Nkumai, so silent and sure in the high trees, were unable to read groundsigns, and I remained quiet and unmoving in the thicket where I lay hidden.

Feet ran by on the other side of the river. No one saw what must have been obvious marks of my climb up the slope, and my followers soon passed on. I slept again, and again that night I slid down to the water and drank, and slept again.

The water was not pure. I began vomiting early that morning, and from the first I was puking blood. I didn't open my eyes, just writhed in agony and panicked as I feared that my fever would lead to delirium, and delirium would call my would-be killers.

I don't know how many days after that I was feverish and unconscious. But I was vaguely aware of walking, always in a stupor, and only the ignorance of the Nkumai saved me—I was careless. Perhaps I walked at night. I don't remember. But I moved from the river to cleaner brooks, and drank; the trees were an endless brown blur; the sun was merely a bright spot in the green from time to time; I knew nothing of what was transpiring.

And I dreamed that as I traveled I was not alone. I dreamed that someone traveled with me, someone to whom I spoke softly and explained all the wisdom of my fevered brain. I dreamed I held a child in my arms. I dreamed I was a father, and I would not, did not disown my worthiest son because of something beyond his control. I dreamed, and then tried one day to set the child down so I could drink.

But the child would not leave my arms. And gradually, as I struggled to push the child away, I realized that birds were singing, the sun was shining, sweat was dripping from my chin, and I was not dreaming.

The boy was whimpering.

The boy was real.

I remembered how the child had cried out in hunger. I remembered now how I had deliriously crooned to him as I walked along, how we had slept snuggled together. It was all so clear—except where he had come from.

It took little investigation to discover. He was joined to me at the waist by a bridge of flesh. Gut to gut, and his food must be the strength he could draw from my body. His legs dangled to within a foot of the ground when I stood erect; his head was only a little shorter than my own; and as I looked into his eyes, I realized they were mine.

Radical regenerative. I could heal anything. And when half my guts were torn away, my body just couldn't decide which was the real me, which to heal. And so it healed both halves, and I stood looking into the eyes of my perfect duplicate, who smiled timidly at me like a stupid but sweet-tempered child.

It was not a child. He had grown quickly, and a faint down of hair around the cheeks and lips hinted at oncoming adolescence. It was thin, starved; its naked ribs protruded. So did mine. My body, unsure which of us to save, had raided my body to give strength to his, and now struggled for a balance.

I did not want a balance.

I remembered the monster lurching toward the troughs in the laboratories, and imagined myself there, ready to be harvested, but not a mere head, indeed no: an entire body. And when I was ripe for the plucking, and they cut the bodies apart, which would be me, and which would they send?

At the moment there was no doubt. I had breasts; I had a small arm still trying to grow out of my shoulder, already with fingers that clasped and curled. I bitterly congratulated my body on having its priorities straight, healing my gut wound before bothering with a surplus arm. Good job.

I would not live with two of me.

Was the new me alive? Human? Intelligent? I didn't think to ask.

I was naked and had no knife. But the connection between us was still only the thin folds of skin that had kept him alive during his gestation. It. That had kept *it* alive. If I let the creature become *him* in my mind, then it was only a short shift to thinking of him as me. And I could hardly bear thinking of *me* as me.

Its hair grew as mine did, the same curls and twists, the same white blond, wild and tangled. I tore at the hair, tried to push it away. Of course it could not go. But it could not stay, either. It was myself, exactly myself, as I had been only a few months ago, before my body had changed to make room for a woman who did not belong there, a woman that they had insisted on saying was me.

Without a weapon, the operation of severance was filthy and painful. It woke as I hacked at our connection with a sharpened stone. It wept, tried feebly to stop me. It did not speak. It merely bled as the skin broke, as I ripped us apart, as I carved my freedom from the burden of bearing myself.

And at last we were separated. I was weak from having created him, but with all the strength I had I brought the stone down on its head, again and again. It stopped crying, and the broken skull poured brains. I noticed that I was sobbing with the exertion, and with the fear at seeing myself die, and I threw down the stone and fled into the forest.

I ate what I could find, trying to gather strength. I saw no more signs of my pursuers—they must have given up the hunt long ago. But that didn't help me escape. If they found me again, my fate would be quick. From where I was, all directions led deeper into Nkumai territory—all but one. And so I calculated a rough northwest from the sun and headed that way.

Travel was hard, for I wasn't strong, but at least now I was conscious. I took the trip in easy stages, each day a little closer, following a brook to a river, the river to, eventually, the sea.

Of course, there was an Nkumai city by the rivermouth, but it was in the trees, except for a few buildings by a rough wharf. They were not sea people, I realized, remembering the huge fleet that had sailed up the sleeve from Mueller, carrying thousands of troops that conquered Huntington in less than a month. From Nkumai no ships would sail.

But ships from other lands might come. And such a ship was my only hope of getting of Nkumai and eventually getting home. (If I still had a home, I remembered bitterly.)

I saw the Nkumai city, and waited until night. Then I walked under it to the sea, and kept to the border of the forest as I traveled only a kilometer or two from the wharf. I could watch for ships from there, and if I could still swim as well as I used to, I could get aboard with no trouble.

And, secure in my hiding place, I slept.

I woke at midday, panting and sweating. I had dreamed that I—but it was not I, it was the child-self I had killed in the forest—I dreamed that I had come to kill me, and I had wakened as knives flashed, and both I and my mirror image had stabbed deep and found each other's hearts.

I vaguely remembered being wakened from the dream by a cry, and wondered if I had called out in my sleep. But when I crept from hiding and looked toward the sea, I saw a ship passing near shore, and the cries were coming from men who were trimming the sails.

The ship put into the port, and for the two days it stayed I tried to calculate how I could attract the attention of the sailors without calling the Nkumai from the city to find me.

I found a rotted branch, and tested it in the water. It would float. Even if I was too weak to make the distance, I would have the branch to support me. The water was cold on my naked skin, but as I saw the ship pull away from the wharf and turn toward me, I splashed out into the water, and then, clinging to the log as if I already needed it, paddled awkwardly out past the gathering breakers into the gentle swells of a calm sea.

Someone on the ship shouted, "Man in the sea! Man!"

I raised a hand and waved.

And in a short time I was picked up from the water, and sat shivering under a blanket in a small boat heading for the ship.

"Thank you," I said.

One of the oarsmen grinned. Not a particularly genial smile. And the rudderman said, "Fine. Take you to captain."

"What nation are you from?"

They seemed reluctant to answer. I wondered whether they had understood.

"What Family? What Family does your ship come from?"

Grudgingly the rudderman replied, "Singer."

The island people from the great North Bay, who had been conquering in Wing when I left Mueller. The ambassador from Wankier had asked my father for troops, knowing his nation would be next, but he had gone away with our sympathy and little else. But at least these sailors were not Nkumai, and they had enough humanity to pull me from the water. I might live.

The captain looked little kinder than his crew, and after I was taken aboard, he spent little time in interviewing me. "Nation?" he asked, and because I thought it prudent not to tell the truth, I said, "Allison. I just escaped from an Nkumai prison camp."

He nodded reflectively, then made a motion. A few sailors came and tore the blanket from me.

"My God," said the captain, "what are those bastards doing to prisoners these days?"

I didn't answer. Let him think what he liked.

"Which is it? Man or woman? Which is real?"

"Both, now," I said truthfully, and he shook his head.

"Impossible," he said. "This makes things very difficult. How will I know how to price you?"

Price me? And then I remembered something else the Wankier ambassador had said. That Singer had a thriving business going. In human flesh.

"Amusement," another officer said. "Put him in a cage and charge money."

"Good," said the captain. "And I think the best market is Rogers. They have circuses. Drop him."

The command had barely been given when I was picked up and carried to a hatch. They opened it, and thrust me down; I landed heavily, and the hatch closed above me. There was no light. There was little air. But I was alive. It hadn't occurred to me to resist. What mattered was that I had value to them; only the dead have no hope.

But Rogers was at the southwest corner of the continent. The trip would take months. Would it then be too late for me to get my information about Nkumai to my father? I didn't know. And there was little enough I could do about it.

Had they noticed the extra arm growing from my shoulder? In the bright sunlight, probably not; staring at my breasts and genitals, they were distracted. But now the arm flexed involuntarily, scratching me on the back. It was going to be a long trip.

singer

It was hard to amuse myself, locked alone in utter darkness, stark naked, with about two square meters of floor space. Sleep took up a large amount of my time, of course, but was hardly restful—it was impossible to straighten my body all at once. As the ship sailed north, cold seeped in; as it went south again, the cell became a sweatbox, with not just my body but also the walls dripping with my sweat. The smell of salt was always with me.

Yet it could have been worse. While I did not see the sun for nearly five months, I was fed. The bucket was lowered to me each morning, filled with water; each evening, filled with food. When I had emptied the bucket, I refilled it, determined to keep the cell as clean as I could without being able to see.

And there were sounds. My only contacts with other people were the cries of the men in the spars, adjusting the endless lashings, furling and unfurling the sails. They cursed at each other, joked loudly; I came to know all their names, and imagined bodies to go with them. I even overhead a plot to mutiny; heard the ceremony as the offenders were cut up and cast overboard.

But there is a limit to how much interest a man can have in the activities of his owners. After a while the darkness caved in on me, and I resented having to wake up, resented having to go to sleep, and above all dreamed of sunlight. I am a horseman, not a seaman. My idea of travel is with surging flesh between my legs, not bounding from side to side and up and down and back and forth with the roll, pitch, and yaw of the boat at sea.

And the effects of my visit among the Nkumai were not over. The massive regenerative effort of my body that resulted in the creation of my erstwhile double did not end with the amputation. Instead, my body seemed determined to regenerate every part of me. The arm already sprouting from my shoulder was long enough and developed enough that I could scratch my back as it dangled, full-size after only a few weeks on the ship. Other limbs sprouted, other growths began. And while there was plenty of food to sustain the growth, I had no chance for exercise, and the energy I took in only had one outlet: growth.

The heat had been unbearable for days when I finally realized that I was losing my mind. I caught myself lying in the grass by Cramer River, watching the light fishing boats skim upstream with the wind. Beside me was Saranna, her robe falling open carelessly (though I knew her careful attention to just how much arousal each centimeter of exposure produced), her finger tickling me unbearably while I pretended I did not feel it. I saw all this, I was doing this, while wide awake, curled in a ball on the floor of my steaming hot prison.

I was doing this while the fifth leg to grow from my hips began twitching awkwardly, beginning to come to life. That was the reality. The sweat dripping on my breasts. The darkness. The destruction of my body. The loss of freedom.

This is how the rads in the pens endure it, I realized. They live another life. They are not wallowing in dirt or grass, feeding at troughs —their bodies are sound and whole again, and they lie by riverbanks preparing to make love to a lover who dares not now remember that they live. And realizing that such madness was my only escape, I determined not to take it.

Determined, instead, to use my mind and keep it awake.

I have a good memory. Not a phenomenal one—I can't conjure up written pages one by one—but I began to use my time to put together all I learned while reading history in Mawa's farthest room.

Mueller—genetics.

Nkumai—physics.

Bird—high society.

These stuck easily in my mind. But again and again I forced myself to go back, let the trances of the madness I could not avoid take me somewhere useful, and I remembered others. Not all, but others.

Schwartz, lost to all human contact on the desert—he had been a geologist. Wasted, on this world without minerals.

Allison—theology. Much good it had done them.

Underwood—botany. And now in the high mountains, what flowers did his children hopelessly grow?

Hanks—psychology, the treatment of the mad. No help for me.

Anderson—the useless leader of the rebellion, whose only gift was politics.

Drew—dreams and their interpretation.

Who had found what to export? I didn't know. But surely in my father's library were the books that would tell what I couldn't remember; books that would fill in the gaps and give us hints of what projects were secretly being worked on in other Families. Some, of course, would have given way to despair, having nothing that on this world could possibly be of value to the Ambassador—the engineers, for instance, Cramer and Wizer. They had been easy to conquer, farmers now, having forgotten lore that could never be put to adequate use on this world. And Ku Kuei, a philosopher whose ideas, obviously, had no wide audience in the Republic.

And iron in Nkumai and Mueller. Physics and genetics. They with ideas, we with products. Our products would never run out; would their ideas? It didn't matter, not if they were getting paid enough iron for each idea that they could overwhelm us quickly.

I would never make it to Mueller in time.

Resist it though I did, I doubt I held off the madness altogether. Because I remember, as if it were real, a creature like myself who came and laughed at me in my cell. He could have been Lanik as I remembered me from mirrors in my early adolescence, except that the side of his head was bashed in and his brains kept sloughing out. Yet he carried on a pleasant conversation, and only at the end did he try to kill me. I strangled him with four arms, tore him apart. I remember it clearly.

I also remember my brother, Dinte, visiting me. He cut me into little pieces, and each grew up into a little Lanik, so small at adulthood that Dinte had great fun smashing them with his boots. Perhaps I screamed then—Dinte fled when someone beat on the hatch above me.

And Ruva came, too, with her curly-headed spawn, her mouth full, but bragging to me as she chewed that she had got my father's testicles at last, had got them and was chewing them up, and I was next. The boy laughed, but at the age of—what, ten?—he still drooled. His wet chin shone in the light. Yet there was never light in my cell except a dazzle for a moment as the bucket was lowered or raised.

And an old woman from the high hills of Mueller kept bringing me arrows until I was half-buried in them.

These I remember like I remember my father teaching me to cut down a man from horseback or giving me grief and wiping the blood on his face as he told me my fate.

In retrospect I have learned to distinguish what could have happened from what could not. At the time I was not so clever.

One day I heard a new sound. It was not unusual in intensity—but I realized I was hearing new voices. The ship had not put into any port. No one had come alongside. Obviously, then, they were letting slaves out of the cells and onto the deck. This meant we were nearing port—atrophied muscles must now be awakened so the slaves would make a good showing in the markets of Rogers and Dunn and Dark.

But that first day no one let me out, and I wondered why.

By the second day I reasoned that because I was to be sold for labor, it didn't matter if I seemed strong. I was to be a freak. I wondered grimly what my owners would think of me now. A new nose was growing alongside and partly joined to the old. On the left side of my head, three ears decorated my profile. And my body was a hodgepodge of arms and legs that had never been taught to walk or grasp. They thought they had a curiosity before. I would be a one-man circus now.

I could never tell anyone I was a Mueller. They might realize then that my condition was a sign of what brought Mueller its wealth in iron. They might realize why it seemed that in battle the Mueller army never seemed to shrink, despite the thousand cuts that even wooden weapons could inflict. I would have to pass myself off as a freak.

Above me, other slaves were walking, could see, could feel the sun and the wind. And I could not.

I began shouting. My voice was unaccustomed. I made little sense, I'm sure. But gradually I increased in volume, and my feeding hatch popped open.

"You want your ass kicked up your chest?" asked a voice I knew too well, though I had no idea who owned it.

"I'll do the ass-kicking!" I yelled back. My voice didn't have quite the effect it used to have on training fields when I maneuvered cavalry troops without the help of a caller. But it did well enough. Instead of a kick, I got another voice.

"Listen, Trash," he said, "up to now you've been a model slave. Don't start giving us shit except in your bucket, if you know what's good for you!"

"I'm grateful for your conciliatory attitude," I said. "I want to go on deck."

"No slaves on deck."

"There are at least ten slaves on deck right now!"

"They're farmers. You're a side show."

"I'll kill myself."

"Naked? In the dark?"

"I'll lie on my back and bit my tongue off and drown on the blood!" I shouted, and for a moment I meant it, though I knew perfectly well that my tongue would heal too damn fast. I must have sounded crazy, though, because a new voice came. It was the captain.

He spoke softly, and the threat in his voice was clear. "There's only one reason we ever let a slave on deck out of turn. It's for punishment."

"Punish me! Just do it in sunlight."

"The punishment usually begins with removal of the tongue."

I laughed. "What do you do for an encore?"

"We finish up by cutting off your balls." He meant it. But that's only a mildly frightening threat to a man who already has a spare pair of gonads. I had three pair now, and the extra testosterone must have given me an over-large shot of courage.

"You can fry them and feed them to me for breakfast! Just let me on deck!"

It wasn't entirely courage, of course. I knew my main value to them was as a freak. No one wants to see a freak that's been mutilated by men. Nature's mutilations only, please. They wouldn't harm me. And the thought of someone being on deck when I was stuck in a hole was the most outrageous provocation I had yet had in my life.

So I was not surprised to have ropes tossed down to me. I took them and held on with four arms as they pulled me up.

The intensity of their reaction surprised me, though I should have expected it: They had put a man with a large bosom into the cell. They pulled out a monster.

I couldn't see anything. The light was too dazzling, and it was hard enough finding my balance on legs that had not really stood up in months. Some of my legs had never stood up at all. I couldn't walk—I could only lurch from one side to the other, struggling for equilibrium.

They weren't helping. Their screams were deafening, and I kept hearing the word *devil* and others whose meaning I couldn't guess, except that the sailors were terribly frightened. Of me. The possibilities that created were enticing. I roared.

They answered with a uniform shriek, and I made some fumbling steps toward the loudest group of screamers. I was answered with an arrow in my arm.

I am a Mueller. The pain didn't stop me, and as for the arm, I had several others just as good—two, in fact, that were much better, since it was not an arm that I used much. I kept on advancing. And now the terror had turned to awe. An arrow had not made the monster pause.

The captain was shouting. Orders, I supposed, and I squinted against the light to try to see. The ocean was dazzling blue. The ship and everyone on it were invisible, shadows that flashed until I had to close my eyes again.

I heard someone coming, felt the vibration of the footsteps on the deck. I turned awkwardly, met the rush. It was then that I discovered I had grown an extra heart—his wooden knife found the one I was used to, and it didn't stop me. I only knew weaponless warfare with my two original arms, but rather than let the sailors notice that fact, I got my extras into the act. They made me fumble at it, but it only delayed me a moment, and in this case delay was rather to my benefit. I took my attacker apart and threw pieces of him to the waiting sailors. I heard vomiting. I heard praying. I heard freedom.

The captain's voice again. But this time conciliatory. Funny, in fact, but I refrained from laughing.

"Sir, whoever you are," he said, "remember that we saved your life from the sea when we brought you aboard."

I only squinted at him and waved my arms. I could vaguely see that he stepped back. They were afraid of me. Had good reason to be. The wound in my heart had already closed up. Oh, what fun we radical regeneratives can have in a pinch.

"Sir," he said, "whatever god you are or whatever god you serve, we entreat you—tell us what you want, and we'll give it to you, if you'll only go back into the sea."

Back into the sea was out of the question. I was a good swimmer

—with two arms and two legs. I had more ballast now, and a bit less coordination.

"Set me on the land," I said, "and we'll be even."

If I had been thinking well, or if I could have seen better, I would have attempted to tyrannize them a little longer and get to more friendly shores. But I couldn't see, until I was in the prow of the longboat, with six petrified crewmen jerkily coming to life whenever the swain commanded them to row, then turning back to stone, their eyes riveted on me. Then my sight came clear—but my back was to the shore.

We touched bottom, and I clumsily lifted myself over the prow and splashed through the water. When I found dry land I looked up and saw where I was.

I turned as quickly as I could, to see the longboat already nearly at the slaveship. There would be no calling them back. I had just cleverly forced them to help me commit suicide.

I stood, naked, on a beach a few hundred meters broad. Behind it rose the craggy, rough slopes of stone and sand that was called by Mueller's sailors "Sandwash." Behind it was the bitterest desert in the world. Better to surrender to an enemy than run aground here, where there were no paths, where boats never stopped, and where walking inland only took you deep into the unknown desert of Schwartz. Nothing lived. Not even the scrub of the wastes on the west shore of the Sleeve. Not even an insect. Nothing.

And it was afternoon, and the sun was hot. My skin, white as the clouds from my long confinement, already was burning. And without water, how long would I last?

If only I had kept my mouth shut in my comfortable, wonderful, well-watered cell. If only I had said things to dispel the crew's fear. If only I had been born a moose.

I walked because there was nothing else to do. Because old stories told of huge rivers in the center of Schwartz that sank beneath the desert before they escaped into other lands. Because I didn't want my skeleton to be discovered right on the shore, as if I hadn't had the guts to at least try to do something.

There was no wind.

By nightfall I was already breathlessly thirsty, excruciatingly tired. I had not got to the top of the rise; the sea looked ridiculously close. With so many limbs, I wasn't much of a climber. But I couldn't sleep, and I forced unready and unwilling muscles to take me farther in the darkness. The darkness was welcome, and cold came to the desert as a relief to the heat of the day. It was summer, or might as well have been, but the night was colder than I had thought possible in such a place, and I kept moving even after I wanted to sleep because movement kept me warmer.

When the sun rose, I was exhausted. But I had reached the top, and could look forward and see endless dunes of sand, with mountains in the distance here and there; I could look back and see, far in the distance, the bright blue ocean. There was no ship in sight. And on land, there was no shade—nowhere I could rest for the heat of the day.

So I walked, arbitrarily picking a mountain as my goal so that I would have one. It seemed to be as close as any, and as impossible to reach. I would die today, I suspected; I was fat from lack of exercise, weak from lack of hope.

Afternoon and I merely concentrated on moving forward. No thought of life or death now. Just step. And again.

And that night I slept in the sand, with no insects buzzing around my head because no insects were foolish enough to try to survive where I was.

I surprised myself. I woke up, and walked on. My point of death was farther off than I thought. But not much farther. My shadow was still on the morning side when I reached a place where the sand gave way to stone and a rough outcropping of rock. Whether it was a shoulder of a mountain I was too incurious to care. It had shade. And as I lay down in the shade my heart stopped beating and I gasped for breath and discovered that death was not so bad after all, if only it would come quickly, if only it wouldn't linger, if only I didn't have to lie there for an eternity before I was free to go.

schwartz

He leaned over me, and my eyes could not focus. But he was a man, and he was not a nightmare of Dinte or Turd or myself.

"Would you like to die?" he asked in a young voice, a serious voice. I considered the alternatives. If living meant another day on the desert like the ones I had already spent, the answer was yes. But then, this person (this hallucination), whoever he was, was alive. One could live on this desert.

"No," I said.

He did nothing. Just watched me.

"Water," I said.

He nodded. I forced myself to rise to lean on two elbows as he took a step away from me. Was he going for help? No. He stopped and squatted on the rock. He was naked and carried nothing with him—not even a water bottle. That meant water was close. Why was he waiting?

"Water," I repeated. He said nothing, didn't even nod this time. Just looked at the sand. I could feel my heart beating inside me—beating vigorously and well. It was hard to believe that just a short time ago it had stopped. Where had this boy come from? Why didn't he get water?

I looked at the sand where he was staring. It was moving.

It shifted sloppily to the left and right, then caved in in small patches, falling down, slipping into something, splashing softly, collapsing, until a circle about a meter and a half across was softly swirling water, black water that blinded me with reflected sunlight.

He looked at me. I awkwardly lifted myself (every muscle aching except my strong, youthful heart) and pulled myself to the water. It was still now. Still and cool and deep and good, and I plunged my head in and drank. I came up for air only when I had to.

At last I was satisfied, and I lifted myself and then let myself drop on the sand beside the water. I was too tired to wonder why sand should come up water, or how the boy had known it would. Too tired to wonder why now the water seeped down into the sand and left a dark stain that soon evaporated in the sun.

Too tired to answer clearly when the boy looked at my body and asked, "Why are you like that? So strange?"

"God knows I wish I weren't," I said, and then I slept again. Slept this time not expecting death but expecting, somehow, through a co-incidence of having been found right beside a spring in this waterless desert, to live.

When I woke again I had forgotten the boy entirely. Until I opened my eyes and saw his friends.

They were silent, sitting around me in a circle, a dozen sun-blackened men with sun-blonded hair, as naked as the boy had been. Their eyes were on me, unmoving. They were alive and so was I and I had no objections.

I would have spoken, would have asked them to shelter me, except that I was sidetracked. I noticed my body from the inside. Noticed that there was nothing to notice. Something was terribly wrong.

No. Something was terribly right.

There was no pulling on my left side where three legs tried to bal-ance two. There was no odd arching of my back to compensate for all the limbs awkwardly under me as I slept. There was no pinch of air painfully being drawn in through an extra nose.

From the inside, all I felt were two arms, two legs, the sex I had been born with, a normal face. Not even breasts. Not even that.

I raised my left hand (only one!) and touched my chest. Rounded only with muscle. Hard with muscle. I slapped myself on the chest, and my arm was alive and strong.

What was real? What was the dream? Had I not been confined in a cell on a ship for several months? Was that, too, a hallucination? If it was, how had I come here, I wondered, and I could not believe that I was, again, normal. It was then that I remembered the boy and the water that had come from the desert. This, too, was a dream, then. Impossible things were happening as I died. Dreams of water. Dreams of a whole normal body. Dreams of the dying. Time was being extended in my last remaining moments of life.

Except my heart was beating too strongly to ignore. And I felt as full of life as I had before I ever left Mueller. If this is death, give me more, I thought, and I asked them, "Did you cut them off?"

They didn't answer for a moment. Then one asked, "Cut?"

"Cut," I said. "To make me like this. Normal."

"Helmut said you wanted them off."

"They'll only grow back."

The man who was speaking to me looked puzzled. "I don't think so," he said. "We fixed that."

Fixed that. Undoing what a hundred generations of Muellers had tried to cure and couldn't. So this was what Schwartz had come to. The arrogance of savages.

I stopped myself in mid-contempt. Whatever they had done, it shouldn't have worked this way. When something was cut off a radical regenerative, it grew back, no matter what. Radical regeneratives grew back every impossible limb and added more until they died of sheer mass and unwieldiness. Yet when they cut my limbs off and my breasts and all the other extras, the wounds had healed without a scar, normally.

Had the water come boiling to the surface *on command?* The thought jolted me, the more because it seemed to have no relation to my previous thoughts. My mind had put it together before I knew. If what I was seeing and feeling was real, these people, these Schwartzes, had something too valuable to believe.

"How did you do it?" I asked.

"From the inside," the man answered, beaming. "We only work from the inside. Do you want to continue your walk now?"

It was an absurd question. I had been dying of thirst on the desert, a helpless monster, and they had saved my life and cured my deformity. Now did they expect me to wander on through the sand, as if I had some errand that their intervention had delayed?"

"No," I said.

They sat, silently. What were they waiting for? In Mueller, a man didn't wait a minute before inviting a stranger—particularly a helpless one—into his home for shelter, unless he thought the man was an enemy, in which case he let off an arrow at the first opportunity. But these people—waited.

Different people, different customs. "Can I stay with you?" I asked.

They nodded. But they said nothing more.

I became impatient. "Will you take me to your home, then?"

They looked at each other. They shrugged.

"What do you mean?" they asked.

I cursed in my mind. A common language all over the planet, and they couldn't understand a simple word like *home*.

"Home," I said. "Where you live."

They looked around again, and the spokesman said, "We are alive now. We do not go someplace to live."

"Where do you go to get out of the sun?"

"At night, the sun goes away," said the man, incredulous.

This was getting nowhere. But I was surprised and gratified that I was physically up to the challenge of conversing with them. I would live—I was whole and strong and talkative again, that was plain.

"I want to stay with you. I can't live here on the desert alone."

Several of them—the ones who seemed oldest, but who could tell? —nodded sagely. Of course, they seemed to say. There are people like that, aren't there.

"I'm a stranger to the desert. I don't know how the hell anyone survives here, but I need help. Perhaps you can take me to the edge of the desert. To Sill, perhaps, or Wong."

A few of them giggled. "Oh, no," the spokesman said, "we would rather not. But you can live with us, and stay with us, and learn from us, and be one of us."

But no visits to the borders? Fine, for now. Fine, until I knew how to survive in this hell where they seemed to be quite comfortable. And in the meantime, I was delighted to live with them and learn from them—the alternative being death.

"Yes," I said. "I'll be one of you."

"Good," said the spokesman. "We examined you. You've got good brains."

I was amused and slightly offended. I was the product of the finest education the most civilized Family in the West could provide, and these savages had examined my brain and decided it was good. "Thanks," I murmured. "And what about food?"

They shrugged again, puzzled. It was going to be a long night.

"I am with you today," said the boy who had found me. "I am told to give you what you need."

"Breakfast," I said.

"What is that?" he answered.

"Food. I'm hungry."

He shook his head. "No. You're not."

I was about to take his head off for impertinence when I realized that, despite having eaten nothing the day before, and for a while before that, I wasn't hungry at all. So I decided not to labor the point. The sun was already hot, and it was barely dawn. My skin, which was fair and burned easily at the beginning of every summer, was already browned and able to endure the direct sunshine. And another day had come with my body as it should be. I jumped up (had I ever felt this good upon rising?) and leaped from the rock where I had slept into the sand below, bellowing. I ran a large circle, then awkwardly turned a somersault in the sand, landing sprawled on my back.

The boy laughed.

"Name!" I shouted. "What's your name!"

"Helmut," he answered.

"And my name's Lanik!" I called back. He grinned broadly, then jumped down and ran to me. He stopped only a meter off, and I snaked out a hand to trip him. I am not used to men anticipating my attacks, but Helmut jumped in the air the exact fraction of a centimeter required to make me miss him. Then he lightly jumped over me, tapping my hip with both feet before I could react.

"Quick little bugger, aren't you?" I said.

"Slow old bastard, aren't you?" he answered, and I lunged at him. This time he let me engage, and we wrestled for fifteen minutes or so, my weight and strength making it impossible for him to pin me, his speed getting him out of my grasp when I had him in holds no one had ever been able to resist before.

"We're a match?" he asked.

"I want you," I said, "in my army."

"What's an army?"

In my world, up to then, that was akin to asking, "What's the sun?"

"What is this?" I demanded. "You don't know about food, about breakfast, about armies—"

"We are not civilized," he said. Then he flashed a broad grin and took off running. I had done that as a child, forcing governors, trainers, and teachers to chase wherever I went. Now I was the follower, and I scrambled after him, up rocky hills and skimming down the faces of sand dunes. The sun was hot and I was pouring with sweat when I finally ran around a rock he had passed only a moment before, to have him jump on my shoulders from above. "Ride, horse! Ride!" he shouted.

I reached up and pulled him off—he was lighter than his size would indicate. "Horses," I said. "You know horses?"

He shrugged. "I know that civilized people ride horses. What's a horse?"

"What's a rock?" I answered, in exasperation.

"Life," he answered.

"What kind of answer is that? Rock is dead if anything is!"

His face went dark. "They told me you are a child, and so I, who choose to be a child, should teach you. But you are too stupid to be a child."

I am not used to being called stupid. But in the last few months I had had ample reason to realize that I would not always be treated like the best soldier in Mueller, and I held my tongue. Besides, he had said *choose.*

"Teach me then," I said.

"We begin," he said instantly, as if he could teach me only as soon as I asked, "with rock." He ran his finger delicately along the face of the rock. "The rock lives," he said.

"Yeah," I answered.

"We stand on his skin," he said. "Underneath he seethes with hot blood, like a man. Here on his skin, he is dry. Like man. But he is kind, and will do good to a man, if the man will only speak to him."

Religion again. Except—and always it nagged at me, though I tried to put it out of my mind—they had cured me.

"How do you—uh, speak to rock?" I asked.

"We hold him in our mind. And if he knows we are not rock killers, he will help us."

"Show me," I said.

"Show you what?"

"How you talk to the rock."

He shook his head. "I can't show you, Lanik-e. You must do it yourself."

I imagined myself in animated conversation with a pebble and consigned myself to the madhouse, where I had recently been. Reality was still up for grabs to me, and I wondered if it was I who was hearing wrong, not he who was speaking foolishly. "I don't know how."

"I know," he said, nodding helpfully.

"What happens when you talk to the rock?" I asked.

"He listens. He answers."

"What does he say?"

"It can't be said by mouths."

I was getting nowhere. It was like a game. Nothing could be done for me unless I asked for it, and even then if I asked in the wrong way, I wouldn't get it. Like food—only as soon as I thought of it, I realized I still wasn't hungry.

"Look, Helmut, what kinds of things will the rock *do?*"

He smiled. "What could a man need from rock?"

"A path up a high cliff," I said, taking the first thing that came to mind. The sheer rock face beside us was formidable—I had wondered, briefly, how Helmut scaled it.

Now he was staring intently at the rock, as he had stared at the sand when I first met him. And as I watched him, I heard a faint rustling sound. I looked around, and sand was pouring from a small pocket on the face of the cliff—in a spot where no pocket had been. The sand stopped. I reached over and brushed it out, put my toes in it, and raised myself. I reached up, could find no handhold above me.

"Hold still," said the boy, and suddenly sand fell away under my fingers, making a handhold. It was as if a hundred small spiders had suddenly erupted from the rock, and I pulled my hand away, brushed off the sand.

Helmut clicked his tongue. "No. You must climb. Do not reject the gift." He was serious. And so I climbed, new handholds and footholds appearing where I needed them, until I was at the top.

I sat, breathless, not from the climb, but from what could only seem to me to be magic. Helmut stood far below, looking up at me. I was not ready to come down. My hands were trembling. "Come up!" I called.

He did not use my handholds. Instead, he went to a face where the cliff was smooth and unbroken, and crawled quickly up it. His toes had little contact with the rock—just his knees and hands. I leaned over the edge watching him, and felt a terrible vertigo, as if gravity had switched directions and he was on level ground, while I clung, incredibly, to a cliff.

"What is this place!" I said, or rather whispered, when he reached the top and sat beside me. "What kind of people are you?"

"We are savages," he said, "and this is the desert."

"No!" I shouted. "No evasions! You know what I'm asking! You do things that human beings simply can't do!"

"We don't kill," he said.

"That doesn't explain anything."

"We don't kill animals," he said. "We don't kill plants. We don't kill rock. We don't kill water. We leave all beings alive, and they also leave us alive. We are savages."

"How can you kill a rock?"

"By cutting him," he said. He seemed to shudder.

"Rock is pretty tough," I answered, feeling superior again. "It doesn't feel pain, or so I've heard."

"Rock is alive," he said, "from the skin to his deepest heart. Here on the surface, he holds us up. Some of his skin he sheds and peels as we do, in sand and gravel and boulders. But it is still part of him. When men cut the rock, however, it no longer falls where it should; they take the rock and make false mountains of it, and that rock is dead. It is no longer part of him. He has lost it until, over the centuries, he can break it back into sand. He could kill you all, by sneezing," said Helmut angrily, "but he does not. Because he respects even evil life. Even civilized life."

Helmut did not sound like a child.

"But he *can* kill," said Helmut, "if the need is great and the time is right. When the civilized men of Sill decided they must own more of this desert, they came with armies to kill us. Many women lived there, the peaceful sleepers, and the men of Sill killed them. So we held a council, Lanik, and we spoke to the rock, and he agreed with us that this was a time for justice."

He stopped. "And?" I prodded.

"And he swallowed them."

I imagined the horsemen of Sill out in the desert sand, suddenly finding the grains heaving and sifting under them, their horses sinking, their footing impossible. And the sand closing over their heads as they screamed and choked on sand and swallowed sand and were swallowed by sand until their bones were rubbed clean.

"Sill has never sent an army into the desert again," said Helmut. "That was when we knew we were savages. Civilized men do not value rocks above men. But then, savages do not kill sleeping women. Do they?"

"Is this true?" I asked.

"Did you climb this cliff?"

I lay back and stared into the blue sky, where not a cloud passed.

"How? Why do *you* know how to communicate with the rock—" I couldn't finish. It sounded stupid.

"You're ashamed," he said.

"Damn right," I answered.

"You're a child. But the rock is easiest to speak to. It's simple. It's large. So large that you can grasp it easily. Our children learned this first."

"Learned?"

"When we had children. Now that no one dies, why should we add to our numbers? We have no need. And some of us have chosen to be children forever, so that the older ones can be amused, and because we would rather play than think deep thoughts."

If someone had told me this while I was safely enwombed in the castle at Mueller, I would have laughed. I would have sneered. I would have hired the man who told me as a clown. But I had climbed the cliff. I had drunk the water. My body had been healed.

"Teach me, Helmut," I said. "I want to speak to the rock."

"Carbon is subtle," he said. "It holds to everything, and builds strange chains. It is softer than the rock, but it can make small lives, where rock can only live in a huge ball that spins around the sun. It's hard to speak to the carbon. It takes many voices to be heard by stone so subtle."

"But you spoke to me?"

"We found the place that had gone wrong. It was on your longest chains, and we taught them how to lie differently, so that they only heal what has been lost, and not what is still whole. We thought at first that you were like us, because your chains were different. We didn't have this healing in our bodies—we had to heal every scratch, one at a time. We liked what you had done, and so we changed each other, too, and now we all heal like you do."

So much for the secret of Mueller, I thought. "Why hadn't you done it before?"

"We don't do very much to the carbon chains. They're subtle. They can cause problems. There are only a few changes we make. But to pay you for your healing change, we gave you the life change."

It was near dark, and we still perched on the pillar of rock, the cliff our only exit to the sand below. "What's the life change?" I asked.

"Civilized men kill because they have to to live. To get energy, they have to eat plants or kill animals. With killing so common, they have no respect for life at all."

"And what do you do?"

"We are savages. We take our energy from the same source as the plants." And he pointed to where the sky was still light from the sun, which had dipped below the mountains to the west.

"From the sun," I said.

"That's why you aren't hungry," he said.

And he talked on into the darkness, and I understood what Schwartz had achieved. A geologist, in a geologist's paradise, and his children after him, with a profound respect for rock, an ever deeper understanding of rock until they awakened, not the earth itself, but that part of their minds which could grasp the structures and change them. The language was mystical, but not a mystery. They understood even DNA as the experts of Mueller couldn't grasp it. And yet the price of their knowledge was savagery. They could use no tools, make no homes, write no language. If they all died and archaeologists came to this desert, they would find nothing but corpses, and marvel that animals with human shape could be so utterly unintelligent.

"How can I learn to speak to the rock?" I asked.

Helmut's voice came from the darkness. "You must leap from this cliff in darkness."

He was serious. But that was impossible. "I'll be killed."

"That's been known to happen," Helmut said. Was he amused? I couldn't see his face. "But you must do it soon. Dissent rises in a few minutes."

"Why will killing myself help me talk to the rock?" I tried to make a joke of it. Helmut was too serious.

"You have killed, Lanik," he said. "You must hold yourself for judgment to see if you were innocent of malice. If the sand receives you gently, the rock will make himself known to you."

"But—" I said, and then could not say that I was afraid because I wasn't sure, even now, if I fully believed all this; because I was unsure whether I was innocent of malice. I had relished the thought of warfare, and while I had never killed a man in battle, I had approved of my father's strategies and longed to be the Mueller and better his achievement. Was that still in my heart? And while I had tried not to kill, two dead men on a road in Allison and a soldier's body beneath the trees of Nkumai and the corpse of my would-be murderer on a Singer ship and the body of my own hapless double all testified that I was capable of murder, or at least of killing. Where were my instincts?

"I should tell you," said Helmut, "that there is no other way down from this tower of rock."

"What about the handholds?"

"They will not hold you. They're already gone. You will jump, or you will stay here forever. And if you wait, and don't jump in darkness now, before Dissent rises, your jump will inevitably be to your death."

"You don't leave much to chance, do you, little boy?" I was angry —I had been trapped.

"I'm a boy in spirit, Lanik, but I was old when your father's grandfather first learned not to piss in the family drinking water. And I tell you that I believe that if you jump, the sand will receive you. But you have to have enough trust in yourself to leap. If you know that you're a murderer, you might as well stay here. You won't starve to death."

I stood. I knew that the edge of the tower was only a few meters away in any direction. But I couldn't step.

"Lanik," Helmut whispered, and his voice was young and innocent again. "Lanik, I believe the sand will hold you." And a cool, gentle hand grasped the inside of my thigh as I stood, trembling, because of what I had to do. "I want the sand to hold you."

"So do I," I said.

"Then jump while it's still dark."

And he took his hand away and I walked briskly toward the edge and suddenly a step in the air and I was no longer in Schwartz, I was in Nkumai and I had stepped wrong in the darkness and now I was falling, endlessly, through the silent trees and everything else was a dream, all these months were a dream and I had fallen in Nkumai and was going to die and I refused to scream but let the wind rush by me and twist me in the air as my stomach rose to my throat and my bladder would not be constrained and death was a thousand knives of soil below me that would carve and break me when I touched them and then I landed in the soft embrace of the sand, which gently parted and sifted and swirled around me, splashed around me warmly, and closed over my head. And there in the embrace of the sand I felt the throbbing heart of the earth, felt the rhythm of the currents of boiling rock beneath me, and heard in the most hidden place in my ears a strange song of eons of itching torment, trying to find a comfortable way to settle down and sleep, while continents danced back and forth on my skin and oceans froze and fell. And while I heard the song of the largest dance, still I could hear the small melodies of shifting sand and falling stones and settling soil. I heard the agony of rock being cut and torn in a thousand places on the surface of my skin, and I wept at the thousand deaths of stone and soil and the plants that thinly gripped life between the stone and the sky.

Armies thundered on my skin, death in every heart, with dead trees carved to make tools to build more death. Only the voices of men are louder than the voices of trees, and where wheat whispers as it dies, the death scream of a man's mind is the strongest cry the earth can hear. I felt blood soak into my skin, and I no longer wept; I longed to die, to be free of the incessant crying.

I screamed.

And the sand sifted by my ears and swept between my legs, and as it pressed against my face I separated myself from the self whose ears had heard for me, and I asked (without words, for there is no mouth that can shape that language) for the sand to lift me to the surface.

I rose through the warm sand and it broke above me. I spread my arms and legs upon the surface of the sand, and it bore me. I had fallen, it seemed, from the pinnacle of rock to the heart of the earth, and now I coasted on the surface, floated on the still wave of sand.

I smiled, and Helmut stood over me, smiling also.

"Did he sing to you?"

I nodded.

"And he found you clean."

"Or cleaned me," I said, and then shuddered to remember the screams of the dying. I looked at the tower of rock I had fallen from. It was no more than two meters high. My eyes widened, and Helmut laughed.

"We raised it," he said. "And if you hadn't jumped, we would have broken it and let you fall."

"Nice folks," I said, but I was too full to be bitter, and it didn't surprise me when Helmut knelt and touched my chest and then embraced me. He wept on my skin, the water standing in drops that soon evaporated. "I love you," he whispered, "and I'm glad you were received."

"So am I," I said, and we slept, his cool skin pressed against mine as the sand had pressed, not to arouse or satisfy, but to express; and as we slept we dreamed together, and I learned Helmut's true voice, and I loved him.

I could have stayed in Schwartz forever. I wanted to. They wanted me to. I learned quickly, and while they had fixed the most obvious signs of my radical regeneration, my body was still determined to be unusual. There is a part of the brain that holds the functions that lets the Schwartzes speak to stone; as I learned to use it, my body developed it, let it grow. My skull bulged a little upward of and behind my ears to make room, and the spokesman finally told me, "You are beyond us now."

I was surprised. "You do things I can't dream of doing."

"Together," he said. "Alone we aren't as strong as you."

"Then make yourselves like I am."

"There are secrets that the carbon chains can keep even from us."

And that was that. Yet it didn't occur to me, not for weeks, that this gave me an advantage that would set me free. For the simple reason that I didn't want to be free.

But when I spoke to the rock, I learned many things that brought me to myself. The wars were continuing, and as I learned to endure the agony of the many deaths, I also learned to study the wars and see where the battles were being fought. When I talked to the rock, the earth's skin became my skin, and I learned to feel where the cries were coming from. And the battles were at first on the plain between Allison and the headwaters of the Rebel River, called Rio de Janeiro. Then the battles moved to the hill country of Robles, and northwest on the confluence of the Myron and the Rebel where the Rebel River ceases to be called Swoop and begins to be called Mueller. And then the war was in Wizer, a land my father had conquered, and that meant that the Nkumai had swept all before them and were at the gates of Mueller.

It didn't matter now that I knew the secret of the Nkumai's iron. It didn't matter that my father had sent me away and my brother, Dinte, wanted to kill me. I was no longer a radical regenerative, and I was twice the soldier my father was and by far a better general than Dinte. I was needed, if my Family was to endure.

At first the thought of going to war was repugnant to me, but my Family's need tore at me, and I began to ask the rock. I asked whether one life could be more important than another, and the rock said no. I asked whether it was right to end one life if by ending it, many others could be saved. The rock said yes. And I asked if loyalty meant anything to the forces of the universe, and the rock wept.

Loyalty? What but loyalty made the rock respond to the call of the Schwartzes? The earth understood trust, and I asked if it was good for me to go back and lead my Family. And the rock said yes.

This conversation was not the product of one night's sleep under the sand, however. It took many nights and many sleeps, and the months passed before I knew that I could go home; that I must go home.

"You cannot go home," said the spokesman.

"The rock spoke to me and told me I should go."

"The rock told you it was good for you to go. Good for you. Good for your family. But not good for us."

"Good for the earth."

"The blood soaks into the earth the same no matter who wields the civilized tools," said the spokesman. "If you can go, it will be good. But I can't let you go, *we* can't let you go, you've taken all we have to teach and now you can use it to destroy and kill in the name of loyalty."

"I swear I'll never use what you've taught me to kill."

"If you kill you'll use what we taught you."

"Never."

"Because every man who dies at your hand will scream into your soul forever, Lanik."

It was something to give me pause.

But when the battle moved to the lowlands of Cramer, not three hundred kilometers from Mueller-on-the-River, the capital, I could wait no longer. Helmut and I were playing in the pinnacles of a knife-like ridge of mountains, doing acrobatics a thousand meters above the sand, when I pulled the rock out from under him and he fell.

The rock caught him on the ledge a hundred meters below me and far above the desert.

"You bastard!" he shouted.

"I have to!" I shouted back. "If you warn the council, they can stop me!"

"You said you loved me!"

I did. I do. But I said nothing. He tried to crawl up the rock. But I forbade the rock to hold him, and I was stronger. He tried to make handholds in the rock. But I was stronger. He tried to throw himself from the ledge to the sand below, but the rock would not let him jump because I said so. And I was stronger.

The ridge pointed northwest, and I went northwest. When it ended, I plunged down into the sand, and ran all day and all night, forbidding my body to sleep. I went by the fastest way any Schwartz could travel, and because none was faster than I, no pursuit could overtake me.

It took eight days (and I slept while running, for my mind had to have sleep even when my body didn't) and I reached a place where clouds skitted through the sky and where occasional clumps of grass poked from crevasses in rocks, and I was out of Schwartz. It should have been a relief, and I was glad enough to see green instead of endless yellows and greys and browns of the desert, but I regretted leaving, so much that I stopped and turned around and almost started back.

I remembered my father's face. I remembered him saying, "Lanik, I wish to God there were something I could do." I heard his voice plead, "The body is ruined. Will the mind still serve me? Will the man still love his father?"

Yes, you land-hungry bastard, I thought. You're against something you're no match for. And I'll come. I'm coming. And I turned back around and headed north into the high country of Sill.

The land had been wasted by war.

Burnt-over fields were accented by the shells of houses and piles of ashes that had once been humbler huts. I walked kilometers of ruin, in what had to be marginal farmland at best, this close to the desert. What purpose could be served by such destruction? No great military objectives lay nearby. All it could achieve was the starvation of the people.

Yet I knew the people of Nkumai (as well as anyone could know them in their endless intertwining lies) and such destruction wasn't in their nature, not the people who stood at the lips of their treehouses and sang in the morning. Even their endless, fumbling bureaucracy and the hypocritical denial that they bought and sold for profit—these were more symptoms of good intention than of deep-seated corruption. And even greed would hold these fields intact. Only vicious, mindless hate could make someone want to destroy the people of a country instead of conquer them.

And who could hate even the simple-mindedly violent people of Sill? My father had let them alone, even when he conquered their two neighbors, because for all their boisterous village life and boastful foreign policy, they were harmless.

I got angrier the farther I walked.

At last I reached land that was watered by rivers and irrigation, and here there were people working to rebuild the canals. New houses were going up, makeshift homes to keep the rain off. I had lost track of seasons—the rains would be coming soon.

And it occurred to me that I was naked, and nudity was frowned on in this part of the world. The idea of clothing seemed foreign to me—I had been without it for a year, at least, ever since I fell from the birdnet in Nkumai. But how does a man get clothing when he has neither friends nor money, and people stare at him and avoid him when they see him coming?

The problem was solved for me. I slept, this time with body as well as mind, in the grass growing along the bank of the River Wong, and when I awoke three women were staring at me. I moved slowly, so as not to alarm them. "Greetings," I said, and they nodded. So much for conversation, I thought. "I mean you no harm," I said.

They nodded again. "We know."

I guess in my unclothed condition it was no secret I wasn't in the mood for rape. I couldn't think what to say to them next, except the obvious. "I need clothing."

They looked at each other in puzzlement.

"I don't have any money," I said, "but I can promise you I'll pay you within a month."

"Then you aren't the Naked Man," one of them murmured.

"Is there only one?" I asked.

"He walks through the fields from the desert. Some say he will take vengeance on our enemies."

So I had been noticed, and word had spread. Not at all odd that such people would take the mysterious and make of it a solution to their problems. "I'm the one," I said. "I came from Schwartz. I'm going to find the army that did all this."

"Will you kill them?" whispered the youngest, who was far along in pregnancy.

"I will stop them from killing," I promised, wondering if I really could. "But in the meantime, I need clothing. It's time for me to dress."

They nodded, and walked away. They were in no hurry, and in the gently rolling country side they were soon out of sight. I plunged into the water to wait for them, and amused myself by lying on the bottom of the river, watching the fish. Everything was ravaged above the surface of the water, but in the slow current of the River Wong the fish never noticed.

I realized I had been underwater a long time, surfaced, and began breathing again. No sooner had I brought my head into the air than a woman nearby screamed, and answering shouts brought others on the run. Again I realized I had fallen into the trap of thinking and acting like a Schwartz. I had to stop doing things that other people couldn't do.

"He was under there all this time," the woman was saying to the two-score people who crowded around her, glancing frequently at me, where I stood in the water. "He was under there all the time and I was here for an hour, for a whole hour."

"Nonsense," I said. "I couldn't have been under there for more than fifteen minutes."

They looked at me with respect and awe (and not a little fear) and the pregnant woman held out an armful of clothing. I walked out of the water, and they stared at me, as if they expected something unusual. I almost laughed to remember the way the sailors on the Singer ship had reacted to the way I looked before the Schwartzes cured me. If they could see me now—in full possession of the sort of power the sailors had only imagined me to have before. Yet the way these people looked at me reminded me of my shyness about nudity when I was young and in Mueller. I dressed quickly, not waiting for my skin and hair to dry.

"Thank you," I said when I was dressed.

"We are honored," said a man who seemed to be in charge—an old man, and I realized that there were no men of arms-bearing age.

"Your sons are all off to war?"

"There is no war anymore," the headman said.

The pregnant woman agreed, soberly. "For Sill, there is no war."

"We're Nkumai now," said the headman.

I looked at them, all nodding in agreement. "Is that so? Then what enemy do you want me to kill?"

They were silent. Until one old woman cried out bitterly, with tears in her eyes, "Nkumai! Kill the Nkumai! For God's sake, if you have any power at all—"

And others took up the cry. "Kill the Nkumai! For our sons, for our homes, for our land, kill the black devils—"

I could hear the song of hate and death in their hearts, and I nodded softly and walked on.

"What's your name!" the pregnant woman shouted after me.

I turned and called out, "Lanik Mueller."

The crying and shouting stopped. They looked terror-stricken.

They silently left me and went to their homes. Except for the old woman, who spat.

Alone, I wondered what in the world there was about my name that should arouse such hatred or fear or whatever had made them leave. I'd been out of circulation for a year, throughout the whole war. There wasn't time to ponder the question, though. I headed north again, bearing a little west, on my way to Mueller-on-the-River.

There were patches the Nkumai had missed, places where the green was deep and the harvest would be rich. But now as I ran I saw no one. Had the word spread ahead of me? (And how had the stories of the Naked Man passed me, since I travelled all day and most of the night? The stories of Rumor as an evil bird that flies faster than sound must be true.) Whatever they feared and hated about Lanik Mueller, it kept them out of sight. A good thing I didn't get hungry (though now as I passed wheatfields and vegetable gardens my mouth remembered the taste and I wished for the food, though I had no need for it); no one was offering handouts.

The River Sill was two days behind me when I saw another person. Or persons. I felt the pounding of hooves before I saw them. They were coming from the north. From Mueller. And when they came into sight, I recognized the banner of the Army of the East. The commander would be Mancik, my godfather. But Mancik wasn't with them, though the commander's banner was there, and I knew he had died. If I'd had a knife, I would have given him grief, but I had no weapon, and after a few moments I had other things on my mind.

I didn't know the commander, nor did I know the soldiers who leaped from their horses and bound me. I consented to the binding partly because I was confused and partly because I was outnumbered. There's a limit to how many body parts even a reformed radical regenerative ran renew. And they looked willing to take me apart.

"I am told," said the commander, "to bring you to the capital alive."

"Then I won't hinder you," I answered. "That's where I was going."

This apparently made them angry. Two soldiers struck me at once, and I dazed for a moment. "I'm Lanik Mueller," I said, spitting out the words, "and I won't be treated like this!"

The commander looked at me coldly. "After the way you've

treated this land, any way we treated you would be far kinder than you deserve." And he looked for a moment, sadly, around the wasted fields.

"I didn't do this," I said, perplexed that he could think I did.

"Of all traitors who have ever lived, Lanik Mueller, there must be a special place in hell reserved for you."

"I've been to hell," I said. "It's a much nicer place than this."

And then they stopped conversing with me, threw me over a saddle, strapped my legs to the stirrups, and left me to find my balance as best I could with bound arms on a galloping horse. They rode madly across the fields, as if they hoped (and I'm sure they did) that my horse would fall, would shatter me, would crush me into the ashes that once had been grain.

The slap of hard leather boots rang out in the stone halls of my father's palace, and I was brought in brutally and thrown down on the floor. I had seen the scene before, but from the other point of view, as men accused of treason were prepared for trial. I knew that the trial was a mere formality. The charge was so serious it was never brought unless guilt was certain.

Yet my thoughts kept wandering. As they marched me through the corridors, held me in the small cell while the court assembled, I had kept looking at the dead stone of the walls, realizing how much death this place had cost the earth. If I said as much to anyone, it would be taken as madness. Living stone? But I spoke in my mind and sang the song of the rock, and felt the resonation. Far under the castle, the stones were listening. They would hear, the living stones would know, if my blood were shed.

The punishment for treason is drawing and quartering the living man. Women are decapitated first. It's grisly, but I always thought of it as a fine deterrent.

I arose from the floor and stood.

"Kneel!" shouted Harkint, the Captain of the Guard (he used to race me on horseback through the streets of the city). I turned to him, and said, coldly, because trials like most of royal life are theatrics, and I could not help but play my part, "I am royalty, Harkint, and I stand before the throne."

This quieted him, and now the court settled into the steady business of hate and fear. What had I done—or what did they think I had done?

My father looked old. It was for his sake I had returned. Now he looked weary and sick at heart, and he said, "Lanik Mueller, there's little point in a trial. You know and we know why you're here. You're guilty, so let's end this shabby business."

I didn't relish dying without knowing what for (and every delay is a promise of life), so I said, "It's my right to hear the charges against me."

"If we listed them all," said my father, "I couldn't stop the people here from killing you."

"Try a brief summary, then.'"

"Brief," said my father, and old Swee read out in a ringing voice:

"The crimes of Lanik Mueller: Leading the Nkumai armies into battle against the armies of Mueller. Destroying fields and homes of citizens in Mueller and dependent Families. Betraying the secret of regeneration so that our enemies now hack the bodies of our soldiers to pieces on the field, so they die. Plotting to undo the succession and take the rightful heir from the throne." Swee looked bitter and the gathered court shouted in outrage as each charge was read.

"I didn't do any of this," I said, looking my father in the eye.

"You've been seen by a thousand witnesses," said my father.

A soldier stepped forward in rage. "I saw you myself, when you cut off both my arms and made me come here to tell the Mueller that you planned to drink his blood!"

I did that?

"There are others who knew you who saw you leading the Nkumai armies. We've heard enough now. You're guilty, and I sentence you to—"

"No!" I shouted. "I have a right to speak!"

"A traitor has no rights!" shouted a soldier.

"I'm innocent!"

"If you're innocent," cried my father, "every whore in Mueller is a virgin!"

"I have a right to be heard, and I will speak!"

They fell silent then, and I tried to say the ideas and explanations as they came into my mind. Because I was realizing things and putting them together as I went along, I sounded as if I were making up a story. But to the best of my knowledge, I told them the truth.

I told them that I had gone to Nkumai, but my subterfuge had been discovered only moments after I found the secret of what they sold to get iron. I told them of my escape, of the disembowelment, and of the echo of myself that had been regenerated from my own gut. I described my imprisonment on a Singer ship and how the Schwartzes had cured me (I said nothing of how, or what I had learned), and how I had come as quickly as I could to warn my father of the danger.

As to the person who claimed to be me and fooled others into thinking he was, I could only guess that he was my double; that he had not died, but had been found by the Nkumai. "I was careless. I should have destroyed the body. But I was not thinking clearly, and most Muellers would have died from those wounds." They must have trained him, I speculated, and he would have had all my native abilities. No wonder people believed he was Lanik Mueller—right down to the genes, he was.

And then I had explained everything I could think to explain, and I stopped talking.

What effect had my explanation had? Little enough. Most of the people were still hostile, openly disbelieving, eager for my death. But here and there, especially among the older men, there was a face that looked thoughtful. And when I looked at my father, I knew (or was it wishful thinking) that he believed me.

But it was not, I realized suddenly, up to my father.

I had hardly noticed Ruva and Dinte, but now they both came up to confer with my father. And Ruva was still talking to him when Dinte stepped forward and spoke directly to me.

"Apparently you think we're fools, Lanik," he said. "But never in all the history of radical regeneration has anyone formed an entire duplicate of himself."

"Nobody's had his guts torn out and strewn across the countryside, either!"

"And how, Lanik, did the Schwartzes cure you? Desert people, yes? And they can do what none of our geneticists can manage?"

"I know it's hard to believe—"

"What's hard to believe is that you could tell us all this with a straight face, dear brother. No one has ever come out of the Schwartz Desert alive. No one has ever done any of these heroic deeds you claim to have done. What people *have* done is see you at the head of the enemy's army. I saw you myself, when I was commanding the Army of the South in Cramer, and you waved to me and shouted some obscenity. Don't pretend you don't remember."

"I'd hardly be the first to shout an obscenity at you, Dinte," I said, and to my surprise there were a few chuckles in the court. Not enough to hint that I had any friends. But enough to prove that Dinte had some enemies.

And now my father interrupted. "Dinte," he said, "you're being undignified." But I heard contempt in my father's voice. The contempt turned to some other emotion when he spoke to me:

"Lanik Mueller, your defense is implausible and the testimony of a thousand men is unarguable. I sentence you to be drawn and quartered alive on the playing field by the river tomorrow at noon and may your soul if you have one rot in hell."

He got up to go. I cried out after him, "Father! If all this was true, why in the name of God would I have given myself up to you?"

He turned slowly and looked me in the eye. "Because even the devil gives some justice to his victims, when they're beyond all help."

And he left the court. The soldiers took me then, and because I had been sentenced to die they spent the afternoon and evening torturing me, and of that I prefer not to speak.

ensel

I was not bleeding anymore, but I was still in pain, and more painful was the memory of the hatred of the soldiers. I knew only a few of them, but those had always been kind to me, and some of them had been my friends since I was a child. Now they delighted in my pain, wanted me to suffer, left (and said) that nothing I went through could equal the punishment I deserved. Their loathing stung, worse because I didn't deserve it and yet had no hope of proving my innocence.

So I lay in darkness in the dead stone cell where they at last let me rest until my death the next day. My wounds healed quickly, and I tried to think of a way to escape. But I admit my thinking wasn't good. I had come too recently from Schwartz, and still found myself as maddeningly disdainful of normal concerns as they were. No one had fed me since I came to Mueller, but I wasn't hungry. No one had offered me water, but I felt no thirst. And since I could ignore pain as it subsided, what was there to remind me that I had to act quickly, act immediately if I was to save my own life?

Save it for what?

My purpose in Schwartz had been to come warn my Family. The warning was a little late, and no one wanted messages from me anyway. And they had locked me in a prison of dead stone, so I couldn't even speak to the rock and sink into the soil and escape.

I could kill myself, of course, but my natural aversion to that was abetted by the fact that I could not bear to be guilty of adding that much pain to the earth. Rock bears enough murders without the scream of the self-murderer's death.·

There was a patter of light footsteps outside the door of my cell. The bar lifted, and the door, with difficulty, swung out.

"Lanik," said a voice in the darkness, and then Saranna was holding me and weeping. "Lanik," she said, "they even put out your eyes."

"They're growing back," I answered. "It's so good to be home."

"Oh, Lanik, we've been so afraid for you!"

It was as if I had never been away. Her hands fit exactly on my back in patterns that long habit told me were where hands that size belonged. She held me with a pressure that I had last felt yesterday (had last felt a year ago) and her breath, her skin as her cheek brushed mine, the scent of her, even the wild wisps of hair tickling my nose—

I held tightly to her because for a moment she took away the nightmare of the last few days and I was Ensel Mueller's son Lanik, heir to the throne and one damned happy young man. Damned.

"Why did you come?" I asked.

"You have friends, Lanik. Some of us believe you."

"Then you must be insane. There's nothing believable about my story."

"This isn't the court. This is a woman who has known you very well for several years and doesn't want you drawn and quartered tomorrow. Come with me."

"You don't think you can get me out of this prison, do you?"

"I can with friends," she said, and so I followed her.

She held my hand and led me through the corridors. She squeezed once when we reached steps going up, twice when the steps went down. We were as soundless as feet can be, and I, for one, didn't breathe. It was easier that way. My eyes were healing well; already they had their round shape; but it would take time for the nerves to heal properly, for vision to be fully restored. It was frightening to be blind and moving, much worse than when I was locked in darkness in the Singer ship. There I had walls close by. Here I never knew what was ahead, had to trust my life to a woman who, until tonight, I had always thought of as being a little flighty. Loyal, of course, and wonderfully exuberant in making love, but not dependably bright. I was wrong, obviously. We met no one on the way.

And then we stopped.

"What are we waiting for?"

"Quiet," she said, and I was quiet. After a few minutes I could hear the distant shuffle of footsteps. An old man, I decided from the sound. And then he was close and I felt arms going around me and an iron grip holding me and hot tears on my neck.

"Father," I said.

"Lanik, my son, my son," he said, and I wasn't afraid anymore.

"You believe me."

"You're my only hope." Always the old bastard regarded me as *his* hope, as if he had first claim on my loyalty, before even myself. Well, he did.

"All four parts of me tomorow," I answered, and he only held me tighter.

"There are times when an honest man has to abdicate, and this is that time," he said softly. "They won't cut you up. I knew you'd never betray me, not permanently, anyway."

"Not even temporarily," I said. "Well, let's get moving before somebody notices that we're holding a convention down here."

"We can't go yet," Father said. "We have to wait."

"Why?"

"Changing of the guard at dawn," he said. "We hope they'll be distracted."

"The guard? You're afraid of the guard? Can't you just hide me and command them to let you through?"

Saranna answered. "It's not that simple. Your father doesn't command the guard."

"Well who the hell does?" I demanded.

"Don't raise your voice," Father said. "Ruva does."

I raised my voice. "The Turd rules in your palace!"

"Quiet, I said. Yes, she does, she and Dinte. They were plotting it before you left the palace, and once you were gone they made their move. I could have blocked them, I suppose, but I couldn't afford to kill my only heir, as I thought, and so I went along, pretending I didn't notice how my prerogatives were usurped, how my friends' offices became sinecures and the real power gathered in younger hands."

"My father tried to warn the court," Saranna said.

"And I had to sign his death warrant."

"Why did you sign it?" I asked.

"For the reason I signed yours," said my father. "He escaped and is living in exile in the north. In Brian, I believe. His agents have already smuggled out half the Family fortune. That was until Ruva caught the leak."

"I see," I said.

"When we heard you were commanding the Nkumai invaders, I was overjoyed. I used my influence, such as I have, to put our stupidest commanders, including Dinte, in the key positions. I opened the doors to the enemy. Thinking, of course, that you were coming to liberate me and the people from that ass I had the misfortune to marry and that child your mother claimed was also mine."

"It wasn't me."

"I knew that when we heard how the armies were destroying everything. You're too wise for that. I knew it was a fraud. But there were so many witnesses." He sighed. "I betrayed my own Family, thinking I was opening the door for my son. Now the enemy ravages from Schmidt to Jones and it's only a matter of time before they cross the river. They'll surely do it soon. The rains will make it impassable in a few more weeks." And suddenly he wept again. "I dreamed of your homecoming, Lanik. Dreamed that you'd come in triumph and lead these people into battle. You could have defeated the Nkumai. And they must have known it. That's why they destroyed the people's love for you. And now we can only run."

"Well, if that's true, let's start running."

"The changing of the guard," Saranna whispered.

"Nonsense. You've already used that strategy once, and Dinte and Ruva will be watching. They probably left me unguarded just so you'd try this and get yourselves killed. You'd better go back upstairs, both of you, and pretend you had nothing to do with this."

"No," Saranna said.

"We have to leave with you," Father said. "Things are intolerable here. We have a few hundred loyal men that I've already assigned to duty in the north. They're expecting us. They'll rally to us."

"To you, you mean. Not a soul alive would rally to me. But we're not going to wait for the changing of the guard."

"Then we'll be caught. Every gate is watched closely."

I could see the flicker of Saranna's torch now. My vision was returning. "I'll create a diversion. The postern gate."

"It's heavily guarded."

"I know. Take me near there, but keep me out of sight. I can see faintly, and I should have full vision soon, but in the meantime I couldn't defend myself against a mosquito. Then you two be ready to spring for the water gate. I'll join you there."

"Blind?"

"I know the way blindfolded. And no one will be looking for me."

"What kind of diversion can *you* create?" Father asked doubtfully.

In answer I opened my shirt and showed them my chest. "Do you remember what was there when I left here?"

They remembered.

"The Schwartzes cured me. As I told you. And they taught me their technique."

Saranna's hand brushed down my chest, like the dream I had lived through a thousand nights, it seemed, on the Singer ship.

"Let's go," I said. And they led me up the stairs and ramps and corridors that would take us to the postern gate. They left me in the window well over the palace door, where, if I could have seen, I would have scanned the courtyard before the postern gate in the palace walls. And I could now see shapes, dimly; though torches were only bright sparks of light, I could see the flames dance.

There was so much dead rock around that I was hampered, but I soon found the voice of the rock. Much was new; the soil, unlike the sand, had too much life in it. It was a barrier, not a channel. But I found the voice, and explained, and asked, and the rock obeyed.

I could not see it. I could only hear the grinding of dead stones as the earth heaved under them and cast them from their piles onto the ground. There were shouts as the men from the postern gate ran to the breach in the wall. The earth kept heaving, and some were thrown to the ground, as others foolishly ran too close to where the walls were dancing and throwing boulders.

I lowered myself from the window and walked the other way, toward the water gate.

Saranna and Father and four soldiers leading seven horses waited in the shelter of a wall.

"What did you do," Father asked, in awe. "It was like an earthquake."

"It was an earthquake," I said. "Just a little one. Big ones take a committee." And then I strode toward the gate. In the light of predawn I could see again, though things were blurry, and with relief I noticed that the gate was unguarded—the soldiers had run off to the breach in the wall.

Unguarded, and so we passed through, Father and Saranna first, and then the soldiers. Which is why I was last and still unarmed when Dinte emerged from the shadows.

I saw the glint of torchlight reflected in steel. "How unequal we are," I said. "A mark of courage."

"I wanted to have no doubt of the outcome," he said.

"Then you should have picked a different target," I answered, and with the speed Helmut had taught me I disarmed him in a matter of moments. It would have been an opportune moment to kill him, but he was screaming for help and he was my father's son, so I merely slit his throat from ear to ear and left him silent and bleeding on the ground. He'd regenerate and recover, as I had from the same wound more than a year ago. But he'd at least know that when he came for me, he'd have to bring friends.

I passed through the gate, still holding the sword, and mounted the horse they had for me. We rode north all day, and at night came to a military outpost that had once guarded Mueller's northern frontier in the old days, when Epson had been powerful and Mueller a peaceful farming Family with some strange breeding practices. The outpost was run down, but a quick count made me estimate three hundred or more horses, which meant as many men at least.

"Are you sure they're friends?" I asked.

"If not, we haven't much hope anyway," Father answered.

"Either way, it would be better if you had this sword, and not I." I handed it to him, and he gasped. "It's Dinte's," he said.

"Good to know he didn't borrow someone else's. He tried to kill me. I persuaded him against it. He's recovering from an extra grin."

"Why didn't you say anything?"

"I didn't want to worry you."

Saranna said, gruffly, "You should have killed the little ass."

"Maybe I did," I said. But I was sure I hadn't. And then we were at the outpost gates and the soldiers let us in and cheered Father, and he explained (very roughly) that it was an imposter and not I leading the Nkumai. I don't know how many believed him. But they were courageous men and cheered appropriately, and then Father ordered them to go to their units and bring as many loyal men as they could find. Wisely, he urged them not to mention that I was with him. Let them rally to the king, not to someone they might still believe was a traitor.

And as the three hundred soldiers rode out to bring an army to us, we changed horses for the fifth time that day and rode on north into the darkness.

"You must have been planning this for months," I said.

"We weren't planning on *you*," Father said, "but we knew that sometime soon I'd have a crisis with my dear younger son and would have to be free to call on the loyal troops. We planned for contingencies."

Dissent had already set for the second time that night when we finally stopped at a farmhouse well off the road. The house was right at the bank of the Sweet River. The wind was cool out of the eastern hills that led to Ku Kuei Forest. The fire in the hearth was hot and fierce, and the host forced us to eat soup before he'd let us go to bed.

The bodyguards slept on the ground floor. And when the host showed me to my rooms, Saranna was already in it, waiting for me.

"I know you're tired," she said. "But it's been a year."

And as she undressed me I looked out onto the wheat-covered rows of hills to the east, where the sun rose out of Ku Kuei, and I felt the breeze playing across my body while Saranna tickled me (nothing forgotten, not even now), and I smelled the reek of horseflesh in my own clothes and the fresh whitewash the host had used a week ago, and it was good to be home.

After three weeks it was clear that ours would be an unnoteworthy rebellion. We had eight thousand soldiers, loyal to the core and some of the finest fighters in the kingdom. But our treasury fed them and armed them to no avail: the rumors were soon verified and we knew we had lost. Dinte had signed a treaty with the Nkumai and there were now 120,000 men against our tiny army. I was a better general, but there are limits to what a general can do.

What hurt us worst, however, was the fact that the Nkumai, apparently from the day I was captured, had put their duplicate Lanik into cold storage and started publicly declaring that I had indeed been with them, but had been captured by Mueller forces and was now a defector with my father's army. And as soon as they started that story going, they ended the policy of wasting the land, claiming that the destruction had been entirely my idea and they were grateful to be able to quit.

It did nothing to make me popular, and troops weren't exactly flocking to my banner. We tried to play down the fact that I was with Father, but some stories can't be kept secret.

And so there we were with eight thousand men, a full treasury, and not one damn alternative except to run away. Of course the Nkumai and dear Dinte chose that moment to join forces on the north side of the Mueller River and head straight for us.

"We'll die heroically," said Harkint, who still didn't trust me.

"I'd rather live," I said.

"We know your preferences," he answered coldly.

"I'd rather all of us lived. Because it won't take long with Dinte in command before people start clamoring to have Father back."

"It wouldn't take long now if you weren't with us," said another soldier, and a murmur of assent came from the others gathered in the large room of the house. Father was worried, but the soldier was right. I was Father's chief liability. Lose me, and he'd be able to raise more of an army. Maybe ten, fifteen thousand more. Still not enough.

"I have a plan," I said. "And it will work."

And the next morning we set out along the Sweet River. We made no secret of our direction and we traveled at a leisurely pace. The river ran southwest, and anyone with half a brain could guess we were heading for Mueller-on-the-Sea, the great port on the Rebel River delta where the fresh water spewed out into the saltwater Sleeve. Strategically it was vital, and the fleet, if we could reach it first, would take us to Huntington, where the troops would still be loyal to Father and would not particularly hate me. It would enable us to wait and prepare an invasion.

Which meant, of course, that Dinte and the Nkumai would race us for the fleet and get there first. I had no objection. After all, even if we got to Huntington safely we would be permanently in exile; with the Nkumai getting both our iron and their own, there would be no resisting them. So when we reached the point where we had to leave the river no matter where we were going, since the river jogged to the west, I ordered our army to begin a doubletime race, not southwest for Mueller-on-the-Sea, but southeast for the Great Bend of the Mueller River, where we would be free to go eastward, gathering strength among the recently conquered and none-too-docile populations of Bird, Jones, Robles, and Hunter. It wasn't the world's likeliest or safest plan, but it was the best I could think of at the time.

We didn't bother galloping—we went at the wagons' best pace, which was still a good deal better, with each wagon lightly loaded, then Nkumai's largely footsoldier army could make. I could only hope that the enemy had got far enough westward, in the wrong direction, so that we could reach the bend before them. If we did, they'd never overtake us heading east, and we'd live to fight another day.

I also had another plan, but it was for the time when we had nothing else to lose.

As we rode southeast, there was little for me to do. Father knew his men and no one was eager to take orders from me. Instead I thought, and one subject that often came to mind was the imposter, the all-too-true Lanik who was now out of a job.

It was an interesting speculation, what his life had been like. His creation had been a nightmare to me—but to him, the first stirrings of consciousness began with someone who looked exactly like him trying to bash in his brains with a rock. And then what had the Nkumai put him through, believing he was me, before they finally caught on to what was happening? If I had been haunted by him before, in dreams, now he haunted my waking hours as I pictured the hatred they must have taught to him. You're no one to them, they must have told him. They'll kill you if they ever know who you are. But if you work with us, we'll install you on the throne and you can show them that you are someone to regard, with fear if not respect.

Had he actually led their armies? Perhaps. Were my memories transferred to him along with my body? If so, he would be a match for me on any battlefield since he'd know my moves before I made them. Surely they'd keep him with them for that purpose if no other.

But if he had no such memories, which seemed more likely, then he was now once again unceremoniously dropped from any important role. Perhaps they've already killed him, I thought. Or perhaps he's feeling as hopeless as I, knowing that there is no one more hated than he in all the West, and yet truly deserving none of the hatred at all.

And I thought of Mwabao Mawa and wanted to strangle her.

No murder, I told myself. No killing. And at such times I would ride off from the army, several kilometers ahead, and lie on the soil and speak to the living rock and stay in contact with myself.

"They've set the Cramers free and they're taking Mueller slaves," one soldier who joined our army told us in horror. The reaction was electric—many of our soldiers had families in West Mueller, where the Cramers might be creating havoc with no one to defend our people. I was not surprised that our numbers began diminishing as soldiers slipped off to head southwest. And I was even less surprised when most of our scouts failed to return. But I insisted that Father stop asking for volunteers for scouting missions—the men who wanted to get away without recriminations were dominating the lists, and we had to have information.

We were only thirty kilometers from the Great Bend, however, when the most important information of all came from someone we had never thought to see again.

"Homarnoch!" Father whispered as he saw the man madly driving a wagon along the road we had just come down. "Homarnoch, here!" he cried, and the old doctor was soon beside us. We called a rest; the soldiers stopped on the road.

"No use," Homarnoch said. "I've killed a brace of horses coming to tell you. The Nkumai didn't take your bait. They only sent Dinte and his force to Mueller-by-the-Sea, and when you turned southeast the rest of them were ahead of you all the way. Not five kilometers off they're waiting for you. They've been at the Great Bend for days."

Father called his commanders and gave them orders to have our men prepare for a much faster march.

"We'll fight them and win," Harkint insisted.

"We'll escape and survive," Father answered, and Harkint went off in a rage.

While the preparations were going on, Homarnoch told us how and why he had come. "They were going to take everything—all our work for thousands of years. I wouldn't have that. Not with those tree-dwelling apes."

I didn't bother telling him that these tree-dwelling apes had given faster-than-light travel to the rest of the universe.

"So I poisoned the rads," Homarnoch said.

Father was shocked. "Killed them!"

"They were five tons worth of iron on the hoof, so to speak, and I couldn't see letting the enemy have that. So I poisoned them. And not even their fingernails'll be worth a gram of iron in trade."

I said nothing, but remembered a time when I had had five legs and an extra nose and still fancied myself a man.

"And then I got the library. The essential records. The theory. It's all in that wagon," he said, "and I burned the rest. And with Dinte's men in charge of the city, nobody even thought to keep me in."

"A master stroke," Father said. Homarnoch beamed with pride.

"And now what the hell do we do," I said.

"Harkint wants to attack," Father said with a wry smile.

"Harkint's an ass," I answered. "But there's nowhere else to go. With Dinte's men between us and the sea, and nothing in the north but Epson. They won't be inclined to provoke Nkumai by taking us in."

"Dinte's no match for us."

"He outnumbers us five to one. With odds like that a jackass could win."

We sat in silence. Homarnoch mumbled something about needing to check the horses. And then Harkint came back. The troops were ready. "And what I want to know is, are we going into battle or running from it."

"Running," Father said. "The question is, which way."

Harkint snorted. "I never thought the day would come when the Mueller would be a coward. I've followed you through everything that's gone wrong, including harboring this class A bastard," meaning me, "but I'll be damned if I turn tail and run from a fight. And there's others that feel like me."

If he'd had any sense of the theatrical, he would have stormed off then. But he hadn't. And so Father answered. "Go through the troops then, Harkint, and ask for all who want to go with you. But tell them that the Mueller is withdrawing, and asks all men to come with him. You tell them that, and take all those who'll go with you."

Harkint nodded and left. And I began scratching out a rough map of Mueller and surrounding territories.

"South and west is out of the question," Father said. "Everyone in Mueller would kill you, and everyone in Helper, Cramer, and Wizer would kill me."

"And north is impossible," I answered, "because Epsin is too weak."

"Everyone's too weak. And we can't reach the East because Nkumai's army is in the way."

"How desperate," said Homarnoch lightly, looking over a sheaf of papers as he returned and stood a few meters off. "We have no hope. Let's throw ourselves in the river and drown."

"There is a direction we haven't tried."

Father wasn't slow. "Ku Kuei. But there are too many legends about the forest, Lanik. The men wouldn't go in."

"I've been through the forest. Not just around the edges. Through it."

"And they'll follow you anywhere."

I laughed.

"And once we got in there, what would we do? Nkumai rules the

East, and the Singer armies are ruining the far north. What do we do in Ku Kuei?"

"Survive. Dinte can't last forever."

"You're serious about us going there, aren't you?"

"What's the story of Schwartz? What do people believe?"

Father knew what I was getting at. "I see. So you hope that there really is a Ku Kuei family, and that they might have something valuable to offer."

"I don't know. But even a faint hope is better than no hope at all."

Father smiled. "The eternal optimist."

"Would Dinte follow us into Ku Kuei?"

"Dinte? He believes all the legends. He closes his windows at night. He won't cross water under a cloudy sky. He sings when a horse's shadow touches him. He's a fool."

"The Nkumai are not fools," I said, "and they don't go into Ku Kuei either. And forests are their native habitat. If whatever it is in Ku Kuei that scares everybody till their snot freezes doesn't get us, we're in good shape."

We formed up the troops, except for the larger-than-we-had-expected group with Harkint, and began to march northeast. It was not a pleasant leavetaking. Some of the troops with us called abuse at Harkint's men for abandoning the Mueller. And Harkint's men cried coward and the march was dismal as we went on our way, only five thousand men or so, with deserters dropping off all along the way. I couldn't blame them, but forced those I caught to get back in line. They didn't mind. They knew they'd get away in an hour or so.

And then we came to the fork in the road where escape to the north would mean following the main way left, while the smaller road east could only take us to Ku Kuei. Father's speech was impressive. But we lost two thousand men right there, just as word reached us that Harkint's forces had been slaughtered within a few hours of our having left. The Nkumai were close behind us, and they had rested for days while waiting for us at Great Bend—they were fresh and we were not.

We filed hopelessly up the narrow road leading through the rough eastern hills. There was little desertion now; in these hills, the best source of food was our wagons, and deserters would have little hope of surviving without giving themselves up to the enemy. Besides, the men who were with us now were the hard core of Father's supporters. The kind, we thought, who would die before they'd abandon him.

"I'm toying with the idea," Father said to me as we headed the column along the twisting road, "of picking a good spot here and going down fighting."

"And I'm toying with the idea of jumping off the next precipice."

Father smiled. But it was a grim smile. "I'm realizing, the closer we get to Ku Kuei, that I'm a bit superstitious, too. Are you sure you got through there safely?"

"I'm here, aren't I?"

"You're here, but you're the only radical regenerative in history to have a remission. How do we know you didn't spend the whole time you were gone in this forest, and now you're leading us into a trap?"

"Yes, Father, you guessed it."

He looked at me sharply. It was unlike him to miss irony. "Lanik, my son, I'm a blathering old man, but unless I'm mistaken, you knocked down a wall of my palace without so much as a small rock or a catapult."

"I'm a man of many gifts."

"What are we going to do in Ku Kuei?"

I shrugged. "Survive."

And then the road veered north and in the distance to the east we could see the trees begin. There was not so much as a path leading toward the forest—it wasn't the usual direction for travelers to go. So I picked out what looked like a reasonably good route, and started overland.

The troops didn't follow.

Not that they said anything, or rebelled. The front ranks just sat there on their horses, watching me, not speaking, not moving.

Then Father left the road and came after me, his horse at a slow walk, and one or two others started, too. But while Father came on until he joined me, the others reined in and stopped a few meters from the road.

"I won't command any man to come," Father said. "But that's where the Mueller's going, and all the Mueller's true men will come with him."

I don't know whether Father's little speech would have been enough to persuade them. Much more convincing, I think, was the flight of arrows that sailed toward our column. The aim was not good—the distance was too great for accuracy. But the message was clear: the Nkumai had flanked us, and the entire length of our column was exposed to enemy arrows.

Father cried out, "To me, Mueller!" and then whispered loudly, "Lead, dammit!" I took off at a totally unwise canter over broken ground; my horse and I were lucky, but others were not, and many horses spilled their riders before they reached the shelter of the woods.

The trees were tall, but the branches were often low, and it was hard to pick a clear path. I had to dismount, and that meant that our forces would also have to pause at the forest edge, exposing themselves to Nkumai archers as they waited for those ahead of them to move under the trees. We lost two or three hundred men there; but when I had led us two hours into the forest, the rearmost men called ahead that the Nkumai pursuit had withdrawn.

The urgency of flight was over, but we couldn't stop there. The trees were so dense that no decent forage for the horses could grow. I decided to lead the men on to the shores of the narrow lake, where the trees broke into enough meadow to keep us for a few days, at least.

Our passage through the forest was silent. I didn't look behind me at the men—it would have made them even more nervous to know how nervous I was about them. When I had come here alone, it was a forest. Trees and soil, and though I had tired out far sooner than usual, there was nothing intrinsically strange about the place. This time, however, nothing was happening to our endurance, but the very silence of the forest and the steady tramping of the horses' hooves and the boots of the soldiers were unnerving. It was as if the sounds were swallowed up in the silence, a bit of ourselves stolen away by the trees and not reflected back to us.

We spent a hard night in the forest. The ground was soft enough, and there was plenty of food in the saddlepacks, but by morning hundreds of men had disappeared. Gone off into the night or turned away first thing in the morning, but gone. We knew they had merely deserted (and more than a few who had stayed were no doubt wishing they had gone, too), but the feeling that men could simply vanish in the night did little to promote calm.

We reached the lake about noon, and sunlight poured down and birds skirted the edge of the water and the horses grazed openly on the meadow and I thought we had made it to safety. I counted the men. Fewer than a thousand. And with this we hoped to return to power in Mueller.

The men bathed in the lake, splashing each other with water like children. They laughed loudly. And Saranna clung to me and told me I must not go. But Father and I had to find the Ku Kuei, and so we left Homarnoch in charge of our peaceful, happy troops, and we left. It seemed wise at the time.

ku kuei

It could have been a holiday in one of the Sweet River woods. Father walking briskly along (he isn't odd at all, I realized) and I following only a little behind, watching as his hands reached up to touch leaves and branches, down to pluck grass or flowers, out in wild gestures as he exuded life and joy. Only now it was incongruous. Now it seemed forced. Now I wanted to weep for him, except that it would embarrass him, shame him. There were things that could be wept for, like long-lost sons come home, but for the losses a Mueller didn't weep. Didn't even give grief for the loss of a kingdom.

We left the lake soon enough, but then it began again, as it had happened when I passed through Ku Kuei before. We walked and walked, and still the sun was high in the sky, hardly seeming to move, and we got hungry and ate, and the sun had not moved, and we walked on until we were tired, and the sun had moved only a little, and at last we had walked until we were utterly exhausted and couldn't walk anymore, and it might have been noon.

"This is ridiculous," Father said wearily as we lay in the grass.

"Not ridiculous. Disturbing."

"All right, you pick the words."

"This happened to me when I came here before."

"What, you gave out after only a morning's walk?"

"That's what I thought, only now I'm not sure." I had learned some things about the world since I last passed through Ku Kuei.

That stargazers in treetops could make the stars dance. That naked savages in the desert could turn rocks into sand. Were we wearing out early? Or was the sun merely a little slow in her travels?

"Rest," I said to Father, and then I lay on the grass under the trees and listened to the rock. Listened through the barrier of living soil and the voices of a million trees, and heard:

Not the voice of the rock, but rather a low, soft, almost unthinkable whisper, and I couldn't understand. It seemed to speak of sleep, or that could have been my own mind. I tried to hear the cries of the dying (though usually I tried to shut them out) and this time I heard, not a crush of voices crying in agony together, but rather distinct, low calls. Tortured, but slow. Tortured and hating and fearing but endlessly delayed and separated and distinct, and against their rhythm my own heart was quick, racing, panicking and yet I was at rest and my heart beat normally.

I let myself fall into the soil, which gave way only reluctantly until I was down, resting against the rock. Stones slid away behind my back; deep roots slithered off to let me by; and then harsh rock gave way and cushioned me gently and I heard.

Nothing unusual at all. The voice of the rock was unchanged, and what I had heard near the surface was gone.

I was confused. I hadn't merely imagined what I heard before, and yet now, next to the rock, all was as it had been in Schwartz a few weeks before.

I rose again, listening all the way, and gradually the song of the earth changed, seemed to slow, seemed to separate into distinct voices. The earth, too, seemed more sluggish to part and let me by. But at last I was on the surface, my arms spread, floating as always on what could only seem to me to be a slightly thicker than normal sea.

Father was standing, watching me, the expression on his face indescribable. "My God," he said, "what's happened to you!"

"Just resting," I answered, because there was little else to say.

"You sank into the earth."

"I forgot to tread water," I said. "Don't worry about it. I had to find something out. I—Father, in Schwartz I learned to do some things. Things that could never be exported through an Ambassador. Schwartz is no competition to us, or to the Nkumai, but I learned how to make rocks and soil behave differently from normal. And they make me behave differently, too."

"You were gone for nearly an hour it seemed, forever it seemed, Lanik. How did you breathe?"

"I held my breath very tight. Father, they've done something with the soil here. Something that slows things down, or makes it seem that way. It's as if—I don't know. As if time slowed for us."

"Why didn't it happen for the army?"

"Maybe we had too much momentum or something. I don't know. But look at the sun." It was only a little past the zenith. "And we're already through for the day."

"I'm not," Father said, and so we went on.

By the sun it was only midafternoon; by my own reckoning, I had done two days' walking since morning; and we reached another lake. I had skirted the southern edge of it on my earlier journey. Now we reached it on its western shore, and we could plainly see the other side, though because it seemed to disappear to the north and south, we supposed it might have been an island or a peninsula.

"I don't know about you," I told Father, "but this is where I stop."

We slept almost before we lay down.

I awoke in darkness. I had never seen night in Ku Kuei on my first journey, and the night before, with the army, I had had other things on my mind. Now I watched the sky. Both Dissent and Freedom had risen, and at this time of year they were near each other. I lay there, still weary with sleep, letting my mind wander, when it occurred to me that Dissent should have passed Freedom by now.

Instead, there was almost no detectable motion.

Could Ku Kuei really have developed a way to slow the sun and the moons? Impossible. Impossible for it to happen here and not be noticed anywhere else.

It was not a change in the earth then, or in the sky. It could only be a change in us. A change that didn't happen when the army was with us; a change that happened when we were alone.

"For once Dissent has learned his place," Father said.

"You noticed, too."

"I hate this place, Lanik." He sighed. "A beggar loves any coin. But I'm beginning to think I would have been happier with Harkint."

"Up to a point, you probably would."

"What point?"

"When they cut your head off and it didn't grow back."

"It's a problem with Muellers," Father said. "We never can believe that death is permanent. I heard once of a man who couldn't think how to get vengeance on his enemy, short of killing him, and he didn't want *that* much vengeance. So he challenged the man to combat and beat him, and while his enemy was lying on the ground, faint from loss of blood, he cut off his arm and sewed it on backward. He liked the effect so well, that he did the same to the man's other arm, and his legs, too, right at the hips, so that the man's buttocks were facing the same direction as his face. And of course he had a tail. It was a perfect vengeance. When all had healed, his enemy spent the rest of his life watching himself shit, while he never knew whether he was lying with a pretty girl or a plain one."

I laughed. It was the kind of tale told by the huge fires in Mueller-on-the-River during the wintertime. The kind of tale that men would lack the spirit to tell now, even if they had the wit.

"I'm never going back, am I, Lanik," Father said. And the way he said it, I knew he didn't want the truth.

"Of course you are," I said. "It's only a matter of time before the Nkumai collapse under their own weight. There's a limit to how much land a Family can absorb."

"No there isn't. I could have conquered everyone."

"Not without me, you couldn't," I said, belligerently enough that he laughed, as he had laughed when as a child I had challenged him to single combat when he ordered me to go to my room for my impertinence. He had laughed, until I drew sword and demanded to be met with honor. He had to cut off my right hand before I was content and would submit.

"I never should have tried," he said. Tried what, I wondered, until he finished his sentence: "Doing anything without you."

I said nothing. He had been forced to send me away, a year or so ago; I had acted with little enough choice since then. A year ago? It was yesterday. It was forever. In the darkness I felt as if I had never been anywhere but here, staring up at the stars.

Father was also looking at the stars. "Will we ever reach them?"

"With long enough arms."

"And what will we find if we get there?" Father sounded vaguely sad, as if he had just realized that he would never find something he had carelessly mislaid a long time ago. "If we of Mueller got enough iron and somehow built a starship and went out among the stars, what would we find? After three thousand years, would they greet us with open arms?"

"The Ambassadors still work. They send us iron."

"If they ever meant to let us off this planet, they would have come here years ago and taken us off. Whatever sins were committed they were paid for a thousand times before I was ever born. Did I rebel against the Republic? What threat am I to them? They have weapons that would let man stand against all of Nkumai's armies and win. While I'm an aging swordsman who once won seventeen archery matches in a single day. I'll wear all my medals and surely they'll bow." He chuckled dismally, and the chuckle twisted off into a groan.

"When you cut their arms off, they don't grow back," I said. "So we do have an advantage over them there."

"We're freaks."

"I'm cold," I said, but the clouds stayed frozen in their places near the horizon, and no wind blew.

"No wind," I said. "They've slowed it all down. Look, father. Across that inlet, see how the grass is lying over? As if a wind were blowing. And yet they stay that way."

Father seemed not to notice.

"Father," I said. "Perhaps we ought to go on."

"Where?" he answered.

"To find the Ku Kuei."

"Off like Andrew Apwiter, then, trying to find the third moon, a moon all of iron that will save us from hell. If we were going to find the Ku Kuei, we would have found them."

"They can't live without making some sign."

"And have we enough years in our lives to search every meter of the forest, hoping for a Ku Kuei dropping or some hair snagged on a low-hanging branch? They can do strange things with us, and yet we never see them. I call it magic. I give up and I call it magic and magicians have no need for us and no help for us and I should go back to my people and die. At least then they'll remember me as the king who fought until he died, and not as the Mueller who ran away into the forest and was eaten by the ogres of Ku Kuei."

"Father—"

"I want to sleep again. I only want to sleep." And he rolled on his side, turning his back to me.

I lay there looking at the stars and wondered what kind of people the Ku Kuei would be. On this world, they could be anything, I thought. As a child growing up in Mueller, I had thought nothing about us was strange. Every child learned his lessons with the threat of dismemberment if he failed his subject. Every child's cut healed a moment after he fell. But now I knew otherwise. Tree people who answer the questions of the universe, desert people whose minds rock the world. On Treason, strangeness was normality and the ordinary were doomed to be forgotten or overrun.

We came to you, I said in my mind to the Ku Kuei, we came to you because there was nowhere else to turn and we hoped for mercy from those who have no need to fear justice.

No one answered my thoughts. No one had heard.

How loud must I shout before you'll notice me, I thought. What must I do to get your attention, even for a moment, however long moments are around here?

The lake reflected the moonlight. Near us the water shimmered a bit, but the shimmering faded and beyond, the lake was still, waves frozen in midfall. And I knew how I could get them to notice us.

After all, water games were the first that I had learned.

The earth sensed my great need, perhaps, or perhaps my powers were stronger than I had thought. But the rocks responded, and the lake sank quickly. Near us there was no time effect; it was as if the power of the rocks superceded whatever subjective games the Ku Kuei could play. The lake level fell; the earth rose to replace it, in part; and when I was through only enough water was left to contain the fish, a scattered group of ponds and marshes, and the lake was gone.

"Sir," said a voice behind me.

"How quickly you came," I answered, not turning around.

"You've stolen our lake," he said.

"Borrowed it."

"Give it back."

"I need your help."

"You come from Schwartz, where they do not kill," said the voice behind me. "But we are not Schwartz, and we are willing to kill."

"Then you're down one lake, aren't you?"

"We owe you nothing."

"You will, when I give your lake back."

Silence. I turned around. There was no one there.

"Sneaky little bastards, aren't they?"

"What?" Father asked, waking up. "What the hell happened to the lake?"

"I was thirsty," I answered. "We had a visitor. He actually spoke to us."

"Where is he?"

"Gone to fetch company to throw us out, I imagine. In the meantime, look at Dissent and Freedom."

Father looked, and saw what I had seen: Dissent moved across the face of Freedom, and the leaves in the trees whispered in the wind.

"Well," he said. "I must go to sleep more often."

We waited on the edge of what had been the lake. But we didn't wait long. Dissent was only a thumb past Freedom when four men came thundering through the underbrush and stood angrily around us. "What the hell!" shouted one man.

"Want to swim?" I asked.

"What right do you have to attack us like this? What harm have we done you?"

"Besides playing with our sense of time?"

They looked at each other in consternation.

"You fooled me on my first trip. But the second time through I caught on a little."

"Why are you here?"

So Father and I told them, and they listened with inscrutable faces. They were all dark-skinned and tall and fat (but there was strength under the fat) and while they didn't look negroid, they didn't look white, either. I speculated on what circumstance could have evolved such an appearance back on the Mother Planet, and gave up. Genetics creates questions, it doesn't answer them.

When we were through with the tale of our sad plight, they looked at us for a while and finally the tallest and fattest, who obviously was in charge (do they choose their leaders by the kilogram, I wondered), said, "And?"

"And we need your help."

"So? Is there some reason we should give it?"

Father was perplexed. "We need it. We're doomed unless you help us."

"That much is plain. But what difference does that make to us?"

"We're fellow human beings!" Father began, but was wise enough to know when to quit. They thought that idea was amusing, anyway.

"I have a good reason why you should help us," I said. "If you don't, you don't have a lake. Mosquitoes breed pretty readily in ponds like these."

"So I promise you everything you want, and you refill the lake," said the leader. "All I need to do is kill you, and there goes our agreement. Plus, we keep the lake. So why not fill the lake and go away, back where you came from? We don't bother you, you don't bother us."

I was so angry. So I removed the soil under their feet and slid it sideways. They fell heavily. They tried to stand up again (and they were quicker than I thought their bulk would allow), but the soil kept dancing under their feet, and at last they gave up and sprawled on the ground and yelled for me to stop.

"For a moment," I said.

"If you can do that," the leader said, pulling himself upright and brushing off his clothes, "you hardly need our help. For all my talk, you know, we don't have any weapons. We don't need them. We haven't killed anybody in years. Not that we have any moral objection to it, though, so don't think you're out of trouble."

"It would be lovely," I said, "if we could have the earth swallow up our enemies. But rocks aren't into mass murder, and so I can only do certain things. Demonstrations. Lake drainings. Pratfalls. Not practical against an enemy. But we don't need you to fight our battles. What we need is time."

They giggled uncontrollably. They laughed. They roared until tears rolled down their cheeks. A clown could retire in five years of working here, I thought. Finally the leader said, "Why didn't you say so? If time's all you want, we have plenty." Which sent them into spasms of laughter again.

Father looked uncomfortable. "Are we the only sane people in the world?"

"Perhaps they think we're grim."

"We can give you time," the leader said. "We've been working with time for years. We can't go into the future or past, of course, since time is one-dimensional. ("Of course," I thought, "everyone knows that.") But we can change our own speed in relation to the general timeflow. And we can extend that change to our immediate surroundings. It takes one of us for every four or five people we want to change. How many do you have?"

"Less than a thousand," Father said.

"How specific," the leader answered, twisting up his mouth as if he were about to launch on another barrage of laughter. "You are right down to the last decimal, aren't you? That would take less than two hundred of us, wouldn't it? But less, of course, if you bunch up, if you share each other's time. So maybe we can do it with as few as fifty."

"Do what?" Father asked, suspiciously.

"I don't know," the leader said, grinning broadly. "Give you time, of course. How long until all your enemies are dead? Fifty years? If we work hard, that means you have to stay in a small area for, say, five days. Is that too long? It's harder the faster we make the time pass for you, but if you need a supreme effort, we can give you a hundred years in a week."

"A hundred years of what?"

"Time!" He was getting impatient with us. "You sit here for what seems to you a week, while outside our forest, a hundred years have passed. You go out, all your enemies are gone, nobody's looking for you, you're safe. Or am I wrong? Do your enemies live exceptionally long?"

Father turned to me. "They can do that?"

"After this last year," I said, "I believe anything. They made us think the moons had stopped."

The leader shrugged. "That was nothing. We had a child doing that. Let us get volunteers to help you, and while we're gone, you fill the lake."

I shook my head. "When you come back, I'll fill the lake."

"I gave you my word!"

"You also told me that it wouldn't bother you to kill me after your word was given."

He smiled again. "And maybe I still will. Who knows? Very chancy world, you have to get used to it." And then, abruptly, he and his friends were gone.

"I'm old," Father said. "I can't cope with all this."

"Can you cope with survival? Maybe we'll survive, after all."

There were only thirty of them, after all, but the leader assured us they were probably enough, and we set off with the lake restored to its pristine beauty behind us. "Maybe now we kill you," said the leader when the lake was full, but then he laughed uproariously and gave me a huge hug. "I like you!" he shouted. All the others laughed. I didn't get the joke.

"Quicktime," said the leader, but to my surprise nobody hurried. Then I realized they meant that their time would pass quickly, while the outside world plodded on at the normal rate. It was early morning when we reached the place where the army was camped, but we had stopped and slept twice on the way, and in all our expedition had taken five days of our time, while to our army it would only be twenty-four hours, or so.

And it would have been, if the army had been there.

From a kilometer away, it was clear something was wrong. We were skirting the shores of the long lake, and we could see far ahead along the meadowland. But where the smoke rose from campfires, there were no large herds of horses. No horses at all. Nothing.

Except corpses, of course. Not too many, but enough to make the story clear. Homarnoch, who had insisted on bringing his wagon into the forest, troublesome though it was, lay dead in front of the wagon's charred remains. Even a Mueller can't regenerate burns over the entire body—but to make sure, they had cut his head off after his death. The other corpses were similarly taken care of.

This we took in after only a few moments at the camp. And then I cried out, "Saranna!" I was not calm. I hoped she wasn't there—better to imagine her alive among the deserters than dead, here. I went on calling for her, and soon the Ku Kuei joined in the search for living among the dead. It was the leader who called to me. "Lake-drinker!" he shouted. "Someone alive!"

I started toward him.

"It's a woman!" he shouted, and I came faster.

Father was kneeling beside her. Her arms and legs had been cut off, and her larynx had been cut out. Her body was regenerating, but she was not a radical, and she still couldn't talk.

The Ku Kuei leader kept demanding to know how she had healed so quickly and why she hadn't bled to death, until Father told him to shut his fat mouth for a minute. We fed her, and she looked at me with an expression that tore at my heart, and the stumps of her arms reached out to me. I held her. The Ku Kuei, puzzled, watched.

"I guess this means you won't be needing us," said the leader after a while.

"More than ever," I said, even as Father said, "That's right."

"Now which of you do I believe?" he asked.

"Me," I insisted. "We don't need thirty men for our army. But there's nowhere we can go now. The three of us. My father, Ensel Mueller. Saranna, my—wife. And my name is Lanik Mueller."

"We've fulfilled our part of the bargain," said the fat Ku Kuei. "So we're rid of you. Shall we carry you to the edge of the forest?"

I had little patience. He landed heavily on his backside, and swore.

"You have the instincts of a bully," he said angrily. "May your children all be porcupines! May your gall bladder be full of stones! May your father be found to have been sterile all his life!"

He looked so serious, so intense that I couldn't help but laugh. And when I started laughing, the leader broke into a grin. "You're my kind of fellow!" he shouted.

It didn't take much to get ahead with the Ku Kuei.

They carried Saranna back with them, amazingly careful for such huge, misproportioned people; but they stopped to rest oftener than Father or I needed, and while Father eagerly ate the immense snacks they constantly offered to share with us, I didn't bother eating. Instead I stayed with Saranna and fed her. We had been traveling for hours on our second day after leaving the camp when Saranna finally spoke.

"I think," she began huskily, "that my voice will work again."

"Oh no!" shouted one of the Ku Kuei. "A woman speaks, and silence is banished from the forest!" The remark brought immense peals of laughter, and several of the Ku Kuei were lying on the ground, unable to sit up because either the laughter or the meal made it impossible for them to remain upright.

"Saranna," I said, and she smiled.

"You weren't gone very long, Lanik."

"Too long, it seems," I said.

"They left me alive to tell you what they thought."

"The only good thing that's been done in a month."

"They were sure you had gone off to kill the Mueller. They knew you planned to bring the terrors of Ku Kuei back on them. They hated you. And so they left."

"Killing on the way."

"Homarnoch forbade them and threatened to kill the first man who left. There were a great many who intended to be first, and so Homarnoch killed no one. Some of the men tried to defend him. They died, too."

"And you."

"They were quick. They wanted to make sure I couldn't travel easily. They thought it would stop you and the monsters from pursuing them."

I looked at the thirty-odd Ku Kuei, sitting like small mountains or snoring in the grass. "Monsters," I said, and Saranna laughed, but the laughter soon turned to tears, her voice sobbing thickly.

"It feels so good to have a voice to cry with," she murmured, when the tears had subsided.

"How are your feet?"

"Better. But the bones aren't hard. Tomorrow I can walk a little."

I unwrapped the bandage the Ku Kuei had improvised around her legs. "Liar," I said. "You're not even halfway down the shin yet."

"Oh," she answered. "I thought I could feel my toes."

"That's the nerve regenerating. Haven't you ever lost a leg before?"

"I always behaved." She smiled.

"All right, we're going, hup hup, hurry, we haven't much time!" shouted the leader, and the others laughed loudly as we started going again. I silently longed to kill the next man who laughed.

The city of the Ku Kuei was in the middle of the lake, on the island we had seen from the shore. If you can call it a city. There were no buildings, no structures of any kind. Just forest, and grass that was rather thoroughly tramped down in a few places.

What was remarkable were the people. The children, mercifully, were thin, but the adults made me suspect that kilo for kilo, the Ku Kuei outnumbered the rest of the population of Treason. The impression I got—and I never had any reason to change it—was one of incredible laziness. No one seemed to do anything that he could avoid doing. "Come hunting with us," many of them said to me, and once I went. They would put themselves into quicktime and walk up to the prey and kill it while it stood motionless, still in normal time. When I suggested it wasn't sporting, they looked at me oddly. "When you want to run a race, do you cut off your feet?" one of them asked me. And another one said, "If I cut off my feet, does that mean I never have to run another race?" Paroxysms of laughter. I went back to the city then.

Yet for all their laziness, their determination to be amused at everything, and their utter unwillingness to take any commitment seriously, I came to love the Ku Kuei. Not as I had the Schwartzes, for I had also admired them; I loved the Ku Kuei as immense self-propelled toys. And they, for some strange reason, loved me, too. Perhaps because I had found a new way to force someone to take a pratfall.

"What's your name?" I asked the man who had led our would-be rescue party.

"What do you think, Lake-drinker?"

"How should I know? And my name's Lanik Mueller."

He giggled. "That's not a name. You drank the lake, you're Lake-drinker."

"You're the only one who calls me that."

"I'm the only one who calls you anything," he said. "And how's Stump?"

When I found out he meant Saranna, I left him. He couldn't understand why I was angry. He thought the name was appropriate.

I suppose the months I passed in Ku Kuei were a sort of idyll, like my time in Schwartz. But in Schwartz I was still exuberant for the future. In Ku Kuei, my future was behind me. And Father was trying to die.

I realized it on the second day of our lessons with Man-Who-Knows-It-All. Saranna and I were lying in the grass, our eyes closed, paying careful attention as the teacher spoke softly and sang occasionally and tried to help us feel his own timeflow as it enveloped us. I don't know what aroused me from the trance (and I roused unwillingly, I'm sure, since Man-Who-Knows-It-All has the gentlest timeflow I ever shared), but I looked over at Father and his eyes were open, staring straight into the sky, and the track of a tear ran down from his eye to his hair.

At the time I put the worry out of my mind. Surely Father had plenty to feel bad about; no reason to try to force him to imitate cheerfulness he didn't feel.

But because of Father, I found it progressively harder to involve myself in the happy-go-lucky mood that unflinchingly gripped the Ku Kuei. Unflinchingly gripped? That was my attitude. Though at times I felt relaxed, felt loved, felt *good*, I was never wholly at peace. Mostly because of my worry about Father. But partly because in all my growing up, I had never had lessons in breaking loose and not caring. I had spent a very difficult year, and its effects were slow to fade. And it is impossible to be uncaring after having heard the music of the earth.

"You're too intense," said Man-Who-Fell-on-His-Ass (the name I eventually gave to the leader I had given several pratfalls to—he loved the name and several of his friends picked it up). "Man-Who-Knows-It-All says you're not making very good progress. You have to learn to laugh."

"I know how to laugh."

"You know how to make silly sounds with a tight belly. Nobody can laugh with a tight belly. And you're too thin. It's a sign of worry, Lake-drinker. I'm telling you this because I think you want to learn timeshifting. You're trying too hard." For once Man-Who-Fell-on-His-Ass looked deadly serious, very concerned. The expression was so foreign to his face that I had to laugh, and he laughed back, thinking he had achieved something. But he had achieved nothing.

Because Father was not paying attention. Even in easygoing Ku

Kuei, one had to pay attention to survive, and Father didn't care. He fell down a lot, once from a rather high hill. That time he ended up with two broken arms. They healed in a few days, but as he lay under a tree during a rainstorm, while I practiced elementary time control by slowing the two of us down a little (very little) so the drops fell with less apparent force, he suddenly held my hand very tightly, which surely caused his arm to hurt worse, and he said, "Lanik, you have the power of the Schwartzes. Can you change me?"

"Into what?" I asked, trying to keep the mood light because a light mood was getting ingrained in me.

"Take away my Muellerness. Take away the regeneration."

I was puzzled. "If I did that, father, that fall might have killed you. And it would take months for these arms to heal."

He looked away from me, his eyes full of tears, and I realized that the fall from the hill might not really have been an accident. It worried me. Father had had reverses before, but this one, admittedly the worst by far, was holding him far too tightly.

Saranna caused me another kind of worry. It began when I found her making love to Bug-killer, so named because he thrashed around so much during sex. She was laughing as he flung out his legs, and she kept laughing even when she looked at me.

Sex under the trees was a common enough sight in Ku Kuei, and I wasn't under any illusion that I had been confining my lovemaking to Saranna because of any overconcern with faithfulness. I just found Ku Kuei women too fat to enjoy. I was a little jealous, I'm sure, but overriding that was my realization that Saranna seemed no different from any other woman in Ku Kuei—amused, detached, easy.

It was Saranna who had begged me to take her with me when I first left Mueller; Saranna who had gashed herself deeply when I refused to let her continue as my lover after I found out I was a rad. And she had been intensely in love with me from the time I came back. Yet now—

"Saranna is a good student," said Man-Who-Knows-It-All.

"I know," I answered. "I can sense her timeflow now almost as well as I sense yours."

"You're unhappy," said my teacher.

"I imagine so."

"Are you jealous because you are the poorest student I've ever had while Saranna is as good as one of our own more gifted children?"

I shrugged. That certainly was part of it. "Maybe I'm more worried because she seems to care less about the things that I care about."

Man-Who-Knows-It-All laughed. "You care about *everything!* How can anybody care about so much!"

"My father cares even more," I said.

"On the contrary, Tight-Gut, your father cares as little as we do. It's just that he tends to despair, while we are full of hope."

"I'm losing Saranna."

"That's good. No one should own someone else." And he went on explaining why it was that my timesense was no good and I needed to *relax* before I got as stiff and hard as a tree.

I wasn't worried all the time, of course. That would be impossible in Ku Kuei. If there weren't the games in the lake or the mad expeditions through the forest, there would be enough to engage a man for a century just walking through the city, pausing to taste the timeflows as people lived their own pace.

For instance, Man-Who-Fell-on-His-Ass was almost constantly in a very fast timeflow. I was so inept at timeshaping that I almost automatically joined the timeflow of anyone nearby; even Ku Kuei of ordinary skills could keep their own timeflow near someone else. When I was with Man-Who-Fell-on-His-Ass, the rest of the world seemed utterly stopped. We walked and talked and the sun never moved in the sky and the people we passed were frozen or (if they had a fast timeflow) they moved sluggishly. No one moved as quickly as Man-Who-Fell-on-His-Ass.

"My friend," I finally said one day, when I felt he was my friend, "you speed through life so quickly. What's your hurry?"

"I'm not in a hurry. I never walk fast."

"I've been here for maybe a month or so—"

He interrupted by giggling. "I don't know how you keep track of the days, as if they meant anything!"

"And you've grown older in that time."

He touched his hair. "Gray, huh?"

"Gray. And wrinkles."

"Laugh wrinkles!" he said triumphantly, as if that answered everything.

His fey attitude was growing in Saranna—but it held her differently. She slowed down. It was not a sudden decision (today I'll be slow), it was gradual. But after she mastered timeshaping I began to notice that when I was with her, caught up in her flow, everything around us moved quickly. Unbearably fast, the Ku Kuei who passed us dancing madly, racing out of sight, jabbering for a moment and going on. When Saranna and I talked, she kept looking over my shoulder, from side to side, watching as people sped by. Now and then she'd smile, an expression unrelated to our conversation, and I'd turn to see the scene that had amused her already gone.

When I met her once early in the morning and after a short conversation found that it was nearly night, I asked her why she slowed down so much.

"Because they're so funny," she said. "Racing along like that."

That would have been reason enough for the flighty girl I had first fallen in love with, but it wasn't reason enough now. I insisted. She balked. "You're too intense, Lanik. But I love you."

We made love, and it was as good as ever, and her passion for me was still warm, not the laughing, amusing affairs she had with the Ku Kuei. I knew I still had a hold on her, yet not enough of one to pull her out of her insistence on letting the world race by without her taking part.

She became notable. The Ku Kuei took to calling her Stump for another reason now; to most of them she was as immovable and dead as a cut tree. She wouldn't change her timeflow for anyone, and so I, the chameleon who changed times with every friend, was the one who most easily could talk to her. Most of the time she stood, frozen impossibly in midstep, and from a distance I watched sometimes for hours as she would complete a step and shift weight to the other foot.

Once for three days every time I saw her she was in the middle of making love to Man-Who-Knows-It-All. The caresses and strokes were as slow, the movement as infinitesimal as if they were distant stars, and I felt as if I had never known her, or worse, as if she were merely a pornographic statue under a tree on Ku Kuei Island.

Saranna and Father were both finding their own way to retreat from life. While I was unable to escape.

The day that Father died he came to me and lay beside me under a tree as a thin drizzle fell. "Play no games with time today," Father said. "You always concentrate so hard that I don't think you're listening to me." And so I lay there and Father put his arm around me and pulled me close as he had when we were on maneuvers when I was a child. He was saying I love you. He was saying good-bye.

"I was a builder," he said, writing his epitaph in my mind, "but my buildings crumbled, Lanik. I have outlived all my works."

"Except me."

"You've been shaped by stronger forces than I can muster. It's a shame when an architect lives to see the temple fall."

No one had built temples in Mueller for centuries.

"Was I a good king?" Father asked.

"Yes," I answered.

"No," he said. "Wars and murders, conquest and power, and all so important for so many years, and then all undone. Not undone by the inexorable forces of nature. Undone because men who live in trees happened to win the game and get the prize faster than we, and it unbalanced us, threw us to the ground. Chance. And it was as much chance when we got iron from the Ambassador, and so I wasn't an empire builder after all, was I? I just used the iron to kill people."

"You were a good ruler to your people," I said, because he needed to hear it and because, on the relative scale by which monarchs must be measured, it was true.

"They play games with us. A dose of iron here, a dose there, and see what that does to the playing field. I was a pawn, Lanik, and I thought I was the king."

And then he grabbed me fiercely, clung to me, whispered savagely in my ear, "I will not laugh!" And to prove it he wept, and so did I.

He drowned himself, and the body was found floating in the tall rushes on the shallow side of the island, where the current had carried him. He had jumped from a cliff into a shallow part of the lake and broken his neck; his body could not regenerate quickly enough to stop him from drowning as he lay helpless on the bottom. He had beaten the regeneration, and I was rather proud of his ingenuity. Suicide had been beyond most of the Muellers for years, unless they were mad and could lie down in flames. Father was not mad, I'm sure of it.

With Father gone, some things were better. He no longer worried me, and when I finally was able to forget the empty feeling, when I stopped turning around, looking for someone that it took me a moment to remember would not be there, I improved as a student. "You are still terrible," Man-Who-Knows-It-All told me, "but you can at least control your own timeflow." And it was true. I could walk within a meter of someone on a different flow, and not be changed. It gave me a measure of freedom I hadn't had before, and I took to changing my flow to a very fast rate when it was time to sleep, so that my nine hours took only a few minutes and to others I seemed to be awake all the time. I saw every hour of every day, and like a Ku Kuei, I found they all amused me.

But I wasn't happy.

No one was happy, I realized one day. Amused, yes. But amusement is the reaction of very bored people when nothing entertains them anymore. The Ku Kuei had all the time in the world. But they didn't know what to do with it.

I had lived with the Ku Kuei for half a year of real time (the seasons, by and large, were unaffected by their games) when I heard that Man-Who-Fell-on-His-Ass was dying. "Very old," said the woman who told me. And so I went to him, and found him, still in his quicktime, racing madly toward death as he lay in the grass under the sun. I sped up to his time, which few Ku Kuei were willing to do, particularly since there was nothing amusing about death, and I held his hand as he wheezed.

His body had grown thinner, though he was still fat. The skin sagged and drooped.

"I can cure you," I said.

"Don't bother."

"I'm sure of it," I said. "I can renew you. I learned it in Schwartz. They live forever in Schwartz."

"Whatever for?" he asked. "I haven't been hurrying all this time just to be cheated now." And he giggled.

"What are you laughing at?" I asked.

"Life," he said. "And you. Oh, Tight-Gut. My Lake-drinker. Drink me dry."

It occurred to me that I was the only person in Ku Kuei who would grieve for him. Death was ignored here, as it had been when my father died. Man-Who-Fell-on-His-Ass had had many friends. Where were they? Finding new friends who hadn't rushed through life and finished up before the others were through.

"It had no meaning for me," he said. "But it means something to you. We say that we are happy because we have hope, but it's a lie. We have no hope. You're the only person I've known in my life who had hope, Lake-drinker. So leave here. This is a cemetery, leave here and save the world. You can, you know. Or if you can't, no one can."

I noticed with surprise that he wasn't laughing.

"You mean this, don't you?" I asked.

"I like you, Lake-drinker," he answered, and then he died. Enough of his timeflow lingered that he had decomposed in a few minutes of real time, and so no one moved his body. He just sank into the earth.

And I also sank into the earth, letting it close above me and listening again to the music of the earth. The war was over; the screams of the dying were isolated now, constant but isolated in space, the deaths all in the random pattern of peace. And yet I did not believe the world was at peace. The world had never been at peace.

Save the world? From what? I had no illusions. I couldn't even save myself.

I could, however, savor the world, and here in Ku Kuei the flavor was thin and bland. With Man-Who-Fell-on-His-Ass dead, and Father dead, and Saranna frozen in time, and Man-Who-Knows-It-All convinced that I would never learn any better control of time than I had now, it occurred to me that it was time to go.

"Don't," Saranna said when I told her.

"I want to and I will," I said.

"I need you." And the look in her eye was frightened. So I stayed a little longer. I stayed with her in her timeflow for another day, another night, and another day of real time and we made love and said many gentle things that would make good memories later and would soften the pain of parting. When I left, she did not cry, nor did I, though both of us wanted to, I believe. "Come back," she said.

"All right."

"Come back soon. Come back while you're still young enough to want me. For I'm going to be young forever."

Not forever, Saranna, I thought but did not say. Young only until the planet is old and is swallowed by a star. Then you will be old, and the flames will wither what time could not. And because you've chosen to hide from time, the flames will burn you infinitely before you die. I thought when I left her I would never see her again, and so, once out of her timeflow, I looked back and memorized her, a single tear just starting to leave her eye, a loving smile on her face, her arms reaching out to bid farewell—or perhaps reaching out to catch me and bring me back. She was unbearably lovely; the pretty girl had been hurt into womanhood. And I fleetingly wondered if I was yet old enough to truly love her.

Then I left, bidding good-bye to no one because my leaving would not have particularly amused anyone. And I set out into the forest with my timeflow sliding naturally along in real time, so that at night I got tired and slept, and woke in the morning with the sun. Normality was refreshing, for a change.

I was a day out of the city when I felt a faster timeflow nearby, and adjusted myself to fit it. I found three Ku Kuei, young girls who were still adolescently thin. They were harrying a stranger who had ventured into the forest. Whatever direction he had been travelling, he was now going south, following the Forest River that flowed outward into Jones. One of the girls left the others and explained to me that they had been with the poor fellow for days. He was nearly insane with worry about why he couldn't seem to travel more than an hour by the sun before he had to sleep. "That's one man that'll never come back to Ku Kuei," she said, giggling.

"You never know," I said. "Someone did that to me my first time through, and I came back."

"Oh," she said. "You're Tight-Gut. You're different." And then she started to undress, a sure sign that a Ku Kuei expects to make love, and I made her laugh uproariously when I told her I didn't want to. "That's what they said, but I didn't believe it! Only that white girl from Mueller, right? Stump, right?"

"Saranna," I said. That made her laugh all the more, and I left her and settled back to real time so that they would go quickly away from me. It was true, though. Before I ever left Mueller, I had spent countless hours plotting to deceive Saranna and sleep with every girl I could find who was willing. And there were few who were unwilling to sleep with the Mueller's heir. Yet since coming back to Mueller, I had slept with no one else. Why not?

Faithfulness had taken me by surprise. I wondered how long the phase would last.

When you walk in it without fear, the forest of Ku Kuei is beautiful enough. But I was bred to farmland and the riding range: when the Forest River broke out of the trees into the high hills of Jones, a tumble of land that led down to the great Rebel River Plain, I sat for an hour on a hilltop, looking at the fields and trees and open land. From here I could see smoke rising from kitchen fires nearby; on the Rebel River far to the south there were sails; but in the great sweep of land men had made little difference after all. I felt philosophical for a few minutes, and then realized that one of the nearby orchards was filled with apples. I wasn't hungry. But I hadn't eaten food in so long that my teeth seemed to tingle just to think of chewing. And so I walked down the hill, forgot the philosophy, and joined the human race again.

Nobody was particularly glad to see me.

jones

The town had a name, but I never knew it. Just another of the villages astride the great highway between Nkumai and Mueller. Once it had been one of the many small roads that let Jones trade with Bird, and Robles with Sloan, but now it had become a large road, heavy with traffic. It was only a year since my father and I had disappeared into the Forest of Ku Kuei and never returned; already we were legend, and Dinte ruled in Mueller and the whole Rebel River plain, from Schmidt in the west to the Starhigh Mountains in the east, was at peace. At peace because it had been conquered, and it was an open secret that while Mueller had all the outward show of independence—indeed, was even larger and stronger than it had ever been before—Nkumai's "king" ruled in Mueller as surely as he ruled in Nkumai.

King? I heard much of this king, but I knew better, and so did others who had reason to know. Like the innkeeper in the town, a man who had once been Duke of Forest-edge but made the mistake of holding back the huge conqueror's tax the soldiers of Nkumai came to collect. He had enough money cached away to buy the inn and stock it. "And now I work here day in and day out, and I make a good living, but boy, I tell you cause you'll never know it, there's nothing like chasing the hounds after a cossie fleeing through the forest-edge."

"I don't doubt it," I said, particularly since I had hunted down many a cossie, too. We surplus royalty made up in memories for what we had lost in station.

"But the king says no more hunting, and so we eat beef and mutton mixed with horse manure and call it a stew."

"The king must be obeyed," I said. In those days, it never hurt to add a plug for loyalty (nobody here but us loyal supporters of Nkumai).

"The king must be screwed," said the innkeeper, and I liked him better instantly. If there had been any other customers, perhaps he would have been more circumspect. "The king of Nkumai is about as prevalent these days as starships."

I laughed. So he knew, too.

"Everyone knows the real power behind the throne is Mwabao Mawa."

The name brought back floods of memories, ending on a dark night when she tried to make love to a sweet young girl in her treehouse. Oddly, the memory stirred me and I thought wistfully of what might have happened if we had made love. Wouldn't she have been surprised.

"And what I know but not everyone knows is that the scientists are the power behind Mwabao Mawa," he said.

I smiled. "Scientists? They're nothing but dreamers."

"Do you think so? Do you think because I've fallen on hard times that I don't have supporters and friends in high places? The same's true of Mueller. The geneticists are running things there—Dinte's just to keep those that love royal blood from rising up in rebellion. It's a sad day when those born to rule are keeping inns while self-appointed wise men oversee things they were never meant to handle."

He went into the back room, then, and didn't come back out until I had finished drinking the ale. I didn't need it, but every now and then it just felt good to drink. And afterward it felt good to piss. People who do these things every day never realize how much pleasure they involve.

"Don't go yet!" he called out, and he strode back into the common room. "Sit back down, and give me your word you'll not tell anybody what I tell you now."

I smiled, and he foolishly took that for assent. He smiled back. "I knew in a minute," he said, "that you're not a common boy. It's not just your white hair, though sure enough that places you in Mueller or Schmidt. You've got the look about you. Even though you're alone, you've known how it was to command men."

I said nothing, just stared at him. He grinned and quieted his voice. "My name's Bill Underjones. Understand that, so that you know that I'm not just a dreamer." *Under-jones* made him only one step removed from royalty. "There are those who still oppose these niggers. We aren't many, but we're smart, and we're stockpiling iron south of here, in Huss. It's a backwater country, but that's the best place to hide. I'll tell you who to see there, and he'll be glad to take you in. It doesn't matter who you are, one look at you and he'll want you. His name is—"

"Don't tell me his name," I said. "I don't want to know."

"You can't tell me you don't hate these niggers as bad as I do!"

"Maybe worse," I said. "But I break easily under torture. I'd give away all your secrets."

He looked at me slantwise. "I don't believe you."

"I urge you to try," I said.

"Who are you?"

"Lanik Mueller," I said. He looked startled for a moment, then laughed uproariously. I often used my own name—it always brought that reaction. "Might as well claim to be the devil himself. No, Lanik Mueller was swallowed up—what a joker. Might as well claim to be the devil."

Might as well. He was still laughing as I walked out onto the street.

The inn faced the main highway, and as I stepped from the inn's wooden frontwalk, a beggar child ran past me, jostling me as he went. I was annoyed, and watched the boy as he ran on, finally colliding head-on with a very important-looking man with clothes of a quality that implied he was not wondering whether dinner would be on the table. The man had been talking to several younger men, and when the child struck him, he gave the boy a vicious kick in the leg. The child fell to the ground, and the man cursed him soundly.

It was foolish of me, but this seemed at the moment to be the crowning injustice of all the million injustices I had seen and perpetrated in my life. *This* time, I decided, I would do something.

So I pushed myself into quicktime, and the people on the street slowed until they were nearly stopped. I threaded my way carefully through the crowd until I stood in front of the man who had kicked the child. His right foot was descending to the ground as he walked along, still in animated discussion with his young friends. It was a simple matter to have the soil of the road sink a dozen centimeters or so right under his foot, and to have a puddle of water form in front of him, extending a full two meters on. With my hands I took one of the stones common on the road and placed it so it would impede his left foot.

Then I walked to the stable where my horse was being fed and groomed, and leaned against the door. I felt more than a little silly to have gone to such lengths to effect such a small thing. It was more a desire for the prank, I think, than any moral principle that inspired the act.

However, now that I was in quicktime among the crowd, I took a moment to relax. No need to put up a facade of ordinariness that few with any perception believed anyway. Instead I could survey the crowd at my leisure. And because I had allowed the child in me to hold sway for a few moments, I toyed with the idea of picking pockets, not because I needed any money, but because it was possible to do it and never get caught.

There is something about knowing you won't get caught that could tempt the most honest man, and I have never claimed to be unusually honest. I looked over the crowd to see who might be a likely target. A little way down the road a large wagon was coming— an Nkumai coach, and judging from the large contingent of mounted Nkumai soldiers, it contained somebody important. It was a warm day; the carriage was open; the sole occupant was a middle-aged man, rather stocky and thoroughly bald. To my surprise, he was white. I immediately supposed he was a Mueller returning from a visit to Nkumai. But the Nkumai don't give mounted escorts to foreigners who are leaving. Either this man deserved unusual honor (in which case, why didn't I know him?) or the Nkumai were letting foreigners high in their own government.

Wondering about him put the idea of picking pockets out of my mind. I slid back to real time, turning to watch the result of my prank. Exactly as planned, the self-important stranger stepped into the rut I had made and fell headlong into the puddle. The splash was formidable, and he arose sputtering and cursing as all the people nearby laughed at him. Even his coterie of admirers couldn't hide their amusement as they solicitously helped him up. And, for all that the gesture was small, I felt a certain satisfaction, particularly when I looked at the laughing child the man had kicked.

And then the moment passed, and people moved to the side of the road to let the Nkumai troup and the carriage pass. I glanced at the carriage and was shocked to see, not the middle-aged man, but Mwabao Mawa.

She was only a little older—it had scarcely been two-and-a-half years—and held herself very importantly in the carriage. I briefly wondered why I hadn't noticed her in the carriage before, and where the bald white man had got to; but I dismissed the thought because it seemed unimportant and didn't admit to any ready explanation except that I had been careless when I looked before. Instead, I let myself remember my days in Mwabao Mawa's house. It seemed impossible to me now that I had once had breasts and passed for a woman. *Been* a woman, rather. And for a moment as I involuntarily reached up to my chest I expected to find softness there, and was surprised to find it gone. I glanced down, cursed myself for a fool, and then looked up to see Mwabao Mawa staring at me, at first in mild interest, and then, as the carriage pulled farther away, with recognition and surprise and, yes, fear. The fear was gratifying, but the recognition could be a disaster.

She turned to give instructions to the driver. I used that moment to step back into the stable and get out of sight. I also pushed into quicktime again—I had to think, quickly. There was no way I could take my horse, since Man-Who-Knows-It-All hadn't been able to teach me to have much effect outside myself. In quicktime I could walk faster relative to the rest of the world than a horse could possibly carry me at a full gallop.

I went to my horse, a huge, stupid beast with all the instincts of a hog but with a price I could afford, and unloaded the saddlebags, selecting as much as I could carry, and taking anything that might give a hint as to my identity. There was little enough of that—I had never been one for embroidered handkerchiefs. Then, carrying the bags, I passed back into normal time and walked up to the stabler, who was talking to his apprentice.

"Sir," I said urgently, and he turned around. "Sir, for the next two days that horse is yours. You bought it from a passing horse trader and got the worst deal of your life because the damn thing won't obey without a kick in the leg. If you tell any other story, or if that horse isn't here when I get back, I'll slit you up from gut to gills, do you understand? But if all's well in two days, I'll pay you the price of a better horse than that."

I imagine my manner was convincing, even if my words had not been. He nodded dumbly.

"You've never seen anyone who answers to my description, right?" I asked.

"Hell no," he said. And I gave him a silver ring and walked out the back way into the corral, shoving my way into quicktime again as soon as I was out of sight. Whether Mwabao Mawa believed him or not, she would be suspicious and would order soldiers to patrol. But I rather thought she wouldn't push the stabler too hard—I had only been standing in the doorway, and there was no particular guarantee that I was actually at the stable on business.

When she didn't find me, she would forget the search and figure she had only seen someone who reminded her of me.

I hoped.

I tossed the bags over the fence, climbed after them, and walked off down a side street. I'd have to stay in quicktime for several days. Which irritated me, because in quicktime, of course, I aged more quickly relative to the real world. I wouldn't end up like Man-Who-Fell-on-His-Ass, but I resented losing days or weeks off my life. How old was I now, anyway? I had gained days and weeks when I was with Saranna in slowtime; I had lost many more days and weeks in quicktime among the Ku Kuei. Was I anywhere near my calendar age of eighteen? Hardly, even if my body seemed that young and strong. I had done enough to feel middle-aged, and as I strode off through the back roads and started on my way to Robles in the south, I decided that quicktime didn't matter anyway. I had no particular desire to live to be old.

Though I had no intention of letting the Nkumai catch me and realize who I was.

The worst thing about quicktime was the loneliness. No one is safer than a man who moves so quickly that he can't be seen. But it's a bit tough to carry on a conversation with someone who won't even know you're there unless you stand in the same place for a half hour.

I crossed the Rio de Janeiro into Cummings before I let myself back into real time. No matter how alarmed Mwabao Mawa was, she wouldn't send troops more than a thousand kilometers to look for someone she had seen only a few meters off that very day.

Why did I go south? I had no particular object. Except that I had lived in a dozen towns under Nkumai control in Jones and Bird during the past six months, and I wanted to get to a place where the enlightened empire of the scientists didn't rule. I didn't want to link up with any rebels gathering in Huss, so I went southeast over the da Silva pass, and found that there was no escape from the imperial committees. A few dozen scientists in Gill ruled from Tellerman to Britton, and no one was free.

I might have gone right back to Schwartz then. Or I might have gone back to Mueller. But I hadn't the weariness yet for retirement from the world, and I hadn't the passion for a dramatic death, and so both Schwartz and Mueller I reserved for the future. Instead I wandered from da Silva to Wood, from Wood to Hanks, from Hanks across the sea to Holt, and finally to Britton, where I found out that it *was* up to me to save the world after all, whether I like it or not.

I didn't like it.

britton

It was wild country on the borders of a calm sea. The steep cliffs and jumbled rocks of the coast were met, not by crashing waves, but by ripples that lapped against the stone as gently as aging dogs greet their master. And the stones also sprouted from the earth, it seemed, on the steep hills and narrow valleys of Humping. A river hunted for a way to the sea, and found it over a forty-foot fall; sheep looked nervous as they picked a safe way to unshorn pastures; and here, a few thousand Humpers tended their sheep and scratched vegetables from the stony ground and lived as independent a life as human beings can live when they still need human company and still must eat.

I didn't need to eat, but the human company was good, for the Humpers asked no questions and gave no answers. It was hard even to find a town in this most isolated section of Britton, for the people tended to congregate in family groups of two or three simple sod houses with thatch roofs. I never found a gathering of more than twenty families within a kilometer of each other.

The isolation was forced by nature, for the meager land could not support much density, and only the uniformity of want made the people think they were not poor. Despite the distances, however, they clung to each other's company grimly, wordlessly coming to the help of the family whose house was blown over by the storm, anonymously leaving a young hegoat among the herd whose sire died the day before, and occasionally gathering at each other's homes for a night of tall and terrible tales or songs of loneliness and silent longings.

I had another impression, subtle but strong: when I came to Humping, as I had come to so many other places in the past year, I knew that I immediately felt comfortable there. Or if not comfortable, at least willing to bear the discomforts because they fit the awkward places in my heart. The people viewed me with suspicion, of course, for I came over the hills from the west, where more civilized folk in easier farms had nothing but contempt for the Humpers, using the name as a mockery for slow-witted children.

But I lived in these hills, speaking to no one, for a week, when my loneliness struck a sympathetic chord. I was standing on the crest of a steep hill, watching as a shepherd far below tried to get his sheep to climb a slope to a saddle that led over to a greener valley. The man had no dogs, which was unusual, and the sheep kept breaking to left or right rather than climbing. When the man finally stopped and sat on a rock to watch his victorious sheep hunt for forage in an already-overgrazed valley, I came down the hill and stood a few meters off from him, watching the sheep. I didn't speak because I had nothing to say; my offer was intrinsic in my presence.

The shepherd accepted. He stood and began prodding the sheep and uttering the low, guttural cries that the sheep could hear clearly but that were inaudible from a good distance off. The sheep began to move, but this time when they broke left there I was, crying them onward; when they broke right, there was the shepherd, grunting. Finally the sheep gave up and shambled up the slope and over the saddle, rushing downhill to graze in the thick grass.

I stayed in the valley with the shepherd all the rest of the afternoon, staying pretty much on the other side of the valley from him, but watching his sheep, and sending back the few that strayed in my direction. He seemed not to notice me, and said nothing (I wondered if by ill-fortune I had stumbled on a Humper who couldn't talk), but when the sun came close to the horizon he stood and began herding the sheep along a fairly easy route home. I did not follow, but when the shepherd crested a rise, after making it plain he didn't need my help on *this* journey, he turned and watched me for a moment, then beckoned. I was to come home with him.

I followed him for several kilometers before we came to a cluster of three low, thatched houses. They looked like small hills, the roofs the color of the summer-yellowed grass, but inside they were warm against the cold night. The sea wind came heavily from the north, even during summer nights, and the deep current that flowed through the Humping Sea was icy—though Britton was as far south as Wong, which sweltered in the summer, no night in Humping was ever warm, and the winters, while snowless, killed any fool who was caught out of doors after sunset.

That may have been part of the reason the shepherd invited me home. It was well-known to the Humpings (for news of any kind travels quickly in lonely places like this) that no one had taken me in; I spent night after night in the hills, yet was still alive. That made me somehow holy and powerful, and they were in awe of me, yet when I proved my intentions were kind by helping the shepherd with his sheep, I was accepted, not as one of them, but as one they would willingly share their small homes and tiny larders with.

Dinner was stew, and since the wife had not known I was coming, the pot was meager enough that I ate little—enough to accept hospitality, but no more. And when the pot had been passed around and scraped clean by the shepherd's wife on her own dish, the shepherd looked to me.

For what? Did these people pray? Or was there some custom a man had to follow when offered food? I didn't know, so I smiled and said, "My name is Lake-drinker, and what good I can do you, I will always do you."

The shepherd nodded gravely, and turned to his wife. She lay her hands on the table, closed her eyes, and intoned:

Sun on wheat,
Baking bread,
Making meat
From the dead.
Good we give
That we live.

Then, reverently, the three children, none older than five, watched as their mother took a spoonful of stew from her own plate and gave it to her husband, who solemnly chewed the bit of meat and swallowed. Then the husband took stew from his own dish and gave it to me, and I also ate. I was unsure what to do next, but the ritual made a kind of sense, and so I took from my dish and gave to each of the children, who looked wide-eyed and surprised, but ate.

The shepherd looked at me with tears in his eyes, and said, "You are welcome here forever."

Then we fell to and the stew was gone in a few minutes.

They made a place for me in the largest bed, a frame filled with straw and covered with blankets. I knew it was the parents' bed, and indeed they were preparing to sleep on the floor of packed dirt. I had slept on the earth in Schwartz and Ku Kuei and many a field maneuver in Mueller; I had no need of comfort when I slept. So I ignored the offered bed and curled up on the floor by the door. A cold draught slipped under the door, but my Schwartz-shaped body coped easily, and the parents, wonderingly, went to bed in the straw.

In the morning, I was one of the family, and the children chattered freely in my presence.

"Glain," said the shepherd, and then, glancing at his wife, "Vran." And from then on, though conversation was never lush, what needed to be said could be said.

His dogs had died in the same week nearly a month ago, and since then he had lost nearly a dozen sheep from random strays that he could not pursue. At first I herded with him; later I stayed at home and tended his vegetable garden while his wife was sick because the fourth child was coming. It disturbed me at first to take the many stones out of the soil and to know that the plants that grew would live to be killed. In the night I asked the earth, and received only indifference. The billion deaths of plants together made a powerful sound, but that death was necessary for life, and what agonized the rock was the cry of the murdered. I heard all the sounds, and all hurt, but I decided that in the world outside Schwartz death was the way of things. I had eaten all my life before the sand accepted me, so there was no murder in farming, and I worked hard and did well for Glain and Vran.

Gradually the other shepherds came to visit, and soon got over their shyness in my presence. I knew that the story of my nights on the hill and the fact that I slept in the coldest part of the floor were known to everyone, and while they called me Lake-drinker to my face, I overheard references to Man-of-the-Wind, a creature who comes either to kill or cure, brought by the cold wind and taken, eventually, by the sea.

Yet because they were unused to people of prestige or power among them, they treated me no differently from each other. In a place where all men lack equally, the only reward is trust, and I received that. I learned to handle sheep, to shear with glass blades without cutting the skin, to help with the foaling, to know when the sheep were nervous and when they were sick. I learned the soil, too, not in the personal way I had known in Schwartz and Ku Kuei, but as a reluctant ally in the war against starvation. I never knew hunger; but I knew the faces of the children when they were hungry, and I worked hard.

Vran began labor a week early, and so I was alone with her and the children when it became clear that the child would not come easily. She was in the house screaming, while the children stayed out with me. Humping mothers bore their children without help, alone —and it was forbidden for a man to come into the house while they were bearing. But as the children sat by the garden, frightened, I lay on the earth and listened to Vran's screams as the earth heard them, and I knew death was near.

There are times for taboos and times to ignore them, and at the end of a particularly terrible scream that signaled a new plateau of pain, I got up and went into the house.

Vran was squatting nude over the straw of her bed, the blankets removed. Her hands were buried in the hard sod wall, where she gripped at the clay and roots in her agony. She looked at me with terrified eyes, and I saw the blood coming in a continuous stream, trickling onto the straw.

I came to her and eased her into a lying position and, as I had done with ewes at lambing, I reached in to see what way the baby was presenting. A hand and a foot were in the birth channel.

With a ewe, it would be simply a matter of pushing and pulling. On a woman, that kind of treatment could kill. But no treatment at all would kill, too, and so I forced the child to a different position, breaking its back in the process, and pulled it out. Somewhere in the operation, Vran fainted.

Work on the genetic level was beyond me, but curing wounds and fractures was normal work in Schwartz. It was no great feat to restore both Vran and the infant boy, and when the sun was setting, Glain came home to find his wife and child in good condition. Better condition, in fact, than Vran usually was in after a delivery.

What she told him I don't know—she had slept through the worst of it. But word spread, and I began to be brought sick animals and injured children, and women would ask for my advice. I had no advice. If there was a problem, I had to come. And the Man-of-the-Wind legend took its full grip.

It was inevitable, I suppose, that even as close-mouthed as the Humpers were to outsiders, word would eventually get out. And one day I was planting in the garden for my second spring in Humping when a man came up on a horse. The mere possession of such an animal made him important; when he identified himself as Lord Barton's servant, Vran immediately rushed out of the house, called for me, urged me to come quickly. I came.

"My master wishes to see you."

"When the planting's done," I said.

"Lord Barton is unaccustomed to waiting."

"It is a custom he should acquire at the earliest opportunity," I said, and I went back to the garden. Soon the servant left.

It was hard to concentrate on gardening that afternoon. For nearly two years I had lived in Humping, and while joy was limited here, so was grief. I had found a place where my talents were useful and where I was accepted. No one regarded me as an enemy; I had hundreds of good people I could count as friends.

But could I afford to meet this Barton? I felt my good life in Humping slipping away: I couldn't afford not to meet him. If I resisted, it would only cause trouble to the Humpers, particularly to Glain and Vran. If I went, it might lead to trouble for me. Almost certainly would lead to trouble. And the only other alternative was to slip off in quicktime and find another place to live.

I didn't want to find another place to live.

And, in fact, as I pushed the wooden spike into the earth and dropped in seeds after it, I realized that I was excited as well as disturbed by the prospect of change. Two years, and what had I done? Saved lives, made some people happier, come to love many, given much of my life to a harsh land. All worthy ways to have spent my time. But I was raised to be the heir of the Mueller, and either that or a drive born with me as my father's son insisted that I must do something that would shake the world or admit that my existence did not matter.

I was ashamed of thinking that going to see Barton might lead to better things than life among the Humpers. I had seen many of the "better" things and the Humpers had no call to envy any man. But there was the drive in me, and I knew that when Lord Barton's servant came again, I would follow him.

Two days later the planting was done, and, as if he had been watching from the distance, that afternoon the servant came, this time leading a second horse. "Will you ride?" the man asked, more humbly this time, and I said nothing, merely mounted the horse.

The children gathered silently in front of the house. Vran looked at me expressionlessly. I raised a hand in farewell. And Vran, violating every custom I had seen among the Humpers, burst into tears in front of me and fled into the house. It frightened me to see how much such independent people could come to lean on someone who offers even the slightest hope of power linked with kindness.

The servant followed no road—there were no roads in the Humping Hills but one, and that the one that led from the lord's house-by-the-sea to the city of Hesswatch a hundred or more kilometers to the south. Instead, he seemed to find his way by riding east to the sea and then following the shore from a respectful distance until the cliff house was visible on a virtual pinnacle that rose considerably above the hills of Humping.

The sky darkened over with clouds, and the rains came as we approached, the wind driving swiftly and the sea, usually so placid, suddenly forming huge swells coming in from the north to break their faces on the rocky coast. The wind whipped at us, and the horses became unruly, so we dismounted and walked. The servant seemed unsure of himself. He was not a Humper, and he cast his way inland, away from the sea, which would seem daunting to any who only saw breakers when the wind was high. Unfortunately, he did not lead us to the road, but instead managed to end up at a ravine, and in the darkness it was impossible to tell which way was north and which south.

He looked at me, his eyes still confident, but the question quite clear: What can we do, now that we're lost? So I led my horse up away from the ravine and found shelter under a steep cliff, where the wind from the north would, at worst, allow only spray to strike us. Then I tied the horses to each other and the servant helped me as I hobbled them.

"I'll keep watch at first," I told him, and he nodded gratefully and curled up to sleep, looking tall and gaunt in the dark red cape that he wrapped around himself.

I was more tired from the day's exertions than I thought, however, and I decided to catch some sleep in quicktime, so that I would be able to stay awake through most of the realtime night.

I slept easily, and awoke after a long time, feeling refreshed. I lay a moment in quicktime, watching how the drops came crawling down from the sky to hover over the horses' backs, finally striking and breaking instantly into pools and splashes. And as I slipped into realtime, I glanced at the servant and was momentarily startled to see him looking much shorter, and wearing a blue cape that barely covered his knees.

The illusion passed immediately. I was in realtime, and he looked as he had always looked. I laughed at myself for having let my vision be fooled by the darkness and my sleepiness, and I watched well throughout the rest of the night, taking a short nap as the clouds cleared just before dawn. The horses stirred occasionally, but were usually docile, and we got under way almost as soon as the sun was up.

The cliff house rose in a jumble of stone from the promontory, and up close it was even more dramatic than its height made it seem from a distance. It must have been constructed in bits and pieces over centuries; there was no clear architectural style, and some of the earliest constructions seemed to have been designed for defense. Now, however, the place seemed brooding and forlorn, and the still-high seas cast spray up to the level of the lower stories, seeming to say that it was only a matter of time before the sea claimed the house.

The servant led me to the stable, where a single groom put the horses into stalls and ignored us as we left. Inside the house, the rooms were cold, and we passed no one. It was plain the place was designed for large companies; the emptiness made the cold penetrate even more.

But coldness was not Lord Barton's manner, and when we appeared unannounced at the door of a large study, I was struck by the contrast. In *this* room, a huge fire burned; in *this* room, the walls weren't stone, but rather were lined with books rising dizzyingly to the ceiling ten meters from the floor. Ladders were strategically placed and their treads were well worn, implying that the books were a building still under construction.

And Barton, an aging man with a smile that overwhelmed his face frequently, welcomed me with a handshake and pulled me into the room. "Thank you, Dul," he told the servant, and we were alone.

"I've heard of you," said Barton. "Heard of you and wanted to meet you for some time, some time. Sit, please, I've moved the softest furniture up here, where I live. It's shabby and old, but so am I, and it all fits nicely when you consider that I'm the decaying remnant of a decadent line. I only have one son." That amused him, and he laughed.

I did not laugh. I looked at the titles on the spines of the books. Habits of the Humpers did not disappear overnight, and when I had nothing of importance to say, it was hard to say anything.

Barton stared at me penetratingly. "You are not," said Barton, "what you seem."

And that awoke my old manner of thought. "So many people have said that that I'm beginning to think that's precisely how I *do* seem. What is it I seem to be that you think I'm not?"

"A sharp tongue, even when speaking to a lord, and a man who refuses to come when bidden until the planting's done. You seem to be a rebel, sullen and silent. But the people say you're the Man-in-the-Wind, and you save mothers in childbirth and heal lame sheep and help simple children find their minds. Miracles, yes?"

I didn't answer, regretting my outburst of Muellerish speech. Enough of that. I was done with that.

"But the reason I asked to see you has little to do with that. Legends come and go among these superstitious folk, and I don't call every passing healer in to speak with me. What intrigued me was white hair like wool, as the Humpers say, and a man who seeks out hardship. A man who seems young in years but old as I am in experience. Whatever became of Lanik Mueller?"

The last question was so ridiculous I couldn't hide my surprise. Barton laughed. "Tricks and traps. I play them even on the wise. There are rewards, you know, for seeming to be a foolish old man. Lanik Mueller has always fascinated me, you know. It's been what, four years now since he and dear old Ensel Mueller vanished into the forest of Ku Kuei, never to be seen again. Well, I don't put much stock in legends. They always seem to have a perfectly natural foundation. And I don't think people who go into Ku Kuei necessarily die. Do you?"

I shrugged.

"I think they come out again. And I think that Lanik Mueller, the scourge of the Rebel River plain, I think he lives."

He looked at me intently. "I met you, boy, when you were eleven."

That forced me to look at him again. Had I ever seen that thin old man before?

"I was a traveler in the old days, and a bit of a historian. I picked up histories and genealogies wherever I went, trying to discover what had happened to the world in the days since the Republic set down our ancestors and their families on this paradise of a world as a punishment for their sins. And when I met you, I thought, 'Here's a boy bound to do something important.' They say you burned and ravaged and raped and killed anything in your path."

I shook my head.

"But what intrigued me most was something that strikes very close to home, Lanik Mueller. I have learned that your younger brother, Dinte, is now ruling where you would have ruled."

"A figurehead, thank God, since the bastard couldn't rule an anthill with any efficiency," I said, admitting what he obviously knew.

"The child of your mother?"

"Incredible as it may seem, yes. I never saw you, Barton."

"I was younger then." He got up from his chair and strode to a ladder, climbed it slowly, and reached down a book that must have weighed five kilos. When he was back to the floor, he gave it to me. "I bought this," he said, "from your father, who was reluctant to part with it. But he had another copy, and when I explained how important genealogy was to me he became convinced I was a doddering old idiot, and he let me buy the book, though he charged me five times what he thought it was worth."

That was my father.

I opened the book. A genealogy of Mueller and a history, kept as a kind of chronicle in the handwriting of a herald. I didn't recognize the hand at the end of the book, but sure enough, the account and the genealogy ended when I was eleven. It was amusing to see what the herald had thought was worth recording. I must have been someone's delight—every clever thing I said as an infant was there.

The expectancy of Barton's silence was pressure enough that I skimmed and rushed through to the end.

"Genuine?" he asked.

"Of course," I said. "Do you doubt it, when you got it the way you did?"

"Not at all. I just wanted your opinion before I point out an omission, a simple but very important thing left out of the book. So obvious it would occur to you to miss it."

I waited.

"Your brother," he said. "Dinte."

Of course Dinte was mentioned. So many of my childhood memories were tied to him. But I glanced back to the time when Dinte was born, and there was no mention. Nor was there any mention of him for the entire duration of the journal.

"Well, maybe the herald didn't like Dinte any better than I did," I said.

"The herald didn't meet Dinte."

"He led a sheltered life in the palace, then."

"Lanik Mueller, I want you to think back to a memory. An unpleasant one, preferably. I want you to picture it in your mind."

I smiled. "No one takes psychology seriously anymore."

"It's not psychology, Mueller. It's survival."

So I thought back to the time I lied about who had lamed Rurik, the horse I was given after I had learned to ride like an adult. I had jumped him stupidly, and he had been injured, and then I walked him home and told my father that the stableboy had lamed him and that I had noticed it as soon as I was away from the stable. The boy had lost his job and had a good thrashing in the bargain, particularly since he had "lied" about it and claimed the horse was healthy when I took it out. I remembered the expression on the boy's face when my father made me accuse him to his face. I remembered clearly how I felt.

"I see from your face that you've thought of something that mattered. How clearly do you remember it?"

"Clearly," I answered.

"Now, think of your clearest memory concerning Dinte from the time you were, say, seven or eight, and both learning from tutors. Did you have the same tutor?"

"Yenwi."

"But did he have the same tutor?"

I shrugged.

"Think of a childhood memory of Dinte."

Easy enough. Until I tried it. But all my memories of Dinte were of the time when I was older. When I was twelve and thirteen and fourteen and fifteen. I simply could not remember Dinte before that, though the unshakeable conviction remained that he was *there*.

"Just because I can't remember details," I began, and then saw that Barton was laughing.

"My own words," he said. 'Just because I can't remember details. But you're so sure. Haven't the slightest doubt."

"Of course not. If I could have made the little bastard disappear, I would have done it years ago, believe me."

"Let me tell you a story, then," he said. "Settle down in the chair, Lanik Mueller, because it's a long one, and being old I shall undoubtedly lace it with details that were best left out. Try to stay awake. Snoring puts me off my form." And then he recounted to me the story of his son, Percy. When he mentioned the boy's name, I immediately recognized it.

"Percy Barton? Lord Percy of Gill?"

"The same. You're interrupting."

"But he's the ruler—or should we say, figurehead—over the so-called East Alliance. And he's your son?"

"Born and raised in this castle, but I shan't ever finish if I can't begin, Mueller." I let him begin.

"It's my penchant for traveling, you see. I made a journey, not all that many years ago, one of my last before travel became out of the question because of my health, to Lardner. You may know Lardner —a land of cold that makes Humping look like paradise, but it has the world's best physicians. If ever I were sick, I'd want a doctor from Lardner. And while I was there, I chanced upon a doctor whom I had known when I was a young man, just married and barely into my own as lord of more than I have now—not just Humping, but of the whole east peninsula. This doctor, Twis Stanly, was a specialist of sorts, women and women's problems, but he was also a damned fine archer and we'd bow together and have the grandest time on vacation in the Spire Mountains. Good friends, but I remembered he had treated my wife only a month after we were married for a rather odd infection. This was, of course, some time before Percy was born."

He paused a moment, as if unsure how to say what came next. "He inquired, of course, after my wife, and I had to inform him, quite sadly, that she had died only two or three years before, of ripe but not old age. She was over fifty, and it stunned me that it had been near thirty-five years before that Twis and I had brought down two harts of the same herd with single arrow each, practically in unison. I mentioned the fact, and then commented on how my son, Percy, had hardly a notion that his father was once handy with a bow.

"We shared a bit of a laugh at that and the foibles of youth, and then he said, 'Well, Barton, you remarried then?'"

"The question seemed odd. 'Of course not,' I told him, 'what made you think so?'

"'Then you adopted the boy? Your son?' asks he, and I deny it. 'A true born son of my flesh, not two years into marriage.'

"He went a bit white then, as we old men are prone to do, and he took down a notebook from his interminable shelves of trivial records, and looked up a particular entry, and had me read it. It recorded the hysterectomy he had performed on my wife a month after our marriage.

"Can you imagine what a shock that was to me? I was sure he was mistaken, but he was a methodical man, you know, and I couldn't shake his surety. He took everything, womb, ovaries, everything, and she damn near died in the process, but it was that or a cancer to destroy her life within the year. So she was doomed to childlessness in exchange for life.

"It was a blow. I insisted I could remember the childbirth, but when I tried to recount the circumstances, I couldn't remember a bit of it. Not the day, not the place, not whether I went in or stayed out, not how I celebrated the birth of an heir, nothing. Nothing. Like you and your brother just now."

I might doubt many men, but in this case I couldn't fathom a reason for Barton to lie. And now the book of genealogy in my lap weighed heavier, and I struggled even as I listened to try to remember something, anything about Dinte from our childhood together. A blank.

"That's not all my story, Lanik Mueller. I went home. And on the way home, I somehow forgot the entire conversation. Forgot it! Something like that, and it simply slipped my mind. It was not until I was out of Britton on my very last journey, this time a visit to Goldstein because of the warmth in the winter. And while I was there, I got a letter from Twis. He wondered why I hadn't been answering his letters. I hadn't known I had been receiving any. But in his letter he said enough to refresh my memory. I was shocked at the lapse that had occurred, appalled that I could have forgotten. And then I realized something. It wasn't old age, Lanik Mueller, that made me forget. Something was doing something to my mind.

"I came home, only this time I thought, steadily, continuously, of how my son was a fraud, a total mountebank. I clutched Twis's letter to my bosom and reread it every few minutes all the way home. I've never had such a struggle in my life. I've never suffered so much anguish of mind. I would finish reading the letter and have no idea what it had said. The closer I got to Britton, the harder it became. But I kept saying, "I have no son. Percy is a fraud," and never mind wondering how anyone could come to a childless man and pass himself off as his son. Suffice it to say that I made it. I came here with my mind and memory intact. And behold, on this very desk, four letters from Twis, opened and obviously read, which I had utterly no memory of receiving. Now I could read them, and each one of them referred to the matter of Percy being an impossibility.

"In the other letters, Twis gave me comments from friends who had come from Lardner to stay with him during his days in Britton,

friends who had met me. I remembered them well. All of them had
clear memories of the fact that I was childless and that my wife and
I knew perfectly well that we had no hope of having children. He
quoted my own witticism to the effect that at least now my wife had
no time of month when she could beg off from her duties in bed.
And as I read Twis's mention of that occasion, I remembered it. I
remembered saying that. And it was as though something snapped
inside of me. I remembered everything, and I had no son. Until I
turned forty or so, and then, suddenly, a nineteen-year-old boy eager
to rule, passionate for opportunity. I made him governor of my
northernmost holding, and it was all he needed. In five years he was,
incredibly, overlord of all of Britton. And only eight years ago he
rose to the head of the alliance and turned it into a dictatorship."

I shook my head. "Not a dictatorship, Barton. A figurehead for a
committee of scientists. The self-proclaimed wise men rule in Nkumai and Mueller, too."

"It's always wise, when discovering figureheads, to be certain who
is manipulating whom," Barton said with a bite that made it clear
he thought me unclever in holding that opinion. "Don't you understand what I'm telling you? Dinte and Percy are the same. Children
who appeared out of nowhere, but no one questions them, no one
doubts them in their own family, in their own country, and now
they have both risen to the highest position of authority in very powerful countries, and everyone is convinced they're mere figureheads."

It did sound rather odd.

"I shall help you be convinced," he said. "When I spoke to you
once about how it felt to be heir to the throne, you said, quite
bluntly—your father was proud of your bluntness, as I remember—
you said, 'Lord Barton, it is only fun to be heir because there is no
other legitimate, unless you count the retarded dwarf Ruva spawned.
If I had a brother, I should have to be more careful of how I
behaved, for they could rid themselves of me thinking that if they
lost one heir, there was always a spare.' I remember the words because your father made me recite them to five or six different people
during my visit, as evidence of your precocity. Do you recall the
words?"

I did. I recalled the words. I recalled the moment I remembered
old Barton, younger then, of course, being much amused and slap-
ping his thigh, roaring with laughter, repeating fragments of the

remark. I had felt much impressed with myself at having won laughter from such a man.

I remembered, and at that moment I knew that Barton was right. I had no brother. I was an only child.

And I remembered something else. I remembered Mwabao Mawa. The servant who had brought me to the cliff house came in with toddy.

I had seen a middle-aged man on the streets in that town in Jones, riding in a carriage. A white man. And then a moment later, I had seen Mwabao Mawa in the carriage, in precisely the same place. She saw me; I fled; and yet in all that time since then, I had never wondered why the man would have left the wagon in mid-travel to let Mwabao Mawa get on. Where was Mwabao Mawa up to then? Where did the white man go?

It fit the pattern. A seemingly powerless figurehead, run by the committee of scientists—but when viewed differently, perhaps the very person who ruled.

The servant brought a toddy to me, at Barton's insistence, and was now carrying the other to Barton.

I had been in quicktime when I saw the bald white man. Then, in realtime, I had seen Mwabao. Was that the difference, then? In quicktime, I saw the reality? In realtime, I was fooled like everyone else?

The servant leaned over Barton and I remembered having caught a glimpse, that very morning as I came out of quicktime, of a blue cape on a shorter man turning into a red cape on the gaunt servant who now bent over Barton, who now watched as Barton took the toddy to his lips.

"Don't," I said to Barton. "Don't drink it."

Barton looked surprised for a moment, while the servant stood, blankly looking at me. Then, suddenly, the servant crumpled and Barton leaped to his feet, ran agilely out the door. I was startled. I was put off. I was slowed down. And then I looked at the servant, lying in a tumble on the floor, and realized it was not the servant at all. It was Barton.

How had I seen the servant fall and Barton leave, and been in error? They had never changed places, not that I had seen. And yet there lay Barton—and his head had been nearly severed from his body, except for the spine, in a single strong whick of a very sharp blade.

It had to be an iron blade, in fact.

No time for speculation, of course. I knelt by Barton and pressed the head against the neck and did as I had done for so many Humpers—I connected blood vessels, I healed torn muscles, I linked the skin together without a seam, and made the body healthy and whole and I even, because I was doing the work and because I cared for the man and because it was easier to do something I *knew* how to do than to think about what to do next, I even found his rheumatism and his feebleness and his lung disease and his dying heart and fixed them, renewed them, made him healthier than he had been in many years.

He was conscious, looking at me. "Man-in-the-Wind," he said, smiling. "The stories are true."

"The servant was one of them," I said, and neither of us had any doubt as to whom the *them* referred to.

"That much I guessed. Dear Dul. How the buggers do proliferate. Tell me, how did you guess?"

I had neither time nor inclination to tell him about Ku Kuei and the manipulation of time. "I just guessed," I said. "You had made me alert."

He looked at me doubtfully, then decided that if I had wanted to tell the truth I would have told it already, and he got to his feet. He arose so suddenly, in fact, that he startled himself and nearly lost his balance forward. "When you heal, you don't play games, do you?" he asked. "I feel like a thirty-year-old."

"Damn. You should feel twenty."

"I didn't want to exaggerate. Lanik, what are you? Never mind. Never mind. Dul must have been listening. They know you know something, or he wouldn't have tried to poison us both. I assume the toddy was poisoned, yes? And then he killed me to shut me up and took off. I doubt we'll find him. He'd probably seem to be an old woman and then slip a knife into our backs as we passed."

"We?" I asked.

"I only lacked your confirmation," Barton said. "I was still, in the back of my mind, more than a little worried that I was going mad and had made it all up. But now, of course, I know I'm right and so do you, and it's time to confront Percy and kill the little bastard."

Kill? Barton? "You don't seem the type," I said.

"Perhaps not," Barton answered. "But there's a sort of anger a man feels when he's been fooled that compares to no other. He made a fool of me, and not over something small, but over my own self, over my own wife, over my own hope of a family. He became my heir, he used me as a springboard to power, and all by pretending, by illuding me into thinking he was my son. I'm very angry, Lanik Mueller."

"He also will think you're very dead. It is wise to disabuse him of the notion so soon?"

Barton paused at that.

"And besides, Barton, what good will killing one of them do? We already have evidence of four of them. Surely there are more. It might be more to the point of the problem if we found out where they're from."

"Does it matter?" he asked.

"Doesn't it?"

He smiled. "Yes, it does. It occurs to me that they have gone a long way toward taking over the entire planet. And Nkumai and Mueller both had iron, yes?"

"And now these people, whoever they are and however they do what they do, control the source of that iron."

"For thousands of years we've competed murderously for something to sell offworld through the Ambassadors in order to be the first to build a starship and get out of here. And now they'll be first, no matter who wins. Now they'll control it all." He scratched his head. "Seems we've all been taken by some pretty fast operators."

"It's not your normal swindle," I pointed out.

"You've taken all this so calmly."

"I'm used to seeing strange things in this world. I'm going to Gill, Barton, and I urge you to stay here. Here, at least, you'll be safe. And I think I have a way of recognizing them. Easily and safely. And getting around their illusions."

He didn't ask, because I think my manner made it clear I wouldn't answer anyway. No need to have someone else, even Barton, know what I could do. Not yet. Not until I knew what I was going to do about it. He promised to stay at the cliff house and I went down to the stable, saddled a horse—the best Barton owned—and set out for Gill. It's a measure of my stupidity that I did not go in quicktime.

As I sat astride the horse walking briskly but not frantically down the road toward civilization, and eventually toward Gill, I saw a Humper driving his flock north, toward the less-civilized and therefore more inviting part of Humping. And it seemed incredible to me that just the day before I had finished Glain's and Vran's planting; that I had seriously thought of spending the rest of my life there among the Humpers. The memory, only a day old, struck me like a terrible ache, a realization that I was not, after all, ready for goodness and peace and happiness, but instead still felt a sense of mission. If there is a purpose to fulfil, I will fulfil it, I thought bitterly (and yet with some pride, for up to now all my purposes had come to nothing) and this time—this time, because in quicktime the illuders stood revealed to me, I was not just a person who could stop them, I was the *only* person who could stop them. I was the only person who could spot them among the normal human beings they imitated and destroy them.

Destroy them. Did I already, so casually, plan murder? But it's war! I insisted to myself, and wondered then who had declared it and why I thought I was on the "good" side. I need not ask the earth on this one, I realized. This time it wasn't a matter of eating vegetables. I meant to kill men, kill them in cold blood, kill them for a noble cause, but kill them just the same.

And was the cause noble? Was I striking a blow for Mueller's independence? From what? Perhaps these illuders were doing something valuable for our miserable planet. They were ending the bloodshed, ending the competition, unifying the planet to achieve a common purpose.

No. Wrong. They were not ending the competition. They were winning it. And that was a different matter.

Ending the competition was a goal I had never really formulated before. It did not yet seem to me to be that important. Far more important was the fact that so many people were being fooled, thinking they were governing themselves or at least believing they understood who ruled them. Yet in fact someone, or rather some ones, were secretly stealing power at its very founts, and that struck me as being unfair.

Which is, after all, the only way any man decides what is right and what is wrong—how it seems to him. And this was *wrong*. Other men's minds were solving the problems of the universe. Other men's blood and genes had gone into winning the iron Mueller had taken from the Ambassador. And those minds and that blood were being stolen without anyone's knowledge that the crime was taking place.

I remembered being a radical regenerative. I remembered standing at the window, observing the pens, identifying, to my terror, with the monsters of many legs and arms who were fed from troughs and denied even the slightest shred of humanity. It was cruel, though how else rads could have been treated God only knew. Yet even that cruelty might have been bearable, or at least partly bearable, because the rads knew that they were doing it for Mueller. Doing it to ensure that their families and their families' families would be the ones to sell offworld, would be the ones to make the starships and go out into space and be free.

If that hope had helped keep them sane, it was a terrible thing to turn that hope into a lie and have their suffering and loneliness and loss of humanity be for a race of strangers who insinuated themselves into families—

I hated Dinte. I had despised him before, but now I hated him. I pictured myself going into the palace at Mueller-on-the-River and walking up to him and going into quicktime and seeing the man who really was Dinte, the man pretending to be my brother, the man who had destroyed my father and robbed me of my inheritance; and when I saw him, I could picture myself killing him, and the picture gave me pleasure.

(I could hear the earth screaming with the cries of dying men, but I shut out that memory. Not that memory. Not today. I had blood to shed before I was ready for that memory again.)

But first, Percy Barton. I had to learn from him where he came from and who his people were, so that somehow they could be destroyed. Or could they? Was there any way to make an end to people who could appear to be something they were not, who could trade places with a man before your eyes and never have you notice, who could pretend to be your brother for years and never give you a clue?

How did they do it? How could I fight it?

And as I descended from the hills of Humping, I felt a terrible sadness, because I knew I was leaving my truest home in order to go out and destroy my peace of mind and cause agony to the earth. I remembered the spokesman of the Schwartzes telling me, "Every man who dies at your hand will scream into your soul forever."

Almost I turned back. Almost I went back to Glain and Vran. Almost.

Instead I rode on for twelve days until I came to Gill, the capital of the Family of Gill, and also the capital of the empire called the Eastern Alliance. In my days of travel, I had figured nothing out and knew nothing more than I knew before. I hadn't even taken elementary precautions, which is why they caught me in Gill and killed me.

gill

Lord Barton's servant, Dul, had reached Gill ahead of me. That had been predictable. What I had forgotten was that if Dul heard enough of our conversation to want to poison us, he also heard enough to know that I was Lanik Mueller.

Did they believe him? Did they suspect that Lanik Mueller had survived, had reemerged from Ku Kuei? Perhaps they doubted it now, but once word reached Mwabao Mawa, there would be no more doubt. She would remember having seen me, and they would be certain.

It was an academic question at the moment, however. Lanik Mueller or Lake-drinker or Man-in-the-Wind, I had discovered the existence of the illuders and I had to be destroyed. I was given no trial—the soldiers recognized me from my description as I came through the gate into the port city of Gill, and I was taken to be executed.

If they killed me the wrong way, it could be disastrous—I might really die from beheading or burning. It would be beyond my abilities to save myself, and so I would have to escape before they performed the execution; and the only methods of escape I had were too demonstrative of my abilities to fail to raise an alarm among the illuders.

I was lucky. Executions in Gill were by squads of archers. Arrows were easily taken care of by any Mueller, unless they were a direct hit to the heart—and as a rad, even a cured one, a hit to the heart worried me very little.

The soldiers were very businesslike. In Mueller every person—stranger, slave, or citizen—had the right to a hearing. In Gill, apparently, strangers were exempt from that particular ritual. I was arrested, carted off in a wagon through the streets of Gill (the people apparently disposed of rotten fruit and vegetables by giving it as a parting gift for those in the executioner's wagon), and put in front of a large pile of straw, so that misses wouldn't result in a lost or damaged arrow.

The archers looked bored and perhaps a little irritated. Was this their day off? They lined up casually, selecting arrows. There were a dozen of them, and all looked competent. The captain of the guard, who had escorted me to the place of execution, raised his arm. There were no preliminaries, no last words, no final meal (a waste of food, of course), no announcement of what the hell I was supposed to be guilty of. When he lowered his arm, the arrows loosed in a commendably uniform and accurate volley—all the arrows landed on my chest, and though two were stopped by ribs, the others all penetrated, with four piercing my heart and the rest wreaking havoc with my lungs.

It hurt. And although I knew I didn't need to breathe and my heart would heal as soon as I took the arrows out, my body still believed it was dead, and I collapsed.

It would not be politic, I decided, to reach up and pull out the arrows at this point. So I went into slowtime—a mild slowtime, that left me stiff to them, while their handling of my body was painfully rough, but not unbearable. I figured they'd probably be rid of my body within fifteen minutes—they showed no tendency to wait around—and that would be about three minutes of subjective time, leaving me a few seconds to remove the arrows and heal before my body started hurting for lack of blood. I could live for some time without breathing, but the blood had to flow.

They cut it close, and for one terrible moment as they carried me by a furnace I was afraid they practiced cremation. Instead, they dumped me in a hole in the ground, and as soon as they had quit shoveling on the dirt, I went into realtime, muscled the dirt out of the way enough that I could remove the arrows, and lay there healing for a few minutes. Once I was in reasonable health again, I went back into slowtime—no point in trying to endure hours of being shut up in a grave if you can avoid it—and only came out when I estimated it would be evening.

It was nearly dawn. I woke the earth around me, and it raised me reluctantly to the surface. I spread my arms, and the earth took its firm shape under me. I looked around to see if I had been observed. I had not.

The graveyard, like the place of execution, was near the southern edge of the city, outside the wall. The sea was nearby, and festering garbage on the shore, mixed with the smell of the normal number of clumsy crabs that couldn't remember which way the water was, made the place unforgettable to my nose, if not to my other senses. This time I planned to enter the city more subtly. I pushed into quicktime and made my way among the hovels clustered around the walls until I found what I dubbed "garbage gate" and went inside.

I had seen only the seamy side of Gill. In the years since then, I've seen many cities, but for slime and sludge Gill is queen of them all. Gill's position at the isthmus between the Landlock Sea and Slashsea won it a role as the largest merchant Family in the East. Yet the wealth didn't show up in Gill itself—people with property moved east into the mountains, building wood or stone mansions that would make princes in other Families jealous.

In Gill, poverty and business made an uneasy division of the city. Warehouses and manufactories and wholesale houses made way for slums and whorehouses and gaming rooms. In the nighttime, the gaiety must have been something to see; in the early morning, the city seemed weary. And still a little drunk.

There were corpses on the road leading to the garbage gate. I passed a wagon loaded with corpses frozen in the middle of the road, several men who looked little healthier than their cargo wearily hoisting another piece of human flesh into the cart for the trip to the graveyard. There are few places where life isn't cheap, but this was the first place I had found where even the poor (especially the poor, who are often kinder to their dead than the rich) had so little regard for the dead that they were cast like garbage into the street.

The palace of the governor of Gill, now the headquarters of the East Alliance, rose from the warehouse district like a wart among the moles: there was no attempt at grace, only a great grey block of stone brooding among smaller yet somehow more inviting structures that stocked cloth, salted meat, and leather.

Gaining entry to the palace was difficult. The doors were all closed, and the guards stood with their backs against them. There would be no subtle way to enter, even in quicktime—not through the doors. It attracts too much attention to knock over a guard. And the force of my passage, in quicktime, would probably kill him.

I would have to wait until later in the morning, when people were passing in and out. So, for nostalgia's sake (and perhaps planning some pretty vengeance) I sought out the gate where I had been taken the day before. As I walked along the streets I became more and more depressed. I wondered if Gill were really exceptionally vile, or if all cities, even Mueller-on-the-River, were as bad. The harsh hill country of Humping was kinder to its residents than this artificial desert of stone and dirt.

I saw in the distance as I neared the gate that the executioner's cart was already in business. What a busy day it had ahead of it! I toyed with the idea of breaking an axle, but decided it wasn't worth the time or trouble. Instead I went on to the gate, hardly glancing at the cart and the hooded prisoner as I ran past, and found what I was looking for. The captain who had silently taken me to my death the day before was in a guardroom whose door was latched. I unlatched it and walked in. Placing myself directly in front of the captain, who was alone, I slipped back into realtime. I had seen the effect often enough in Ku Kuei—from his point of view, I simply materialized out of thin air.

"Good morning," I said.

"My God," he answered.

"Ah, first question answered. You can speak. It was quite irritating not even to be greeted yesterday before you took me off and killed me."

His look of terror was delightful. I am not a vengeful man, but now and then this kind of thing does wonders for the soul. "I won't bother you long. I'm just checking up on this murder business you have here. For instance, who decides who's going to die?"

"P-Percy. The king. It isn't my fault. I don't decide anything—"

"Never mind all that, I don't do the judging around here. How many people a day do you take from the city gates straight to the graveyards?"

"Not very many. Honest. You yesterday, Lord Barton today, and I can't remember anybody for months before that. And usually they're taken as they're leaving, not as they arrive."

I tried not to look shocked. Barton! He'd ignored all my advice and come here anyway!

"You handle it very efficiently," I said.

"Thank you," he answered.

"What happens to you if something goes wrong?"

"Nothing does."

"But if it did?"

"I'd be in trouble," he said. He was beginning to act a bit more confident with me, and I suspected that in a moment he'd reach out a hand to see whether I was solid or spirit.

"Then you're in trouble," I said. "Because Barton isn't going to die. And if you should succeed in killing him, I'd be back for you within the hour. No matter how much trouble you get in for his failure to die, just remember it's better than what you'd get if you actually killed him. Now have a wonderful morning." And I slipped into quicktime, pausing before I left to turn an inkwell upside down on his head.

I ran down the streets in earnest, and soon found the executioner's cart. If I had looked closely before I would have recognized Barton's clothing—he was dressed as he had been that day in the cliff house. I climbed into the cart, then slowed to normal time long enough to say, "Don't worry, Barton, I'm with you." Then I was back in quicktime and out of the cart. The driver hadn't noticed me, and if any passerby saw me, he'd only blink and wonder whether the alcohol from the night before was still in his blood.

I got to the place of execution and waited out of sight among the stacks of straw. It took a half hour for the cart to arrive, and then the routine of the day before was followed—the archers lined up, very casually, and their leader, not the captain from the gate, raised his arm. I slipped into quicktime and walked out into the space between Barton and the archers. I paced back and forth (I become visible when I stay in the same place too long) until the leader's arm fell and the arrows were loosed. Then I collected the arrows in midflight, took the hood gently from Barton's head, and stuck the arrows through the hood into the straw directly behind Barton's chest. Then I walked back to my concealed observation point and watched.

It took a second in realtime before the archers realized that Barton's hood was off and no arrows were sticking into his chest. Then, angrily, the leader of the archers told them to go collect their arrows, furious that they had missed. When they found the arrows sticking through the hood in the straw, however, even the leader became a little less outspoken. There was no natural way those arrows could have got directly behind him.

Barton was smiling.

"I don't know what kind of tricks you're pulling," the leader said furiously (yet there was fear behind his voice), "but you'd better stop 'em."

Barton shrugged and the leader formed up his archers for a second try. I pushed into quicktime and, in order to put an end to this quickly, I took the arrows in midflight and this time shoved them through the pulling wrist of each of the archers. For good measure, I took a few more arrows out of one archer's quiver and impaled the leader's hand, fastening it firmly to his thigh, while similarly sticking the three men lounging around watching the execution. Then I was back to my observation post and into realtime.

A howl of pain from a dozen throats told me that my work had been effective. The archers dropped their bows, clutching at the arrows in their wrists. The pain was nowhere near as bad as the shock. It isn't every day that you fire an arrow and have it turn around and hit you.

Barton's presence of mind was astounding. He haughtily said, "This is your second warning. There won't be a third."

"What's going on!" shouted the leader.

"Don't you know me? I'm the emperor's father. I'm Lord Barton of Britton. And it's a crime for commoners to shed royal blood."

"I'm sorry!" cried the leader. Several of the archers chimed in—most were trying to stanch the bleeding.

"If you're sorry, you'll go back to your quarters and cause me no further trouble today."

They were sorry. They went back to their quarters and caused him no further trouble that day. As soon as they were gone, he looked around for me and saw me lying against a pile of straw, laughing. He came over looking a little upset. "You didn't have to wait until the last minute, did you?"

"I told you not to worry."

"You try not worrying with a dozen arrows pointed at your heart."

I apologized profusely. He forgave me and we headed out of the place of execution, toward the city. "The one thing they won't expect us to do," he said, "is come into the city after they've tried to kill us both." Then he laughed. "It *was* funny. I wouldn't like to be the soldier who has to report this to my dear son Percy. What *are* you, anyway?" he asked.

"Man-in-the-Wind," I answered.

"I don't know what's going on in the world," he said. "Everything seemed so reasonable and scientific until I discovered my son was a fraud with the ability to hide my own memories from me. And now you come along. The captain at the gate told me you were executed and buried yesterday."

"He spoke to you? He didn't say a word to me," I said.

"I'm accusing you of violating the laws of nature," he said, irritated at my failure to respond.

"Nature's virtue is intact," I reassured him. "I just know some different laws." And then we were at the garbage gate. The guards weren't too bright, and, not surprisingly, no alarm had yet gone out. However, we looked conspicuous, Barton in expensive clothing and I dressed like a Humper, which meant I appeared quite countrified, even in the poorer sections of Gill. I had to get him off the streets while I carried out my original intention of paying a visit on Percy. So I led him to a whorehouse I had noticed on my earlier trek up the street.

The manager was a crusty old man who looked more than a little irritated at being disturbed in the morning. "We don't open until afternoon," he said. "Late afternoon."

Barton had money—quite a bit of it. I was surprised the executioners hadn't removed it. Maybe they had planned to wait until he was a corpse, so he wouldn't know he was being robbed. It was a touch of delicacy I hadn't previously suspected the soldiers of having. The money, spread on the table, served to open the house for business a little earlier than usual.

"Full-service?" The manager asked.

"Just a bed and silence," I said, but Barton glared at me. "I feel like a thirty-year-old, and you expect me to sleep all day in a place like this? I want your youngest girl who doesn't have any foul diseases," he said, then caught himself and said, "but of course she must be of age." The manager looked as if he were trying to figure out what age he meant.

"Over fourteen," I said hopefully.

"Sixteen," Barton said, horrified. "Do they really offer them younger?"

The manager rolled his eyes heavenward and led Barton off. As soon as they were gone, I pushed into quicktime and made my way back to the palace.

I was lucky. When I arrived someone was just passing through the door. It was tight, but I skinnied through beside her and passed on into the palace. I followed the path that the most guards impeded

and soon found myself in an impressive throne room. Then I made
my way to an unobtrusive corner and watched. I tried to look carefully at every face in the room, so that if anyone changed I'd know
it. And then I slipped into realtime.

The old woman sitting on the throne became a youngish man
with a remarkable resemblance to Barton. Most of the officials
around him remained unchanged, but I recognized Dul among the
crowd. He had been a young man in a plain brown tunic. A few
other faces changed, too. I passed back and forth from realtime to
quicktime several times to make sure I had spotted them all. There
were eight of them.

I had come with the full intention of killing them after finding
out where they came from. Now I wondered how I'd manage either.
I couldn't talk to them in quicktime, which meant exposing myself
to the dangers of a realtime confrontation. And how could I kill
them without attracting the attention of all the other illuders?
Warned against me, they might be able to defend themselves.

At least I knew that I could spot them by switching from realtime
to quicktime and back again. But killing them in quicktime—that
would not be easy. Oh, of course, it would be simple enough to per-
form the act itself. But it would be a far different thing for me to
plunge a knife in an unaware man than to do the petty tricks I had
played in quicktime up to now. I was trained for battle; I had fought
and killed before. But always my enemy had as good a chance of
hurting me as I had of hurting him. I had no stomach for striking
when a person was utterly helpless.

The Ku Kuei had killed animals by hitting them on the head in
quicktime. And I had condemned them for it. But they were right—
you don't cut off your feet when you're starting a race. I would
have to kill the illuders if they were not to take over the world.
There was no hope of treating with them—they had already proved
their determination to get and keep power at any cost, even blood.
Justice would not be offended by their deaths. And if the only way
to kill them was to creep up like a coward. . . .

It was an unproductive line of thought, and anyway, Dul was moving away from the crowd in the throne room. I waited until I saw
which door he was headed toward, then pushed into quicktime and
passed through the door ahead of him. Murder was not on my mind
—only information. As he walked through the door, I, in realtime
again, stepped out and took him by the arm. "Dul," I said, "what a
pleasure to see you."

He stopped and looked at me, his face registering only mild surprise. "I thought you were still in Britton," he said, and then, though I could clearly see both his hands at his side, I felt a knife plunge deep into my chest. My poor heart would have to regenerate again, I realized. I also realized that there were going to be difficulties about dealing with illuders face to face. When a man can kill you without you noticing that he's moving his hands, he's a dangerous opponent.

Quicktime, of course, and I saw him just pulling his hand back from the knife sticking in my chest. I took out the knife, stepped away, and waited while my heart healed. I could not push myself too hard—there were limits to what my heart could take without rebelling and insisting I spend a few days in bed. Finally, though, I was through, and came back to Dul, who had brought back his hand and was already registering surprise that I was gone. I took the knife and, in order to convince him that I was serious about the need for his cooperation, I pushed the knifeblade (iron of Mueller manufacture!) deep into his arm. Then I slipped back into realtime, watching him transform at the last moment from the young man I had stabbed into the taciturn servant. The taciturnity didn't last long, however. He looked startled, gripped his arm, and in that moment the illusion flickered, faded, he changed back and forth before my eyes, until finally he resolved as himself, the young man.

He leaped at me, dragging me to the floor. The knife was already out of his shoulder, was slicing toward my throat. I stopped it, and wrestled him for control of it. He was strong and young—I was younger and a good deal stronger. Also, he was quite unskilled in the use of the knife. He probably had never had to use it where his enemy could see it coming.

I had him pinned to the floor and was demanding that he tell me where he was from before I killed him when I heard a sound from the door. I looked and saw no one—but the door was still swinging open. If the illuders could do all I had already seen them do, they could probably make me think I saw no one: I was sure someone else was in the room. Interrogation would be impossible with an audience of illuders, and now they were warned. I had had one chance, not a very good one, to find out where they were from. Now I had lost it.

I pushed into quicktime and arose from where my erstwhile opponent lay on the ground. Not one but three illuders were already heading toward where I had been, knives ready. It was pointless, but

I took the knives out of their hands and brought them with me into the throne room, where the old lady who was pretending to be Percy Barton sat on the throne, looking bored. I placed the knives in her lap, blades pointing toward her, and then walked out of the palace. The message would be clear—she could have been killed. But it was only a message, only a could-have-been, and I didn't know what to do next.

Kill them all? Pointless, utterly wasted if I didn't know where they were from. They would only be replaced by fellow illuders, and the plot would hardly be thwarted, only mildly delayed. And I did have some time to plan my next move, in quicktime, at least—it would be a week before riders could get from Gill to any other capital of any size, and with a week in quicktime I could accomplish a lot.

I left the palace. They would hardly leave records lying around saying, "The imposters in this palace come from the following Family." I would have to use reason alone to determine their homeland. And when it came to reasoning, I had come to respect Lord Barton.

"You weren't gone long enough," he said after I sent the girl out of the room. "You impose on our friendship."

"I need your advice."

"And I need solitude. Or dualitude. Do you realize that I was on the verge of accomplishing something that I haven't achieved in thirty years? Twice in a row. Twice in ten minutes."

"There'll be other opportunities. Listen, Barton, I've been to the palace. I've met your son. He's a woman, older than you by some years, and she's surrounded by fellow illuders, including your former servant. But I can't get anything out of them. They're a bit alarmed, in fact. They know that I know them; they've had a taste of what I can do. Within a week they'll be able to notify others, and I'll never be able to stay ahead of them. Do you understand the situation?"

"You bollixed it up."

"I took a chance and it missed. So now, since you were stupid enough to come here after you promised to stay in Humping—"

"Humping," he said wistfully.

"You might as well make yourself useful. I need to know where they come from. I need to know their homeland. Because unless we strike there, first and hard, we'll never stop them."

He settled down to work.

"Well, Lanik, it's plain enough that we can't just pull numbers out of a hat and hope to find them. There are eighty Families—it could be any of them."

"There are ways to narrow it down. I've got a theory, a good one, I think, about what the Families are doing. In Nkumai I found a history of sorts; it listed what the different Families' founders specialized in. Nkumai, for example, was founded by a physicist. Their export product is physical and astronomical theory. In Mueller we exported the product of genetic research—the first Mueller was a geneticist. You see?"

"How constant is that?"

"I haven't visited that many countries and been informed what their export product is. But it held true for Ku Kuei and Schwartz."

"A philosopher and a geologist."

I must have looked startled.

"I don't know why the information should surprise you. Britton was founded by a historian. Not a very likely field to turn into a viable export product, but we are fanatics about keeping records. The list of the original eighty traitors is memorized by every schoolchild from Anderson to Wynn, along with their occupations and brief biographies. We're very thorough. I can also recite my genealogy from Britton himself to the present. I haven't done so because you haven't asked me to."

"I never will. You're a man of iron, Barton."

"The question is, what occupations could possibly have become illuders? Psychologists would be most obvious, wouldn't they? Who was a psychologist? Drew, of course, but they live in the hovels in the north and have dreams of killing their fathers and sleeping with their mothers."

"That could be an illusion," I said.

"Only last year they attacked Arven across the mountains and were humiliatingly defeated. Does that sound like our enemy?"

I shrugged. How could we tell anything about the illuders?

"Besides, they've made little secret of what they've been working on for centuries. Somewhere along the line, the people we're looking for would have to have become secretive. Don't you think? Another psychologist, the only other one, was Hanks. I know nothing about them except that they rebelled against the East Alliance two years ago and my loving son went in with an army and burned the whole country to the ground. The stories said that only one in three people survived, and they lived by getting over the borders and living on charity in Leishman and Parker and Underwood. There is no charity in Gill. Again, it doesn't seem to be a likely spot for the illuders' homeland."

Again, he was right. "No more psychologists?"

"No."

"What other professions then?"

"Maybe they're an exception to your theory, Lanik. Maybe they came up with something new."

"Go through the list. We've got to try to find the most likely prospects, anyway."

So we went through the list. It was tedious, but he wrote it down in a beautiful script that gave me even more respect for his education, though I could hardly read it. Our guesses were long shots. Tellerman was an actor, but that Family was well known to have literary pretensions. The Ambassador had rejected every book and play and poem they had offered in thousands of years. Their persistence was remarkable. There were no magicians among the group, of course—the whole rebellion had been a revolt of the elite against their exploitation by the democratic tyranny of the masses. With a few exceptions, the exiles on Treason were the cream of the cream, the prime intellects of the Republic. Which meant that except for the psychologists and a few other peripheral ones, most of the rebels were experts in a science.

And when he had spent more than an hour exhausting, as we thought, every possibility, the answer suddenly seemed so obvious I couldn't believe we had overlooked it until now.

"Anderson," I said.

"We don't even *know* what he did," Barton said.

"As a profession, we don't. And yet he was head of the rebellion, wasn't he?"

"'Of traitors, traitor most foul,'" Barton intoned.

"Leader of the intellectuals, and yet not an intellectual himself."

"Yes. One of the inscrutable facts in history."

"A politician," I said. "A demagogue who got himself elected to the Republic Council, and yet the same man was able to win the trust of the finest minds of the Republic. Isn't that a contradiction?"

Barton smiled. "You have something there. Of course he wouldn't have any ability like our current enemies. But he was able to make people think he was what he wanted them to think he was. And, except that they're better at it, isn't that what the illuders are doing now?"

I leaned back on my chair. "You at least admit that it's plausible, then?"

"Plausible. Not probable. But none of the others are even possible, so far as I can see. Which makes Anderson the best bet, at least to try first."

I got up and started out the door.

"Isn't this a bit rude? Aren't you going to invite me along?"

"I'll only be gone a couple of days," I said.

"Anderson's a two-week ride across rough country in Israel, and then you have to get a boat to cross the sea in the nastiest bit of water in the world—the Quaking Sea, unless you're fool enough to try the Funnel. And that sounds like at least a month's absence."

"Trust me. Have I let you down yet?"

"Only when you sent the young lady out of the room. Don't worry, though. I won't try to follow you. If you say two days, I'll wait two days, or even more. A man who can make arrows turn in midflight can fly to the moons, if he wishes."

I had another thought. "Maybe you ought to wait somewhere else," I said.

"Nonsense. It's more risky to go out on the street. Besides, I have unfinished business. I want to set a record for myself. Three times within one hour. Send her back in here."

I sent her back in when I left.

It was infuriating that I arrived sooner when I walked the distance in quicktime than when I rode it in realtime on a horse—all because I hadn't learned more in Ku Kuei. It took me nine long days' worth of walking to get to Anderson in the quickest quicktime I had ever attempted since leaving Ku Kuei; it was unnerving that all that traveling was over before sunset the day I left.

I was weary to the bone when I reached the promontory of Israel overlooking the Funnel, the narrow strait between Anderson and the continent. The waves of the sea were frozen, of course, in the middle of their furious rush northward into the slightly lower Quaking Sea. The crests of the waves reached nearly to the level of the promontory where I stood, like hills rising from a cataclysm of the earth.

There were few things I hadn't done in quicktime, but swimming in a realtime sea was one of them. In Ku Kuei, when I swam in quicktime I was always with someone whose timeflow was strong enough to carry a portion of the lake, not to mention me, along with it.

I gingerly stepped into the water. While air caused me no resistance at all, the water was sluggish and bore my weight much better than it did in realtime. In fact, my passage across the Funnel was not properly swimming at all. I crawled, after a fashion, up the slope of a wave as if it were a muddy hill after a rainstorm. Then I slid easily down the other side. After a while it became exhilarating, if exhausting. And it was still afternoon when I reached the other side and scrambled out of the sea onto the rocky shore of Anderson Island.

Once out of the reach of the giant seas, I looked around. The land was grassy, if strewn with boulders, and sheep grazed here and there —it was settled land. But it was hot and dry and bleak. The grass was not thick, and each sheep that was moving at all had a small cloud of dust around it.

I walked along the crest of the slope down to the rocky coast, wondering how I would now go about discovering if this were indeed the home of the illuders. I couldn't very well go up to someone and say, "Good afternoon, is this where the bastards who are trying to take over the world hail from?" I had to have some plausible reason for being there. Remembering the sea I had just crossed, shipwreck seemed a likely possibility. All I had to do was make sure to struggle ashore conveniently near some shepherd's house. From there I could, I hoped, play it by ear.

When I came to a house only a few meters from the beginning of the rocky littoral, I scrambled back down the rocks to the sea. Recognizing how high the waves really were and how violent they must be in realtime, I prudently climbed to the crest of the first wave away from the shore. And then I slipped back into realtime.

I should have stood on a rock and let the spray get me wet.

anderson

The wave didn't wait around for anything. I was immediately dropped sickeningly toward the rocks of the coast as a new wave came after and slammed down on top of me. I met the rock with a sickening crunch of bone and then was lifted again to be slammed down again.

The pain of my shattered right leg was excruciating. For the first time in quite a while I had met up with a force of nature I couldn't cope with, and I feared for my life. My father had died by breaking his spine in water, and as I sank rapidly toward the rocks a second time, my urge for survival took over and I scrabbled through the water toward the shore, caught at a rock, and then the wave that hit me tore loose my grasp and pulled me out again.

The third time I was able to keep my hold and drag myself farther from the waves. I was still soaked by spray every time a wave came to shore—which seemed to be every second or two—but I was relatively safe. I waited for several minutes for my leg to begin to heal enough that, if necessary, I could walk on it. And, when I was satisfied that it could bear my weight, I began calling out.

"Help!" I bellowed above the din of the waves. It was hopeless—I couldn't possibly be heard. I had to get closer to the hut and farther from the sea. I clambered less than nimbly among the rocks. It was then that I saw her, a girl who couldn't have been older than twenty, dressed in a simple garment that didn't come to her knees. She was winsomely beautiful, and the light breeze tossed her black hair. This was hardly the moment to feel amorous, but I was immediately attracted to her. Attracted to a woman for the first time since leaving Saranna in Ku Kuei.

I called out again, and she came delicately down among the rocks until she reached me. She smiled; I smiled back, but let the pain I still felt show clearly. I stumbled—not hard to manage—as she led me up to the plateau. And as she led me to her house I burbled out a story of getting caught up in the current heading up the Funnel, my father and I in a fishing boat; how I was sure he had been drowned, since the mast when it broke struck him in the head. She, in turn, told me how the sea had snatched her old father from the rocks not three years ago, and she was struggling on to keep a flock of sheep and retain her independence.

"Surely you don't lack for marriage offers," I said.

"No," she answered shyly. "But I'm waiting."

"For what?" I asked.

"The right one, of course," she said playfully, and then led me to her cottage.

From a distance, when I had first seen her house, I hadn't noticed the flowers growing around the walls. They made a pleasant contrast in this land of desolation, and I found myself liking her. She offered me food, showing me a cold stew that she could soon heat up.

Before I could say anything the earth began to shake and I was thrown to the floor. I had heard enough about earthquakes to know that indoors was not a good place to be during one—I scrambled on all fours to the door and watched as the earth visibly heaved and a crevice opened in the ground not ten meters off. It was wide, and the earth groaned as it opened and closed again.

And when the quake was over, and I got up, sheepishly, and dusted off my clothes. They were still wet from the sea—mud clung to them.

"I'm sorry," she said, and I realized she seemed more vexed than terrified by the quake. "We have such inconvenient weather here, between the earth, the sky, and the sea." And as if to prove her point, the sky, which up to a moment ago had been cloudless, suddenly began to pour down rain as clouds roiled across from one horizon to the other.

The flowers were quickly drenched, and seemed to stand a little straighter.

"Your clothes," she said. "I can wash out that mud, if you want to take them off. And the salt from the sea, too."

I trust my blush was convincing—I was convinced, anyway. She seemed so innocent and shy that it was impossible not to be shy with her.

"I'm not wearing anything under these," I admitted.

"Then go into the bedroom—I have two rooms, you know—and pass the clothes out to me. I'll clean them while the stew warms."

I didn't have to be urged. I stripped off the trousers and shirt, reminders of Glain and Vran and Humping, and handed them to her, then lay on the bed (which was surprisingly soft—luxury like Mueller, here in sheep country!) naked, spreadeagled, to dry out and relax. It felt good, after a month of relentless travel and a grueling few hours with the sea.

And I slept.

What woke me, I'm not sure. I couldn't have slept long—the sky was virtually unchanged, still dark with clouds but not with night. The smell of the stew was strong in the house. And then the door opened.

She stood in the doorway, naked. Her body was young; it reminded me achingly of Saranna's body when we were children in our teens before I left Mueller too many years ago. I wanted the girl. And from her smile, she wanted me to want her.

Wanted me to want her. Was this the shy woman who made me blush?

Something didn't fit. Many things didn't fit. As she came into the room and knelt on the bed, I realized how terribly unlikely it was that such a creature could live unmolested in such isolation, so near the coast. I realized how odd it was that the rainclouds appeared from nowhere, that she hadn't been bothered by an earthquake that nearly shook her house down, and that as sweet and shy as she was, she now knelt straddling my body, her arms crossed over her breasts.

I pushed into quicktime. The knife was only a handspan away from my throat. And the nude young girl was now a vile, ugly old man, with perhaps the most vicious, hate-filled expression I have ever seen on a human face. His eyes were deepset and watery, his face gaunt with poverty. I had no doubt what he was after. His skeletal body cried out for meat. By comparison to him, I was fat.

The bed I was on was not soft, either—it was a board, and so hard and ungiving that when I slid awkwardly out from between his legs, he hardly bounced. And then I stood for a moment, wondering what to do. The door to the kitchen was still open. I went in and found that the stewpot, far from being full of cold stew, was actually dusty from nonuse. None of the interior finishing that had made the place look homey and inviting was real—it had made way for rough sod walls, a dirt floor, and filth everywhere.

The dirt, in fact, was indescribable. It was as if, because the man could choose to live in illusion, he didn't bother to make his real surroundings even tolerable. Yet did his illusions really fool him? Perhaps. Yet, I realized, he had already put on my clothes, and I could find no trace of his own. Had he been naked then, before? The poverty was appalling. I had never seen a human being live in such relative savagery outside of Schwartz, and there the poverty had dignity, since the Schwartzes truly owned all the earth.

Outside, even the flowers turned out to be brambles and dusty grey grass. And the hut was tilting, slipping toward collapse. There was no trace of any crevice in the earth, and the rain, like the quake, had been an illusion.

There could be no doubt, then, that Anderson was the place I was seeking. And no doubt that my decision was correct. If there was an opposite to what the world should be, Anderson was it: all seeming beautiful, and the truth being, instead, vicious and squalid and murderous.

I went back into the house, back to the tiny lean-to that in the illusion was a bedroom, and I took the knife out of the old man's hand. Then I slipped into realtime. He turned into the girl again, but suddenly she pulled up and held one hand with the other because of the pain of my having pulled away the knife so quickly. She looked to where I was, and her face registered shock. I kicked her squarely in the groin, and suddenly she was an old man lying on the floor, writhing.

"Who are you!" he demanded. "Whose dream are you!"

"Yours," I said.

Recovering somewhat from the pain, he nastily said, "I come up with better dreams in my sleep. I thought you were real, the way that quake scared you."

I reached down with the wooden knife and stroked his throat with the tip. And then, suddenly, hands were around my throat from behind. I cursed myself for a fool and shoved into quicktime. The man disappeared from the floor in front of me and now leaned over my back, trying to strangle me. I broke his hold, then got behind him. As soon as I was in realtime again, I picked him up and pushed him from the bedroom and into the kitchen. He screamed all the way—I had broken all his fingers in getting him loose from my neck in quicktime.

But illusions extended even to the sense of touch, and suddenly he was behind me again, this time with the knife, this time stabbing through my back to my kidneys. By now I was tired of pain, and so instead of trying to fight him, I ran out of the house. An earthquake began instantly. It took tremendous force of will, but I walked right across a crevice that yawned in front of me. It was solid ground. And then, a few dozen meters from the house, I lay on the earth and as quickly as I could forced an earthquake that swallowed up the house in a huge collapse of land.

I was lying on the surface of the earth, and it shook beneath me. But it was not the quake that swept through me like a harrow through fine soil. It was the scream of death. Not the scream of a man murdered by a weapon in battle, nor the scream of the countless men and women and children taken by disease or famine or fire or flood. It was the scream of someone murdered by the earth, unwillingly, and the cry was amplified a thousand times until it filled me and I, too, screamed.

I screamed until my voice could no longer fill my ears. The pain was not physical. When it ended, there was no residual aching in my muscles or tension that would not release. The pain was in that part of me which had been in communion with the earth, and as it shattered me I wondered, briefly, if I would die from it.

I did not die from it. But when my own scream fell into silence and I looked and saw that the earth had closed again, leaving no trace of the house and its sad, nonexistent flowers, I wanted to call it back, call back the hideous old man, let the life of him continue even though the self of him could not live. He deserved to die except that nothing deserves death, and I might have gone mad at that moment, needing the house and the man and the life to return and knowing that it had to be destroyed, except that for some reason I thought of my father bloated by the water of the lake; I thought of the thousands of soldiers and civilians of the Rebel River plain killed or left homeless as the Nkumai, led by an Anderson illuder ravaged and ravished their way across the earth. I thought of the million deaths they had caused and would still cause, and this balance, this sense of the utter rightness of the destruction of Anderson, preserved my sanity and let me get up from the ground and weakly, wearily walk back to the rocks leading down to the sea.

Yet the questions were not so easily resolved. I had heard the scream of the earth at being forced into complicity in murder, even a just murder. It would strip the structure of my soul forever. I had never believed I had a soul until then, when it was laid bare a hurt more deeply than any other part of me could bear.

And I grieved all the way across the water; all the way in quick-time back to Gill; all the way until I came to the whorehouse and mounted the stairs and found Lord Barton's body cut into dozens of small pieces, already rotting in the heat coming through the south-facing window.

treason

How they had found him I didn't know, but it couldn't have been hard. The integrity of the manager was suspect at best; stories of our odd midday arrival might have circulated up through the symbiotic chain of criminals and police until it reached the attention of someone who was aware of Barton's odd salvation from execution. The mutilation of his body was probably because, having seen me again after I seemed thoroughly dead, the illuders and their unwitting assistants wanted to make sure there was no chance of error.

I was still in quicktime as I surveyed the destruction of my friend. It had been, to me, a month since I left Anderson, two months since I had left Barton. It was early evening of the same day, in realtime. And I couldn't help wondering if I could have saved Barton by coming back a little sooner, or leaving a little later.

There was no confusion in my mind on one point, however. His death caused me no guilt. Guilt I knew from the earth's scream in Anderson; and guilt for Barton's death belonged, not to me, but to the illuders. It had been too long since I last lived in Mueller for me to feel a need to give him grief in that fashion. I would give him another kind of grief.

With Barton dead, I had no reason to delay the next stage in my journey; I had every reason to hasten it. None of the illuders would escape. No matter what it took, Treason would be free of them before I was through. Any doubt about the rightness of my intended killings was gone. I was beyond thought, and intended only to carry out the decision I had so reluctantly made, yet was now grimly glad to fulfil.

There was a matter of priorities. Before moving against the Andersons who were running things in other Families, I had to see to it that the home island was depopulated. No replacements, no angry and deceptive and irresistible army from Anderson should be able to rescue the rulers. And the population of Anderson could be as much as a million; certainly was no less than a hundred thousand. That would be long and weary work in quicktime, with me armed only with my iron knife and forced to go from person to person. It would use up my lifetime before I was half through.

I needed help, and there was only one place I could get it. But could I persuade the people of Schwartz to kill, even when that killing would save other lives—and, perhaps more importantly, make millions of lives more worth living? There was no room for value judgments in the Schwartzes' thinking, I knew too well. Life was life. Murder was murder. And I, who had left them still innocent, was coming back to them with blood on my hands, asking them to help me with my killing.

For weeks I had lived utterly alone in quicktime, neither eating nor drinking, neither speaking nor hearing another human voice except that of the beautiful girl in Anderson. And for another thirty days I traversed the whole southland of the continent, from Wood to Huss.

The trees gave way to lush grassland. The grass gave way to brush that could survive the low rainfall. And finally the brush gave way to endless sand and sun-broken rocks.

I stopped, in quicktime, by the last bush I could see, and there slipped into realtime. I could not find the Schwartzes. They would have to find me. And find me they would, I knew.

For a moment I toyed with the thought of turning back. My reunion with them would not be happy. They couldn't possibly kill me, but when I had lived with them I had known the kind of love they give. I had depended on it. It would not be there now.

I had walked for a day when the first Schwartz began paralleling my path, visible from time to time a few dunes away, or at the crest of another rockpile. The second morning there were three others, and by evening, when I stopped in the shadow of a rise of rock, there were nearly a hundred all around me, more than I had ever seen at one time when I lived among them.

They were silent, all watching me. I did not eat, of course, but sat before them and in my mind reached into the sand, found the water far below, and pulled the water to the surface. It glittered in the reflected light from rocks that still caught the sun. I leaned down to drink. The water withdrew, sank away from me.

I stood, then, and spoke to the Schwartzes.

"I need your help."

"You'll get nothing from Schwartz," said an old man.

"The world needs your help."

"The earth needs nothing but life." And someone murmured, "Killer."

"I didn't say the earth!" I answered, sharply. "I said the world. Men. You know what men are—they're the ones who still have to eat to live, who still worry about dying."

"Who still fear murderers," said the old man. "We heard the faint echoes of that scream, Lanik Mueller. You performed the act, so only you heard it clearly, but we know what you did. We taught you, and you used the knowledge to kill. You forced the earth itself to be your sword. If we ever longed to kill, you would be the one whose death we'd seek. Can I say it plainer? Leave us. You'll get nothing from Schwartz."

"Helmut?" I asked, recognizing him, though I didn't know how.

"Yes," the old man answered.

"I thought you wanted to remain young forever."

"A friend betrayed me, and I grew old."

Then he turned his back on me, and so did the others. Yet none of them left.

The darkness came in then, swiftly as it comes to the desert once the sun is down, but soon Dissent passed through the sky, casting little light but at least providing a reference point so that the vertigo of utter darkness did not overtake me. The silence was unbroken, however, until at last I could stand it no longer. My memory of my months among the Schwartzes was too acute. I took off my clothes and lay upon the sand and wept.

I wept for myself, who had betrayed the trust of the rock and killed. I wept for Barton, whose wit and courage in trusting a stranger had opened up the possibility of saving the world. I wept for the thousands of people I had passed in my journey here, none of them even suspecting that their fate was passing by, that their future would soon be hanging in the balance.

And I wept because I knew that in the end it would be largely futile. Even when the Andersons were gone, if I could destroy them, how free would anyone on Treason be? The Muellers would again make iron swords and attack their neighbors; the Nkumai would again descend from the trees and overrun those who fought with wood and glass. Killing the Andersons would open up a flood of death on the earth. Unfree as the world was, they didn't really know it, and they were at peace.

Who was I to think that this peace was worse than war?

The real enemy was not the Andersons. The real enemy was iron. Not iron for starships to escape from Treason and return to the rest of the human race. Iron to bring blood from soldiers and make them die—that was what was destroying us. Because what choice did anyone have? If they had something, anything that could be sold to the Ambassadors for iron, then a Family had an advantage over all the others. And so it was necessary for a Family to protect its independence by striking down all other Families that might develop or had developed something the Ambassadors would buy.

As I lay in the sand, my head resting on my arms, I realized that killing the Andersons would accomplish nothing, unless I also killed the Ambassadors. As long as dead iron could be sent from other worlds to shed blood on this one, the dying would go on.

"You taught me," I said, "that there is iron in the earth."

They didn't answer me, had not turned even when I wept, supposing, probably, that I wept the tears of the guilty and the damned.

"Why is none of this iron on the surface?"

No answer.

"There was some iron on the surface, wasn't there? That's why the first Schwartz came here, wasn't it? The geological survey was enough to show that there weren't any easily accessible iron deposits. But there was iron *here*, wasn't there?"

Helmut spoke: "No one will ever find iron in Schwartz."

"But it was here, wasn't it? It was here, and you knew, or your ancestors knew, what iron could do, didn't they? They knew the iron would kill. They knew that in the scramble for supremacy, so much blood would be shed that any victory would be meaningless. Didn't they!"

Helmut turned to me, a strange, twisted expression on his face. "No one has ever left Schwartz believing that."

"You had the iron! And you decided not to use it! Didn't you!"

Helmut stood, angry. "Don't you know anything? Haven't you seen the mountains? Why do you think we never let it rain here? If we let the rain fall in Schwartz, the rust in the rocks would be visible for miles! We'd have no peace, not here, not anywhere in the world! We have kept the iron hidden, and you will *not* bring the world in here to take it and kill with it!"

Others were facing me now, and they looked angry, too.

"You don't understand. I don't want to tell anyone about it. I want to finish the work your fathers started. You live here in Schwartz protecting mankind from iron, but out there iron is shedding blood anyway. Don't you know that?"

"Of course we know that," said Helmut. "But we're not responsible. It isn't our fault."

"Your hands are clean, aren't they? Out here where the sun keeps everything pure. But you're not pure! Because if you could stop the suffering and dying, and didn't stop it, then you *are* guilty. It *is* your fault."

"We can't stop men from killing each other. We only refuse to help them."

I had the thread of an argument, though, and I pursued it. "If you help me, I can stop the iron from coming here. I can completely stop the flow of iron from the Republic, and I can end the mutual fear and the competition that has been causing these wars. But I can't do it without your help."

"You're a killer."

"So are you!" Helmut's eyes widened. I pressed the point. "In Hanks, hundreds of thousands of people died at swordpoint or from the famine when the land was scorched by the armies of Gill. On the Rebel River plain, hundreds of thousands died when the armies of Nkumai destroyed every living thing in their path. Had any army ever done that kind of thing before? Ever?"

No, they agreed. Never. "And the sound of it was terrible," Helmut said faintly.

"The reason that kind of war was waged was because of iron. Was because the Nkumai and Mueller were both getting iron, and it seemed inevitable that one of them would become supreme among the Families. But there was another Family, one that had a product they could never export. The Ambassador would never give them iron. But what they *could* do, what they *have* done, is go out and take the iron the other Families got."

"What do we care what happens to Mueller and Nkumai," Helmut said scornfully.

"Nothing at all. But you should care what happens to mankind, for the sake of the rock if for no other reason. Because this Family is Anderson, and their power is to lie, not just to tell someone something that isn't true, but to make them believe it, against their will, to make them so sure that the lie is true that it never occurs to them to question it." And I told them about Dinte, about Mwabao Mawa, and about Percy Barton.

Helmut looked concerned at last. "And these are the people who have been killing so many?"

"They are."

"And what would you do? Kill them all?"

My pause was answer enough. Helmut's look changed to loathing. "And you want *us* to help. You were never my friend, not if you can believe we would do it."

"Listen to me!" I shouted, as if sheer volume would make him open his mind. "The Andersons are irresistible. No man can fight them. They've come subtly this time, insinuating themselves in governments and ruling people who don't know they're ruled by them. But if they are aroused, they can come from their island in force, and no army could resist them, because they would come appearing to be terrible monsters; or they would come invisibly in the night; or they would fight openly, and yet when a man struck at them his enemy would no longer be where he seemed to be, and every soldier would be killed before he ever put his sword to good effect."

"I know what warfare is," Helmut said contemptuously, "and I reject it."

"Of course you reject it. Who can kill *you*? You'll never die. But out there are millions of people who *can* die, and when someone comes up to them with a sword in his hand and says, 'Obey me or I'll kill you and your wife and your children,' what does he do? He obeys. Even if he's a hero, he obeys, because he knows that anyone who has the power to kill and is willing to use it will defeat his enemies unless they are just as eager to kill. The power to steal life is the ultimate power in this world, and before that power every other man is weak."

"We aren't weak."

"You aren't men. Men are mortal. You can laugh at a soldier and throw up a wall of rock that will keep him out forever. You can stand on that wall and watch as he and his children and his grandchildren grow old and die, and you'll never understand why it is that they're so constantly afraid. They're afraid because the rain might not come and so they might starve; because floods or earthquakes can snatch away their lives without warning; but most of all because in the night another man can come and lift a sword and cut them off completely from the world. They're afraid of *death!* Can you at least imagine what that means?"

"We fear death, too," Helmut said.

"No, Helmut, you resent death. You regret death. But as for your own life, you know perfectly well that no one can threaten it at all. Death is something that happens to someone else."

"And because of that you want us to kill people? You want us to do the same thing?"

"No, I don't. I want you to help me stop everyone on this planet from having the power to be irresistible. I want to destroy the Ambassadors so that no Family will ever be able to raise iron weapons against wooden ones. And I want to destroy the Andersons because they, like iron, kill wantonly and cannot be withstood."

"And how would we be different from them, killing those whose actions we don't like?"

"I don't know! Maybe there's a measuring rod somewhere in the universe where men's acts are judged, and those who kill other men for the sake of power will be judged more harshly than those who kill those power-hungry men for the sake of freedom. But if there's no place in the universe for a man to resist the thieves of freedom and still be called a good man, then I don't think there is any good or evil in the universe, and it all means nothing, and I couldn't bear that!"

There was no way to convince them. I saw that now. They watched me impassively, and I despaired. "All right. I can't compel you. Nobody can force you to do anything." And, bitterly, I hurled insults at them. "You hold freedom like a prize, and it's in your power to help others be free, but you're too damned selfish to reach out and give them freedom, too. Keep your freedom, keep your immortality, but somewhere along the line I hope you figure out what you're living forever *for*. What noble purpose you mean to achieve. Because you're no good to anyone here, not even to yourselves."

And I turned and walked away, back the way I had come, toward Huss and civilization and hopelessness. I walked for hours, and then I realized that someone was close behind me. It was Helmut, and he looked different. It took me a moment to realize why, but it was because his hair was no longer white with age.

"Lanik," he said, and his voice was younger. "Lanik, I must talk to you."

"What for?" I asked, not daring to believe that my words might have had an effect on him.

"Because you love me. And hearing you talk like that, I realized that I love you, too. Despite everything."

So I stopped and sat in the sand, and so did he.

"Lanik, you have to understand something. We aren't deaf to other men. We heard you. We understood. And we *want* to achieve the goal you set out. We *want* to destroy the Ambassadors. We hate the Andersons and their murders and their deceptions as much as you—nothing is worse to us than those who murder, not for anger or hurt or revenge or because they believe it is their duty, but for profit. Do you see that? We hate what you hate. And we long for it to be destroyed.

"But Lanik, we *can't do it*. Did you think our hatred of killing was just an opinion, just an emotion, just a wish that no more suffering take place? We *cannot* kill. It's that simple. We suffer from the song of death among the rocks even now. But you heard the scream of the earth when you made the earth kill that man in Anderson. You *heard* it. What was it like?"

I answered honestly, "It was the worst thing in the world."

"Well, Lanik, you have more ability with the earth than any one of us. We told you that years ago, before you left. And so you heard that scream more clearly than any of us could ever hear it.

"But if we were to destroy Andersons, we'd have to swallow up the island in the sea and the earth, to take it completely from the surface and you know as well as I do that there isn't one of us, alone, that could do that."

I nodded. "I hoped the council—"

"That's the problem, Lanik. The council is a collection of individuals. Weak ones, like me. Together, we can twist and turn the earth in ways you couldn't imagine. We could sink Anderson into the sea in moments. We could build a mountain range from one end of the world to the other in an hour. We could, if it were ever necessary, take this entire planet and twist it in its orbit until it was cooler or warmer, farther from or closer to the sun.

"But if we should kill everyone on Anderson by sinking the island under the sea, the scream you heard from one man would be magnified hundreds of thousands of times. Can you comprehend that? And those hundred thousand screams would be borne by a mere three or four hundred of us. Each of us would bear a scream hundreds of times more terrible than what you heard. And worse, because we would be the council, we would have penetrated deeper into the heart of the earth than you could ever pierce, yet we would still be individuals, and there where the rock's voice is loudest, we would be individually less able to resist. The scream would penetrate us deeper, and we would be drowned in it as surely as the sea would drown the people of Anderson.

"Do you understand, Lanik? To do that would destroy us. And who would control the anger of the earth then? Who would absorb the hatred of the rocks? Who would control it? No one. We would destroy the earth because we would no longer be able to contain his wrath. That's why we can't agree to what you propose."

I hadn't known that. I hadn't understood the price they would have to pay. "Fine," I said. "I'll do my best without your help."

I got up to leave. Helmut got up, too, and after looking into his eyes a moment, I turned away.

"Lanik," he said.

"Yes," I answered.

"They asked me to tell you the way."

"The way to what?"

"The way to do what you want to do."

I turned and stared at him. "You just said it is impossible."

He shook his head, and tears came to his eyes. "I said it was impossible to us. But there is another way, and I didn't want to tell you, Lanik, for fear you would accept it, because it would destroy you, and I love you and don't want you destroyed."

"If there's a way, Helmut, I'll take it, even if it destroys me. God knows every alternative destroys me anyway."

"You have so little love for your own life?"

"Helmut, you don't know, you've never been alone like I have, but in my solitude I've discovered something. That I'm passing through the world invisibly. Even when people see or speak to me it's as if I didn't exist, as if I had no right to exist. I tread across their land and they don't see me. I act and act and act and nothing makes any difference in the world. But they touch *me*. There's a family in the hills of the poorest part of Britton, and they needed me, and their very need became the most important thing in my life. There's a woman frozen in time by a lake in Ku Kuei, and she needed me, but we have been torn apart and if I could do anything to take her from the eternal death she's consigned herself to I'd do it. And a man who wasn't old enough to die killed himself in Ku Kuei, and when he died I realized that half of me was him, and that half died with him, and the other half will never stop mourning. I'll do what it takes, Helmut."

At other times and on other days, both before and since, I couldn't have said those words. Heroes and victims are as much the product of the mood they were in when opportunity came or when circumstances were at their worst, and had I not walked three thousand solitary kilometers only to be met with refusal and despair, I do not know if I would have said so easily, "I'll do what it takes."

But I said it, and I meant it, and Helmut embraced me and he explained, "When we act together, we don't all have to go into the earth. We can send one, and he lies among the rock and sings all our songs with his voice, and he hears all the earth's song with his heart. It can be joyful, and we honor our greatest men by sending them for us on such occasions. It can be painful, and we also honor our greatest by entrusting them with the pain for all of us. But there's not a man among us who could bear this. And so we can't send any of us into the earth. You, however, are stronger than any of us. How much stronger, we don't know. But if you went into the earth for us, we could hope you might survive. And if you died, and the fury of the earth continued, we would still be alive to contain it and keep the world safe."

We lay together in the sand, all with our arms spread; I lay in the middle, curled into a ball, and as I sank into the sand I felt them join me, one by one, until all their songs were ringing in my mind as the sand swallowed me up and bore me down.

Always I had stopped at bedrock before. But now the rock only softened and flowed out around me, like cold mud, closing again over my face. And the deeper I went the warmer the rock became and the faster it seemed I fell, until the heat was as much as I could bear and even when I stopped the rock seethed and twisted around me.

With the knowledge of the hundreds of Schwartzes above me, I easily found Anderson Island, this time not an aberration of the surface but instead the leading edge of a plate of rock floating on a sea of melted granite. The flow was incredibly slow, but once I found the island I began to draw the magma out from under it.

The settling was slow where I was working, of course, but the damage was done on the surface in the first instant. The rock sank abruptly, and every building and living thing on the island tumbled to the ground. And then, as the rock continued to fall, the sea rushed in from both sides and met in a great wave in the middle of the island, along its length from north to south.

And because of the interruption of the plate of rock, hot magma surged up to the surface, striking ocean and leaping still higher until it shot into the sky, throwing hot ash and steam and mud and lava out of the ocean. The water boiled, and anything left alive in that part of the sea was killed as thousands of hectares of the sea turned to steam.

All this happened because I, with the strength of all the Schwartzes to sustain me, had forced the earth to act. And the earth, ignorant of time and so of consequences, obeyed. It was not until the screams of death began that the earth rebelled, and in that moment the Schwartzes left me. Now they had to work to keep the earth from tearing apart, to keep the crust of the earth from shrugging off the irritating life that had caused it so much agony and so little joy. They had to stem the tide of molten rock that seethed to escape and win its way to the surface at every point that had felt the trembling when the island fell.

I, however, knew nothing of their work. There were other matters at hand, because the earth was screaming at the murder of half a million men, and I was the only listener.

Undoubtedly many of those that died were innocent. These were the ones that would haunt me from then on—the fishermen innocently fishing in Britton's Bay when the huge wave struck the shore; the people in tall buildings in Hess and Gill and Israel who were killed when the structure couldn't bear the shock wave riding out from Anderson; and the people on Anderson itself who, even though they were illuders, were not murderers and meant only good to other people.

As for the earth, however, there was no distinction between the innocent and the guilty, between those whose deaths achieve no purpose and those who had to die if mankind on Treason was to mean anything. All death was the same, and the rocks groaned horribly as if to say, "We trusted you, we gave you power, we obeyed you, and you used us to kill!" The rocks seemed to scream, "Traitor!" as the head swept back and forth across my body. And in a moment I lost all moorings, all connections with reality, all sense of time, and where the scream of the man I killed in Anderson lasted for seconds, the scream of the earth this time lasted forever. It had no end because there was no time, and for an infinity I felt an agony of infinite magnitude and I longed for only one thing. Not to die, because death would only add to the scream of the stone, but rather to be annihilated, to have never existed, to have never lived because my life had reached this point, and this point was unreachable, unendurable, impossible.

"Treason," screamed the earth forever.

"Forgive me," I pleaded.

And when the infinity was over the rock spewed me out, the sand vomited me up, and I was thrown into the air and rushed headlong toward the stars.

I rose, and then the rising stopped, and I fell back toward the earth, and it was the same feeling I had had when I stepped off the precipice in the darkness before Dissent rose, and I wondered whether the sand would receive me, after all, or whether this time I would strike the surface and simply stop, spread out for my blood to soak into the sand and for the sun to dry my flesh to leather and then to dust.

Yet even in the air, I exulted. Even if I died now, I had done the first and greatest work, and had lived through it, if only for a while; I had heard the most terrible scream of the earth and had lived.

But as I fell I listened and realized that the scream was not over. I could still hear it. I would hear it forever. I hear it now. It will never end.

I reached the sand and it gave, it bore me up yet let me sink slowly, and at last I lay on the earth's surface again, at rest, though never to be at peace again. The earth would never (the rock *could* never) forgive me for having betrayed its trust. But while it did not forgive, it could still endure me. It would bear my life. As long as I wished to keep on living, the earth would permit me to live.

The Schwartzes lay around me. After a long time I realized they were weeping. And then, strangely, I remembered Mwabao Mawa singing morningsong from a perch high in Nkumai. The melody played endlessly through my head. And for the first time I understood the haunting beauty of the song. It was the song of a killer who longed to die. It was the song of justice yearned for but not yet done.

And the vast cloud of vapor from the sea that had poured into the sky above the sinking of Anderson came over Schwartz, and for the first time in millennia it rained, and water touched the iron-rich mountains and water bled into the sand and cooled it and water mingled with the tears on the faces of the people of Schwartz and erased and washed away their weeping and Helmut arose and walked to me in the rainstorm and said, "Lanik, you lived."

"Yes," I said, because he was really saying, "Lanik, I love you and you still live," and I was really saying, "Helmut, I love you and I still live."

"We've done what we've done," Helmut said, "and we won't regret it because it was necessary if not good. But even so, we ask you to leave. We won't thrust you out because without you worse things would have happened, but please, Lanik, leave us now and never come back."

"I have more work to do."

"I know. I hope that someday the blood will wash from your hands."

"Guard your iron. Keep it safe. Don't let it rust."

He smiled (a grisly thing, at the moment, and yet more surprising and refreshing than the rain) and he embraced me and he said, "I thought you had betrayed me when you left before. I just didn't understand, Lanik. I thought that when I trusted you, that meant you would always act the way I wanted you to. I think perhaps I'll be young again after all, and let someone else be spokesman. I've had enough responsibility for a lifetime."

"And I for ten," I answered, and he kissed me and embraced me and then sent me away. I walked eastward toward Huss, and somewhere along the way I found my clothes, neatly folded and placed in my path, and on top of them my knife. It was the Schwartzes' benediction, absolution in advance for the murders I had yet to commit, and I put on the clothes and held the iron knife in my hand and shoved into quicktime, and for the next three years of my own time I spoke to no man and heard no man's voice, and spent my time walking between murders, listening to the cry of the dying and dead and hearing the earth's scream and knowing that someday I would have found them all, and they would all be dead, and I would never have to kill again.

Percy Barton I killed willingly, for that old woman had deceived and murdered my friend. But her voice harrows up my soul as loudly as that of Mwabao Mawa, who, even though she (no, he, a bald white man ruling a nation of proud, unknowing blacks) had been an illusion, had sung the beautiful morningsong. There was no distinction. The hated and the loved died the same, and in the end my knife went no more easily into Percy Barton's throat than into Mwabao Mawa's.

Killing the Ambassadors was easier, for the earth made no protest at their death. They were machines. Already dead. All I had to do was break the seal where it said, "Warning, tampering will result in the destruction of this machine and the death of anyone within 500 meters of it," and then walk away in quicktime faster than the explosion could follow.

I killed along a path radiating outward from the ruins of the lands bordering Anderson, visiting every capital of every Family to make sure I found all the Andersons and killed every one, and to make sure that no Ambassador survived. Because I was in my fastest timeflow, all this took a week of realtime. I was ahead of every messenger. So far as the people of the world knew, a sudden scourge removed the rulers from their world, and the Ambassadors, too. I wondered what the people thought, who found an old woman's corpse sitting on Percy Barton's throne. Would they make a connection? Or always wonder who it was they found, and never know why or where their king had disappeared?

There was no point in keeping a calendar during my long journey of assassination. By the end of it, a week after it began, I was, as closely as I can guess, about twenty-four years old. When my father was twenty-four I was already alive, and he had played with me in the morning and gone out and led his men into battle in the afternoon. I had no child, but neither could my murders weigh as lightly on my soul as my father's did. He knew no better, and thought the killing would make him a good king. I hadn't even the faint right of kings, and I knew exactly how much murder cost. I was twenty-four in years, but at heart I was unbearably old, and my body was weighted down and weary.

There was one place, however, where I had not yet gone, and when all the other Andersons and all the other Ambassadors were dead, there was one yet to kill: the one who had been my brother Dinte; the one who had destroyed my father; the one who had robbed me of my inheritance; the one that I had hated and rivaled and resented in all our years together; the one who, inexplicably, was still my brother regardless of how much I knew he really was not. Could Lord Barton really have killed the man he once believed was his son? Could I really kill Dinte? I had had the opportunity once before, at the gate in the wall when he attacked me, and instead of killing him I had only slit his throat, knowing that it would quickly heal.

This time, however, I wouldn't see my brother's shape. I would see a stranger, and the stranger I could kill. I would kill. And so I came at last to Mueller-on-the-River, and for the first time in years I entered a city, not hidden by quicktime, but openly. I was Lanik Mueller, and this place had been my home, and whether I was welcome here or not, I would come openly and proudly and declare, at last, when all the others were dead, the work that I was doing and the work that I had done. The world thought of Lanik Mueller as a monster back when I still wasn't one; now that I was, I wanted them to know it. Even those regarded as evil want their deeds to be known.

I walked into the court where Dinte sat upon the throne and strode firmly to the middle of the room, and while many there did not recognize me, for even those who had known me had last seen me as a fifteen-year-old boy, enough did recognize me that the whisper, "Lanik Mueller," ran through the room and every eye was upon me and, for a moment, everyone feared to act.

My brother Dinte arose from the throne and held his arm stiffly out, and in an unnaturally loud voice he said, "Well, brother. Have you come at last to take your throne?" And he stepped aside to let me sit where by right I should sit, and he commanded the people there to kneel as I mounted the dais. They knelt. And Dinte waited, smiling, welcoming.

lanik in mueller

In all the possible versions of this scene that I had imagined, this one had never occurred to me. Yet for one long moment it seemed exactly right. The usurping brother, confronted by the wanderer who has at last come home, willingly steps aside in order that the more lawful heir may take his rightful place.

I had planned to come in, name Dinte as a traitor and a murderer, and in front of everyone in the court stab him to death. Nothing secret: This was not to be Lake-drinker, Man-in-the-Wind, or the Naked Man performing justice on an Anderson illuder. This was to be Lanik Mueller performing justice on his brother Dinte, the usurper who drove his father into the forest of Ku Kuei where he died.

Now Dinte has robbed me of that. Having so willingly (though I knew it was a lie) stepped aside for me, if I killed him now, openly, it would only add to the legend of Lanik Mueller as Andrew Apwiter come to life to recreate chaos and end the world. So, reluctantly, before the Anderson who hid behind Dinte's face could kill me unaware, I pushed into quicktime and stepped forward, which meant that to all intents and purposes I disappeared.

But Dinte did not turn into the Anderson I expected, the crusty, middle-aged man or woman I had supposed waited for me in quicktime. Instead he turned into a creature with four arms and five legs; two sets of male genitals contrasted absurdly with the three breasts that dangled in middle-aged sags. If I had seen such a being in the pens, I would not have been surprised. But I had been expecting an Anderson, and this was either an incredible monster or a radical regenerative from Mueller. And who from Mueller could ever have become an illuder?

Then I looked into the creature's face, frozen, staring at the spot where a moment ago I had been standing. And I recognized the monster, and everything changed.

The face was mine. Lanik Mueller's head topped the bizarre assortment of limbs and protuberances. It was I who stood beside the throne, but through an incredible cruelty it was not the Lanik Mueller who was cured in Schwartz. It was Lanik Mueller the radical regenerative, the monster, the child.

It was my double, who was born in the forest of Ku Kuei.

Impossible! my mind cried out. This creature didn't exist until after Dinte had lived with us for years. This creature could not possibly have been Dinte.

At first I tried to tell myself that he was obviously a secondary illusion; that this Anderson had found a way to fool me in quicktime, too. But that was nonsense—if any Anderson could have fooled me, another would have done it long before.

And so I walked in quicktime to the throne, sat down, and slipped back into realtime.

The effect was one I had rarely been able to show off before: suddenly I disappeared in one place and appeared in another. The murmur of the crowd was frantic. But Dinte (now with the normal number of arms and legs, as I had always known the little bastard) did not seem surprised.

"Dinte," I said. "All these people are startled to see me sitting here, but you and I know that Lanik Mueller has been sitting on this throne for years."

He looked at me a moment, and then nodded slightly.

"And so, Dinte, I will meet you, privately, in the room where I kept my snail collection when I was five." I pushed back into quicktime and left the throne room.

I had kept my snail collection in a long-unused attic in one of the older parts of the palace, a place never locked but, because it was accessible only by ladder and winding corridors, never visited. I headed there in quicktime, then slowed down nearly to the flow of realtime, and waited. I kept just enough edge of speed that if Lanik/

Dinte had ideas of treachery, I could react faster than he could attack.

And if he was a fraud, he would not know what room I meant.

I waited for fifteen minutes, and then he came along the dusty attic walkway and sat before me on the floor. It was hard for him to walk, with his awkward arms and legs, and sitting was ludicrous, but I didn't laugh. I remembered my struggle up a not-too-difficult slope in Schwartz after I was set off the Singer slave ship.

In realtime now, I spoke softly. "Hello, Lanik."

"Hello, Lanik," he answered, smiling ruefully.

"Last time we met, I tried to kill you," I said.

"Many times since then I've wished you had succeeded."

And then we sat in silence for a few moments. What do you talk about when you meet yourself after so many years?

"How did you come here?" I asked. "How did you learn to be an illuder?" Though I already had guessed much of the story.

He told me. How he had lain half-dead as his already weak body tried to regenerate the skull and skin and keep the brain tissue from degenerating. How he had been found by the huge search party the Nkumai had sent after me. "If they hadn't found me," he said, "they would certainly have kept searching until they found you. When they realized what had happened and tried to follow you again, they traced you right to the seacoast. You wouldn't have escaped."

Then he told me of days and weeks with Mwabao Mawa in her treetop house. My body, in constructing him, had given him all my memories. It took Mwabao some time before she realized that he was only a duplicate of me. "And by then she had learned enough that she was certain I was from Mueller—I had spoken Dinte's and Father's names in my delirium, and her fellow Andersons were already here, as you seem to know." She immediately seized the opportunity my double represented and fanned his hatred of me, his feelings of worthlessness because he would always be the monster, the horrible one, the creature that had no right to exist. And so he consented to lead the Nkumai armies and their allies into battle against Mueller.

He exacted a price, however, that Mwabao was only too willing to pay. He asked for training in the Anderson deception, and Mwabao Mawa taught it to him. While I was in Schwartz learning to control the earth, he was learning to control men's minds.

"People's beliefs don't exist in isolation," he explained. "Everyone's firmly held beliefs exert an enormous pressure on everyone else. Not opinions, of course—*beliefs*. We—they—could make anybody think the sun was blue and had always been blue. But, of course, the farther you got from the place where other people believed intensely in the deception, the less you would be influenced. However, by then the work would have been done. Once someone honestly believes something to be a fact, he'll never doubt it without pretty convincing evidence." Which is why Lord Barton was able to learn the truth separated from Britton by a thousand kilometers, but had to struggle to remember it when he returned to his home.

He had not consented, he told me, to the wasting of the land by the Nkumai army on its passage through the Rebel River plain. I could never have done that—and so neither could he.

"And then you reappeared," he said, "and we didn't know what to do. Until, of course, you and Father escaped to Ku Kuei. Then it was clear that I had to disappear so that the monster they had made of me would color other men's perception of you, ruining your effectiveness. And at the time, Lanik, I was glad of it. You can't know how much I hated you. Because you had hated me, not for who I was, but because I *was* at all."

At first they didn't know what to do with him now that Lanik Mueller was officially an exile in Ku Kuei. "Until word reached us that Dinte had disappeared. Mwabao Mawa panicked. How could anyone have known about Dinte and killed him—and yet not publicly raised the cry about who he was? Whoever killed him would surely have seen him change before their eyes from the young heir to a much older man."

And then I realized what should have been obvious to me long before.

"I must have killed Dinte," I told my double. "I slit his throat as I left the palace. I assumed he would regenerate."

He smiled at me. "So you got your wish, didn't you? You killed Dinte, and in the process you saved my life. Because I was the only one who knew Dinte well enough to impersonate him without making waves. I stepped in and began to play the role I've played ever since."

His voice grew soft (as mine always grew soft when I was afraid I would show fear or pity or grief) and he said, "The role I've played ever since. You know—*you* know how much I hated Dinte. And yet I had to *be* him, and talk to his covey of traitors who had plotted your death and Father's death and—God, Lanik, how I survived that time I'll never know. But always I kept telling myself, 'I'm Lanik

Mueller, not this bastard,' and I endured the sycophants and the traitors and the petty criminals and Ruva and all the rest. Because it was common knowledge that you had gone with Father deep into Ku Kuei and would never come back. Father was dead, you see, and I loved him, and the more people here in Mueller abused his memory and yours, the more I felt free to identify with you, to become you in my heart. I stopped hating you long ago. I just longed for you to come back and set me free.

"Lanik," he said, "I go every two or three months to a doctor and have my arms and legs cut off. I'm almost due now. The doctor never knows I'm me, never remembers that he performs these operations until it's time for the next one. But you—you're whole. You're right and normal. You haven't lived this sick deception for these long months, these years. Let's go back out to the throne room. I'll appear in my true form and tell them that you're not the monster you were believed to be. You can take your place, and I'll be free."

"And what will you do then?"

"I'll plead with you to kill me. I've lived for years now as a radical regenerative. It doesn't qualify as life. If you won't kill me, I'll drown myself."

I shook my head. "I came here to kill you."

"Me? Did you know who I was, then?"

"No. Not then. I came to kill the Anderson who controlled Mueller, the one pretending to be Dinte."

He was shocked. "You knew before you came? Then the Andersons' secret is out?"

"The Andersons," I told him, "are dead. A rainstorm reached you" (I groped for the real time) "a few days ago. A drenching rainstorm. And the sky is still overcast." He nodded. "That rain was caused a week ago when Anderson sank into the sea."

He was surprised. "Just like that? Sank into the sea?"

I heard the scream still ringing inside me. "Not just like that. But they have disappeared from the earth. And not just the island. All the others, too, in every Family. You're the last who knows the technique. You and any who worked with you here."

"How did you do it?"

"Never mind how. What matters is the why." And I explained to him.

"And so the Ambassadors are gone, too," he said. "No more iron. Do you realize what you've done?"

I laughed. "I have a good idea."

"We—the Andersons knew every secret in the world, Lanik! Do you realize what was being achieved on this world? Incredible things. Things to make you proud to be a resident of this godforsaken prison planet! And you've stopped it. Without the Ambassadors, do you think that level of invention will continue?"

I shrugged. "It might. The Andersons didn't know all the secrets in the world."

"Stupid! Shortsighted and stupid and—"

"Listen, Lanik!" I shouted back, and the act of using my own name in reference to another person surprised me. "Yes, Lanik. You are me, aren't you? Me as I should have been. Me, captured by the Nkumai and induced to learn Mwabao Mawa's tricks—and I would have learned them, just as you did. I would have let myself become their tool; to a point, and there you sit, as I would have sat, a monster in a body trapped inside an even more monstrous illusion. No, Lanik, you're not the one to judge me as shortsighted or stupid. And I'm not the one to judge you. You called this a godforsaken planet, but you're wrong. Thousands of years ago the Republic decided to be God. They decided to put the finest minds in the universe on a hopeless, ironless planet and then held out in front of them a reward —the first Family to build a starship and come out into space would receive unheard-of riches and power and prestige. For three thousand years we believed that, and spent our souls working to do what—to give to the bastards who keep us here the best we could develop. Our own flesh! The finest products of our minds! And what have we had in return? A few tons of a metal that's cheap everywhere but here. So we can build a starship?

"We'll never build a starship with Republic iron, never. And if we did, do you think they'd let us all come out and take part in human life? Don't you realize the miracle this planet is? If they realized what's *really* going on—if they could spend a few days in Ku Kuei, or a week in Schwartz—if they understood what our potential really is, Lanik, they'd be here immediately, they'd bomb this planet out of existence, wipe us out of the universe. That's the only hope and promise we have from them.

"And what would we do if we joined them? Persuade them to be nice? If they were going to be kind, they wouldn't be keeping the hundredth great grandchildren of great men imprisoned on a hopeless planet like this. Would we then do as our ancestors did, and dissent from the course the human race is taking?"

"No," he said. "No. And I know that. I've often thought about the hopelessness of it, too, Lanik. Dissent accomplishes nothing. It's something I told a young man who had been arrested for protesting against a law. I took him out by the river at night, without his guards, and I pointed out some facts to him. That if he kept his mouth shut, the law would leave him alone and he'd be free. 'I don't want to be free,' he said, 'while that law exists. I will dissent until you take it away.' 'No,' I told him, 'you'll dissent until you die in prison, and what will you have done?

"'It's like the moons,' I said to him. 'See how Dissent moves so quickly and brightly? The most spectacular thing in the sky. But it's spectacular because it's so close to Treason, and so small. Freedom is a much larger moon, much farther away. It doesn't make half the show. But Freedom makes the tides go,' I said. 'Freedom raises and lowers the sea.'"

I was filled with a strange feeling. Recognition. The man thought as I did; and though that was only logical, still it was a surprise to me. No one ever meets a man who thinks exactly as he does, not normally. But now it was as if I could say his words (my words) along with him.

"With Anderson gone, and the Ambassadors," he (I) said, "we're cut off from the Republic. We're free. And when the universe hears from us again, we'll be making the tides."

Silence. And I realized that I had said the last few words, not he. He smiled at me. We understood each other. Not everything, but the thought, the *why* we thought was clear to both of us, and, so help me, I felt affection for him. If the ability to communicate well has something to do with love, there is no one a man can love quite so well as himself.

"Lanik," we said in unison, breaking the silence together. And then we laughed. "You first," I told him.

"Lanik, please take the throne. If you know me, you know how I feel in this body. You know from what I've told you that I've done unbearable things. Set me free."

Unbearable things. I didn't tell him, didn't try to explain the unbearable things I had done, didn't try to communicate the scream that underlay every thought I had. Instead, I closed my eyes and began to do for him what the Schwartzes had done for me.

It had taken only a handful of Schwartzes to change me, to cure my radical regeneration, and so I hoped I could do it alone. I had nothing like their knowledge of the carbon chains, but I could sense them and compare. Any difference between his DNA and mine I changed in him until we matched, perfectly. It meant that not only would his regeneration be cured, but also he would have the gift of never hungering and thirsting again, of being free of the need to breathe, of taking his energy directly from the sun.

But I couldn't give to him the abilities that I had learned, and wouldn't have if I could. He was the real Lanik Mueller, not I. He was Lanik Mueller as I should have been: ruling in Mueller, and ruling well; lonely, but living where he ought to live. And now, without the curse of radical regeneration, he would be free to achieve a measure of happiness that would always be beyond me.

It took hours. When I was through, he lay asleep on the attic floor, his body whole and correct and healthy. He was naked—there were no tailors to clothe the deformed bodies of radical regeneratives. And I looked at his body as I had never been able to look at my own. The skin was young and smooth—for he was younger than I—and the muscles were good and the body well-proportioned. For a moment I saw myself as Saranna must have seen me, and for all that I have no love or longing for other men, I understood why she so often told me that my body was sweet. It had irritated me—an adolescent boy does not seek sweetness. But she was right.

It was the face that made me ache inside. He thought he had known pain, and he had, to a degree greater than many men. His face showed maturity beyond his years, and kindness, and compassion. But I had seen my own face in mirrors, had studied what time and my own acts had done to me, and my face was not kind or compassionate. I had seen too much. I had killed too often. And so there was no sweetness left in me, not to look at, and I yearned to be as relatively innocent as he.

Impossible, I reminded myself. That choice was made years ago in the sand at the border of Schwartz. And I began to suspect that the ultimate sacrifice isn't death after all; the ultimate sacrifice is willingly bearing the fullest penalty for your own actions. I had borne it, and I couldn't hope not to have the scars show in my face and my body.

He awoke and looked at me and smiled. Then he realized what had happened to his body, and he touched himself incredulously and wept and kept asking me, "This isn't an illusion, is it? It's real, isn't it?"

Yes, it's real, I told him. "And when I've destroyed the Ambassador, there'll be no more need to keep rads like cattle. So do this for me. Make it a law that rads be sent to Schwartz, all of them, as soon as they're identified. Have them go into Schwartz and when the desert people come to them, have them say they come at Lanik Mueller's command. The Schwartzes will know what to do after that. They'll send them home, whole. Or if they don't come home, it's because they freely chose to stay."

"And what about you?" Lanik asked.

"I don't exist," I answered. "In the forest of Nkumai it wasn't you who became the extra Lanik Mueller, it was I. You're the real one. Over the next few years, Lanik, change the illusion. Gradually make Dinte's face become your own until you can end the deception. You want to anyway, I know that much. End the lie, except for the name, and live and rule with your own face."

"And you?"

"I'll find someplace else to live."

And then I pushed back into quicktime and left him in the attic and went back to the court, where quite a few people still milled around, chattering about what had happened. It took me only a few minutes to spot the Andersons among them, the last of their Family to survive. I had left Lanik feeling sad and yet better than I had felt in a long time. But that didn't stop me from killing the Andersons and making my way out to the Ambassador and blowing it up.

I had planned, before meeting the other Lanik, that when the last Ambassador exploded I would stay there in realtime to die with it. But now I knew that the real me was still a sweet-bodied boy who would make a good king, and though he wasn't the me-that-I-am, he was the me-that-ought-to-be, and I gained a little respect for myself and no longer wanted to die.

But where would I go? I had no more purpose in my life. What was left to me I could live as I chose.

And as I walked through the fields east of Mueller-on-the-River, I knew where I would have to go. On an island in the middle of a lake in Ku Kuei, Saranna had said, "Come back soon. Come back while you're still young enough to want me. For I'm going to be young forever."

I wasn't young anymore, not by any definition of the word. But I wanted her. Perhaps I only wanted the innocence of the children making love beside the river, oblivious of the pain that could and surely would come to them. But I wanted her more than I wanted anything else in the world, not because my passion was so overwhelming, but because all the other things I wanted were either painfully accomplished or so hopeless that I had given up on them. Only she was left. She and a strange and quiet land of poor yet kindly people who tended sheep among the rocks by the Humping Sea.

humping

I came to Ku Kuei in realtime and laughed a bit when several of the young ones, not knowing who I was, tried to play quicktime games with me. I easily coped with their timeflows and stayed in realtime despite all they did. They must have got worried then, and called on someone older and more skilled. Which is why it was Man-Who-Knows-It-All who came to greet me.

"Lake-drinker," he roared as he came into view, laughing and holding out his arms. "Gone forever! My worst student, the bad example I hold before all the children who come to me to learn. You stayed away so long, however long it's been, who can keep track of time? But it's been a long time, you old bastard, and come on, come on, come on, hurry!"

We hurried, the fat Ku Kuei leading the way briskly, and I drank in the air of the forest. Forest isn't the kind of land I call home, but this forest was my father's cemetery and the last place I had been when someone still loved me as a son and as a lover.

"Saranna," I said, and Man-Who-Knows-It-All looked puzzled. "Stump," I reminded him, and he laughed. "Oh, her. Her, what an incredible thing. A good student, for an outsider, and yet we don't call her Stump anymore. It's Stone now, Lady Stone, because there she stands in the slowest damn slowtime anyone's ever done. Do you want to see her?"

Did I want to see her? I didn't know how much until I stood there and realized that she was standing just as she had stood when I left, six subjective years and three real years before. Her hands were still reaching out to me. Her lips were still parted with her last words. The tears in her eyes had overflowed, and yet the first drops hadn't reached her chin.

I gazed at her and the last six years fell away and it was only a moment ago that I had left her; and I slowed my time, slowed it beyond anything I had ever experienced before, slowed until even the trees seemed a blur, and then, at last, her tear began to move, and her eyes saw me, and her expression changed to hope, and she said, "Lanik. I've changed my mind. I don't want to be young forever. Take me with you."

She embraced me, and I embraced her, and I kissed her cheek where it was wet. "I've been away for six years," I said.

"Hush," she said.

"I've done terrible things."

"I don't need to know it."

"I'm not a good person," I insisted.

She only kissed me, and whispered, "Good enough for me." And she smiled and I smiled and gradually we slipped out of slowtime and the world ceased to be a blur and we were in Ku Kuei again. There were hundreds of people gathered around us. I recognized none of them.

"Why are you watching us?" I asked.

"Because," one fat man said, "everyone told us the Stone Lovers were speeding up to realtime, and we had to come to see."

"Stone lovers?"

"People have been born, grown old, and died, and only seen the two of you move an inch or two, or smile or seem to speak a single word. You looked so intense. Whatever you were saying, you seemed to mean it, and it wasn't amusing at all. Started quite a fashion. People keep looking for purpose now. Complicates everything."

"How long?" I asked.

"Two, three hundred years, I figure," he said. "But now I expect you'll be just ordinary people."

"I hope so," I said, and Saranna smiled.

We left the forest and traveled east until at last we reached Britton, and in the easternmost part of Britton's east peninsula, we came to Humping. In the last two centuries nothing had changed. A new lord ruled from cliff house, but he called himself by the hereditary name Barton. Glain's and Vran's house was now a garden and some-

one else's house stood a few meters off, but the house was full of
children and nothing had been changed. The people were still poor,
still taciturn, still good to the heart.

Saranna and I built a sod house near the sea, and in a few weeks a
shepherd came to see what we were up to, and I healed his goiter
and cured a sick lamb, and they knew who I was. "Man-in-the-
Wind," they called me, and Saranna became the Wind's Lady, and
soon Windlady, and though the people of Humping loved us, they
couldn't have loved us as we loved them. The legend of Man-in-the-
Wind was well known—how he had come from nowhere and lived
with Glain and Vran, healing and doing good for everyone until
someone told the lord in cliff house and Man-in-the-Wind went
away and never came back again. This time, they vowed, it would be
different. And in all the years we've lived here, the lord in cliff house
has never sought us out.

The Humpers aren't surprised that though they grow old and die,
we don't grow old. We have lived to cure the ills of children whose
grandparents' broken legs we fixed. It's a quiet life, but a good one,
and sometime soon Saranna and I plan to have children. When we
have children, though, we will stop changing ourselves, and will grow
old and die when our grandchildren are growing up, just like anyone
else. Children don't need their parents to live forever.

But we're not quite ready for that now. Life is still sweet enough
for us without children, though I look at Saranna and see that it
won't be too long now; and I look at myself and see that I'm nearly
ready. And that will be good, too. Even death will be good, I think,
not because it ends old bitterness, but because I believe it will come
as the last of the many sharp tastes that have taught me I am alive.

Under everything I still hear the scream of the earth, but it no
longer taints the things I see and do. Instead, it heightens my pleas-
ures, and sunrise is brighter because of the dark place inside me, and
Saranna's smile is kinder because of the cruelty I have known, and
healing the animals and children and adults that come to me is
sweeter because once, against my own instincts but because of my
own sense of right and wrong, I killed.

Whether Treason is a better place to live now I'm not the one to
judge.

Whether we are progressing as well as we did before the Ambassadors were destroyed I don't know. It's not up to me to evaluate how
well we've done with our opportunity. It was only my task to create
that opportunity.

And sometimes I marvel that I accomplished it at all. "You don't exist," Saranna often says after we make love, "you can't be real." She means it one way, but I believe it another, and for all the planning and plotting that I did before I acted, I know that I was shaped more by circumstance than by my own will. And I wonder sometimes if I'm not, after all, a piece in some other player's game, following blindly his grand designs without ever knowing that my path along the board is only a feint, while the important matters are played out elsewhere by other men.

But whether there's some grand design really matters little to me. My only hope was this. To see what could be, and to believe that it should be, and then to do all I could to bring it to pass, whatever the cost. And when a life ends as mine will end, no one can persuade me that the cost was not worth what it has brought me at last.